The
OPEN DOOR

The
OPEN DOOR

*and Other Stories of the Seen and Unseen
by Margaret Oliphant*

Edited by

MIKE ASHLEY

THE BRITISH LIBRARY

This edition published 2021 by
The British Library
96 Euston Road
London NW1 2DB

Introduction © 2021 Mike Ashley

Cataloguing in Publication Data
A catalogue record for this book is available from the British Library

ISBN 978 0 7123 5354 0

Cover design by Mauricio Villamayor with illustration by Sandra Gómez

Typeset by Tetragon, London
Printed in Malta by Gutenberg Press

CONTENTS

INTRODUCTION
The Seen and the Unseen

During the Victorian period in Britain there seemed to be no end of married women who produced a number of wonderful ghost stories, their sheer volume establishing the vogue for the medium. There was Catherine Crowe, who more or less started it all with *The Night Side of Nature* in 1848, Elizabeth Gaskell who, when not writing novels of social and industrial life such as *Mary Barton* (1848) and *Cranford* (1853), produced a number of strange tales collected as *Curious, if True* (1861), Charlotte Riddell, one of the most prolific of Victorian writers of weird tales with such titles as *Fairy Water* (1872), *The Uninhabited House* (1875) and *Weird Stories* (1882), and so on through Ellen Wood, Amelia B. Edwards, Isabella Banks, Mary Molesworth, Henrietta Everett, Louisa Baldwin, Mary Elizabeth Braddon, Edith Nesbit, Marie Corelli… and so on, and that's not including those who never married, like Rhoda Broughton or Vernon Lee, or their American cousins like Edith Wharton, Mary E. Wilkins Freeman, Hildegarde Hawthorne or Gertrude Atherton. I'll stop there. Suffice it to say that the ghost story was safe in the hands of many Victorian women whom one could count on to produce stories that were atmospheric, full of character and hauntingly memorable.

One might ask why there were so many women, and I don't think it's because they were left at home on their own while their husbands thought they were running the world. There's more to it than that, and I think one answer lies in the life and work of Margaret Oliphant, one of the most prolific of all Victorian novelists who turned to the ghost story in moments of need, which wasn't until she was in her fifties.

Margaret Oliphant was born Margaret Wilson on 4 April 1828 in Wallyford, near Musselburgh, not far from the shores of the Forth estuary in Scotland. She had two elder brothers, Frank and Willie. Her father, also Frank, was an office clerk constantly changing jobs including being a bank clerk and in customs and excise. Although he provided for the family, he seemed remote from young Margaret and was socially inept, almost reclusive. She was much closer to her mother, also called Margaret, who was a prodigious reader and encouraged her daughter to read. Indeed, the young girl had a decent education, though it was thwarted by the family moving in connection with her father's work. They moved twice in Scotland before settling in Liverpool in 1838, when she was ten, and even then continued to move house in Liverpool and Birkenhead. They occasionally returned to Scotland and she never lost her Scottish heritage, or accent. She spoke with a Scottish lilt all her life.

It was while in Liverpool that she started to write a novel set in Scotland and influenced by the division of the Church following the so-called Disruption of 1843. Her feckless brother Willie appropriated the manuscript and sent it to the entrepreneurial London publisher Henry Colburn. Colburn had long had an eye for burgeoning talent—he had, after all, "discovered" Bulwer Lytton, G. P. R. James and Captain Marryat—and he promptly bought the novel for £150, close on £20,000 in today's spending power. It was published under the somewhat tedious title of *Passages in the Life of Mrs Margaret Maitland of Sunnyside* in 1849 and proved very popular. Colburn asked for more and Margaret obliged—*Merkland* in 1850, *Caleb Field* and *John Drayton* in 1851, and many more, often three novels a year and others in preparation.

Published anonymously some of these early novels became attributed to Margaret's brother, Willie, who used to copy out her manuscripts in a fair hand. Alas, although training for the church, Willie had become an incurable alcoholic. Margaret was sent to London to help look after him and it was there, in 1851, that her cousin Frank (the family seemed to have a limited selection of names) proposed to her. Margaret hesitated for some months but eventually accepted and they were married in May 1852. At that same time Margaret sold her new novel, *Katie Stewart*, to the prestigious Scottish publisher William Blackwood who serialised it in *Blackwood's Magazine* during the summer and autumn of 1852. Her association with *Blackwood's* would last for the rest of her life and it was in their magazine that most of her ghost stories appeared.

Frank Oliphant was an artist, mostly in stained glass, and he worked as a designer for the noted Augustus Pugin, at that time working on the new Houses of Parliament. Margaret was, even then, earning more money than her husband and it seems it was not the happiest of marriages. Indeed, the 1850s proved a difficult period for Margaret, who was still in her twenties. She had two baby daughters, Maggie born in May 1853 and Marjorie in May 1854. Her mother died in September 1854 and her youngest child died in February 1855. Her memory of Marjorie's death, though recorded over thirty years later, shows how grief-stricken she had been and, over the years, remained:

> My little Marjorie was always pale and delicate, but with glorious eyes— to think of an eight months' old baby having these! But I remember that as she died she opened them widely and seemed to fix them on me as she lay on my knee, giving up her little soul in that look of consciousness, as it appeared to me. That was in 1855, thirty-six years ago, but I have never forgot the look with which that baby died.

You need look no further for the start of Margaret Oliphant's moods and memories that she would build into her supernatural stories.

The catalogue of misfortune continued. Her next child, a young boy born in November 1855 died the next day. A fourth child, Cyril, known as Tiddy, was born in November 1856 and thankfully survived, but the next summer her husband developed tuberculosis and by late 1858 found it difficult to work. He closed his studio and the family travelled to Rome for the climate. Frank kept from Margaret his doctor's verdict that his case was terminal and when she learned this she was furious, feeling betrayed. Life in Rome was not good. Frank died in October 1859. Margaret was seven months pregnant and had to stay in Rome until she gave birth to a boy. He was also christened Frank, though known as Cecco. She was not ready to return home until the following February, now with three children and still having to support her brother Willie. One benefit of Rome, though, is that they had met a family who took care of Willie, though Margaret continued to pay for his upkeep.

Once settled back in London, Margaret threw herself into writing and began a series of novels under the general title, The Chronicles of Carlingford which, like Anthony Trollope's Barchester Chronicles, proved highly popular and established her reputation once and for all. She broadened her output to writing biographies which caused her to travel and she returned to Rome in November 1863. Tragically her daughter, Maggie, caught a gastric bug and died at the end of January. She stayed in Europe but was lured back by the astonishing offer of £1,500 for her new novel The Perpetual Curate, equal to almost £200,000 today. Such was her popularity.

Returning to England in September 1865, she settled in Windsor, where she was able to send her sons to Eton School. She had a loyal circle of friends, and she was always generous and kind, bearing the loss of her daughters with grace and fortitude. Those who knew her remarked on her soft, kindly eyes. She was, perhaps, too kind. Already having to pay for Willie's upkeep in Rome, she found herself becoming responsible for her brother Frank's two oldest children. Frank had never had much business acumen and in 1868 he became bankrupt. Soon after

Frank's wife died and he became incapable of looking after his younger children, so Margaret found herself their foster mother. Margaret loved children and found the younger two, Madge and Denny, a delight, but they were all a burden on her purse.

Her lifestyle also became expensive but for several more years she was able to command high payments for her books. This locked her in to an endless cycle of writing. Her popularity gradually waned, but never completely. She always had a solid readership, and there was interest in her spiritual and supernatural stories which Blackwood encouraged.

She had already experimented with a slightly weird story, "A Christmas Tale", which *Blackwood's* had published in January 1857, but it was not until 1876 that she returned to the supernatural with more interest. "The Secret Chamber" was inspired by a legend that Glamis Castle had a secret room where an evil earl had been trapped by the devil. Walter Scott noted the legend in his *Letters on Demonology and Witchcraft* (1830) and Margaret drew upon this along with her own imaginings when a discussion about the legend arose at a gathering in her home in November that year. The telling of the story had a dramatic finale because at the climax there was a terrific crash beyond the door of Mrs Oliphant's drawing room which made everybody shriek. It was later discovered that a picture had unaccountably fallen from the wall just at that moment.

Margaret now turned to the supernatural with more fervour. The short novel "The Beleaguered City", published in January 1879, is one of her best known works. Set in a French town, the dead rise up and eject the living until they mend their blasphemous ways. Like many of her weird tales it has strong moral overtones, but it is full of atmosphere and it cemented her use of the phrase "A Story of the Seen and Unseen", which alerted readers to her work, even when published anonymously—which she preferred. She believed at the time that she had "wasted a good deal of time upon it, which is foolish, but the subject struck my fancy." Yet, when most of her work went out of print in the early twentieth century, it was this that recaptured some of the interest when anthologised in *Six Novels of the Supernatural* in 1944.

The story includes an episode when one of the characters mourns for the loss of their child, which feels as if reproducing Mrs Oliphant's grief at the loss of Maggie. It is more than likely that her increasing passion for the ghost story served as therapy for dealing with so much loss in her life. At the start of "Earthbound" we find a couple mourning for the loss of their son. "The Open Window", which also tells of a poorly child, links to the ghost of another child.

In 1882 Margaret began work on her Little Pilgrim series. These stories tell of the experiences of a soul arriving in the Afterlife and the wonders they discover. At one point the soul meets a friend's daughter, Margaret, Mrs Oliphant's own daughter Maggie. I have not included any of the Little Pilgrim stories here because they need to be read as a whole, and despite their popularity in their day, there is a cloying sentimentality about them which today reads rather too sanctimonious. But I have included another of her stories of the Afterlife, "Dies Iræ", one of her last tales from 1895, which has kept much of its power.

Margaret Oliphant continued to experience loss, both amongst her circle of friends, and within her family. Her brother Willie died in 1885, her son Cyril in 1890 and her other son Cecco in 1894. Cecco had written a couple of ghost stories of his own, one of which, "The Ghost Baby" (1890) was an attempt to make light of the death of a child. The death of Cecco, though, broke her emotionally. She was now sixty-six, worn out by the constant demands of writing and caring. She had been making notes for an autobiography over the years, but she could not continue. She ended it with the words, "And now here I am all alone. I cannot write any more."

But, she did continue to write. It was now she produced "Dies Iræ" and what many consider her best ghost story "The Library Window", again involving a young child. She still had family around her, her niece Denny, and with her she moved to a house in Wimbledon in April 1896. It was there, a year later on 25 June 1897 that Margaret Oliphant died of cancer of the colon, but worn down by sheer exhaustion. Six months earlier *Blackwood's* had published her last story of the seen and unseen, "The Land of Suspense". It is the story of her son Cyril, and his journey into the Afterlife to meet his family, and what he needs to do to achieve that end. The story includes Cecco, but above all it was Margaret Oliphant preparing herself for her own journey into the Great Beyond.

On the surface, Mrs Oliphant's stories collected here may be seen as typical of the Victorian ghost story, but they have to be read from her own experiences of life and death. In the Victorian era death was everywhere and people, parents and children alike, had to come to terms with it in their own way. Margaret Oliphant was able to keep the memories of her children alive in her stories and provide them with their own literary afterlife. She was their mother not only in life, but for eternity.

MIKE ASHLEY

THE SECRET CHAMBER

[Dedicated to the inquirers in the Norman Tower.]

CASTLE Gowrie is one of the most famous and interesting in all Scotland. It is a beautiful old house, to start with,—perfect in old feudal grandeur, with its clustered turrets and walls that could withstand an army,—its labyrinths, its hidden stairs, its long mysterious passages—passages that seem in many cases to lead to nothing, but of which no one can be too sure what they lead to. The front, with its fine gateway and flanking towers, is approached now by velvet lawns, and a peaceful, beautiful old avenue, with double rows of trees, like a cathedral; and the woods out of which these grey towers rise, look as soft and rich in foliage, if not so lofty in growth, as the groves of the South. But this softness of aspect is all new to the place,—that is, new within the century or two which count for but little in the history of a dwelling-place, some part of which, at least, has been standing since the days when the Saxon Athelings brought such share of the arts as belonged to them to solidify and regulate the original Celtic art which reared incised stones upon rude burial-places, and twined mystic knots on its crosses, before historic days. Even of this primitive decoration there are relics at Gowrie, where the twistings and twinings of Runic cords appear still on some bits of ancient wall, solid as rocks, and almost as everlasting. From these to the graceful French turrets, which recall many a grey chateau, what a long interval of years! But these are filled with stirring chronicles enough, besides the dim, not always decipherable records, which different developments of architecture have left on the old house. The Earls of Gowrie had been in the heat of every commotion that took place on or about the Highland line for more generations than any but a Celtic pen could record. Rebellions, revenges, insurrections, conspiracies, nothing in which blood was shed and lands lost, took place in Scotland, in which they had not had a share; and the annals of the house are very full, and not without many a stain. They had been a bold and vigorous race—with much evil in them, and some good; never insignificant, whatever else they might be. It could not be said, however, that they are remarkable nowadays. Since the first Stuart rising, known in Scotland as "the Fifteen," they have not done much that has been worth recording; but yet their family history has always been of an unusual kind. The Randolphs could not be called eccentric in themselves: on the contrary, when you knew them, they were at bottom a respectable race, full of all the country-gentleman virtues; and yet their public career, such as it was, had been marked by the strangest leaps and jerks of vicissitude. You would have said an impulsive, fanciful family—now making a grasp at some visionary advantage, now rushing into some wild speculation, now making a sudden sally into public life—but soon falling back into mediocrity, not able apparently, even when the impulse was purely selfish and mercenary, to keep it up. But this would not have been at all a true conception of the family character; their actual virtues were not of the imaginative order, and their freaks were a mystery to their friends. Nevertheless these freaks were what the general world was most aware of in the Randolph race. The late Earl had been a representative peer of Scotland (they had no English title), and had made quite a wonderful start, and for a year or two had seemed about to attain a very eminent place in Scotch affairs; but his ambition was found to have made use of some very equivocal modes of gaining influence, and he dropped accordingly at once and for ever from the political firmament. This was quite a common circumstance in the family. An apparently brilliant beginning, a discovery of evil means adopted for ambitious ends, a sudden subsidence, and the curious conclusion at the end of everything that this schemer, this unscrupulous speculator or politician, was a dull, good man after all—unambitious, contented, full of domestic kindness and benevolence. This family peculiarity made the history of the Randolphs a very strange one, broken by the oddest interruptions, and with no consistency in it. There was another circumstance, however, which attracted still more the wonder and observation of the public. For one who can appreciate such a recondite matter as family character, there are hundreds who are interested in a family secret, and this the house of Randolph possessed in perfection. It was a mystery which piqued the imagination and excited the interest of the entire country. The story went, that somewhere hid amid the massive walls and tortuous passages there was a secret chamber in Gowrie Castle. Everybody knew of its existence; but save the earl, his heir, and one other person, not of the family, but filling a confidential post in their service, no mortal knew where this mysterious hiding-place was. There had been countless guesses made at it, and expedients of all kinds invented to find it out. Every visitor who ever entered the old gateway, nay, even passing travellers who saw the turrets from the road, searched keenly for some trace of this mysterious chamber. But all guesses and researches were equally in vain.

I was about to say that no ghost-story I ever heard of has been so steadily and long believed. But this would be a mistake, for nobody knew even with any certainty that there was a ghost connected with it. A secret chamber was nothing wonderful in so old a house. No doubt they exist in many such old houses, and are always curious and interesting—strange relics, more moving than any history, of the time when a man was not safe in his own house, and when it might be necessary to secure a refuge beyond the reach of spies or traitors at a moment's notice. Such a refuge was a necessity of life to a great medieval noble.

The peculiarity about this secret chamber, however, was, that some secret connected with the very existence of the family was always understood to be involved in it. It was not only the secret hiding-place for an emergency, a kind of historical possession presupposing the importance of his race, of which a man might be honestly proud; but there was something hidden in it of which assuredly the race could not be proud. It is wonderful how easily a family learns to pique itself upon any distinctive possession. A ghost is a sign of importance not to be despised; a haunted room is worth as much as a small farm to the complacency of the family that owns it. And no doubt the younger branches of the Gowrie family—the light-minded portion of the race—felt this, and were proud of their unfathomable secret, and felt a thrill of agreeable awe and piquant suggestion go through them, when they remembered the mysterious something which they did not know in their familiar home. That thrill ran through the entire circle of visitors, and children, and servants, when the Earl peremptorily forbade a projected improvement, or stopped a reckless exploration. They looked at each other with a pleasurable shiver. "Did you hear?" they said. "He will not let Lady Gowrie have that closet she wants so much in that bit of wall. He sent the workmen about their business before they could touch it, though the wall is twenty feet thick if it is an inch; ah!" said the visitors, looking at each other; and this lively suggestion sent tinglings of excitement to their very finger-points; but even to his wife, mourning the commodious closet she had intended, the Earl made no explanations. For anything she knew, it might be there, next to her room, this mysterious lurking-place; and it may be supposed that this suggestion conveyed to Lady Gowrie's veins a thrill more keen and strange, perhaps too vivid to be pleasant. But she was not in the favoured or unfortunate number of those to whom the truth could be revealed.

I need not say what the different theories on the subject were. Some thought there had been a treacherous massacre there, and that the secret chamber was blocked by the skeletons of murdered guests,—a treachery no doubt covering the family with shame in its day, but so condoned by long softening of years as to have all the shame taken out of it. The Randolphs could not have felt their character affected by any such interesting historical record. They were not so morbidly sensitive. Some said, on the other hand, that Earl Robert, the wicked Earl, was shut up there in everlasting penance, playing cards with the devil for his soul. But it would have been too great a feather in the family cap to have thus got the devil, or even one of his angels, bottled up, as it were, and safely in hand, to make it possible that any lasting stigma could be connected with such a fact as this. What a thing it would be to know where to lay one's hand upon the Prince of Darkness, and prove him once for all, cloven foot and everything else, to the confusion of gainsayers!

So this was not to be received as a satisfactory solution, nor could any other be suggested which was more to the purpose. The popular mind gave it up, and yet never gave it up; and still everybody who visits Gowrie, be it as a guest, be it as a tourist, be it only as a gazer from a passing carriage, or from the flying railway train which just glimpses its turrets in the distance, daily and yearly spends a certain amount of curiosity, wonderment, and conjecture about the Secret Chamber—the most piquant and undiscoverable wonder which has endured unguessed and undeciphered to modern times.

This was how the matter stood when young John Randolph, Lord Lindores, came of age. He was a young man of great character and energy, not like the usual Randolph strain—for, as we have said, the type of character common in this romantically-situated family, notwithstanding the erratic incidents common to them, was that of dullness and honesty, especially in their early days. But young Lindores was not so. He was honest and honourable, but not dull. He had gone through almost a remarkable course at school and at the university—not perhaps in quite the ordinary way of scholarship, but enough to attract men's eyes to him.

He had made more than one great speech at the Union. He was full of ambition, and force, and life, intending all sorts of great things, and meaning to make his position a stepping-stone to all that was excellent in public life. Not for him the country-gentleman existence which was congenial to his father. The idea of succeeding to the family honours and becoming a Scotch peer, either represented or representative, filled him with horror; and filial piety in his case was made warm by all the energy of personal hopes when he prayed that his father might live, if not for ever, yet longer than any Lord Gowrie had lived for the last century or two. He was as sure of his election for the county the next time there was a chance, as anybody can be certain of anything; and in the meantime he meant to travel, to go to America, to go no one could tell where, seeking for instruction and experience, as is the manner of high-spirited young men with parliamentary tendencies in the present day. In former times he would have gone "to the wars in the Hie Germanie," or on a crusade to the Holy Land; but the days of the crusaders and of the soldiers of fortune being over, Lindores followed the fashion of his time. He had made all his arrangements for his tour, which his father did not oppose. On the contrary, Lord Gowrie encouraged all those plans, though with an air of melancholy indulgence which his son could not understand. "It will do you good," he said, with a sigh. "Yes, yes, my boy; the best thing for you." This, no doubt, was true enough; but there was an implied feeling that the young man would require something to do him good—that he would want the soothing of change and the gratification of his wishes, as one might speak of a convalescent or the victim of some calamity. This tone puzzled Lindores, who, though he thought it a fine thing to travel and acquire information, was as scornful of the idea of being done good to as is natural to any fine young fellow fresh from Oxford and the triumphs of the Union. But he reflected that the old school had its own way of treating things, and was satisfied. All was settled accordingly for this journey, before he came home to go through the ceremonial performances of the coming of age, the dinner of the tenantry, the speeches, the congratulations, his father's banquet, his mother's ball. It was in summer, and the country was as gay as all the entertainments that were to be given in his honour. His friend who was going to accompany him on his tour, as he had accompanied him through a considerable portion of his life—Almeric Ffarrington, a young man of the same aspirations—came up to Scotland with him for these festivities. And as they rushed through the night on the Great Northern Railway, in the intervals of two naps, they had a scrap of conversation as to these birthday glories. "It will be a bore, but it will not last long," said Lindores. They were both of the opinion that anything that did not produce information or promote culture was a bore.

"But is there not a revelation to be made to you, among all the other things you have to go through?" said Ffarrington. "Have not you to be introduced to the secret chamber, and all that sort of thing? I should like to be of the party there, Lindores."

"Ah," said the heir, "I had forgotten that part of it," which, however, was not the case. "Indeed I don't know if I am to be told. Even family dogmas are shaken nowadays."

"Oh, I should insist on that," said Ffarrington, lightly. "It is not many who have the chance of paying such a visit—better than Home and all the mediums. I should insist upon that."

"I have no reason to suppose that it has any connection with Home or the mediums," said Lindores, slightly nettled. He was himself an *esprit fort*; but a mystery in one's own family is not like vulgar mysteries. He liked it to be respected.

"Oh, no offence," said his companion. "I have always thought that a railway train would be a great chance for the spirits. If one was to show suddenly in that vacant seat beside you, what a triumphant proof of their existence that would be! but they don't take advantage of their opportunities."

Lindores could not tell what it was that made him think at that moment of a portrait he had seen in a back room at the castle of old Earl Robert, the wicked Earl. It was a bad portrait—a daub—a copy made by an amateur of the genuine portrait, which, out of horror of Earl Robert and his wicked ways, had been removed by some intermediate lord from its place in the gallery. Lindores had never seen the original—nothing but this daub of a copy. Yet somehow this face occurred to him by some strange link of association—seemed to come into his eyes as his friend spoke. A slight shiver ran over him. It was strange. He made no reply to Ffarrington, but set himself to think how it could be that the latent presence in his mind of some anticipation of this approaching disclosure, touched into life by his friend's suggestion, should have called out of his memory a momentary realisation of the acknowledged magician of the family. This sentence is full of long words; but unfortunately long words are required in such a case. And the process was very simple when you traced it out. It was the clearest case of unconscious cerebration. He shut his eyes by way of securing privacy while he thought it out; and being tired, and not at all alarmed by his unconscious cerebration, before he opened them again fell fast asleep.

And his birthday, which was the day following his arrival at Glenlyon, was a very busy day. He had not time to think of anything but the immediate occupations of the moment. Public and private greetings, congratulations, offerings, poured upon him. The Gowries were popular in this generation, which was far from being usual in the family. Lady Gowrie was kind and generous, with that kindness which comes from the heart, and which is the only kindness likely to impress the keen-sighted popular judgment; and Lord Gowrie had but little of the equivocal reputation of his predecessors. They could be splendid now and then on great occasions, though in general they were homely enough; all which the public likes. It was a bore, Lindores said; but yet the young man did not dislike the honours, and the adulation, and all the hearty speeches and good wishes. It is sweet to a young man to feel himself the centre of all hopes. It seemed very reasonable to him—very natural—that he should be so, and that the farmers should feel a pride of anticipation in thinking of his future speeches in Parliament. He promised to them with the sincerest good faith that he would not disappoint their expectations—that he would feel their interest in him an additional spur. What so natural as that interest and these expectations? He was almost solemnised by his own position—so young, looked up to by so many people—so many hopes depending on him; and yet it was quite natural. His father, however, was still more solemnised than Lindores—and this was strange, to say the least. His face grew graver and graver as the day went on, till it almost seemed as if he were dissatisfied with his son's popularity, or had some painful thought weighing on his mind. He was restless and eager for the termination of the dinner, and to get rid of his guests; and as soon as they were gone, showed an equal anxiety that his son should retire too. "Go to bed at once, as a favour to me," Lord Gowrie said. "You will have a great deal of fatigue—tomorrow." "You need not be afraid for me, sir," said Lindores, half affronted; but he obeyed, being tired. He had not once thought of the secret to be disclosed to him, through all that long day. But when he woke suddenly with a start in the middle of the night, to find the candles all lighted in his room, and his father standing by his bedside, Lindores instantly thought of it, and in a moment felt that the leading event—the chief incident of all that had happened— was going to take place now.

CHAPTER II

Lord Gowrie was very grave, and very pale. He was standing with his hand on his son's shoulder to wake him; his dress was unchanged from the moment they had parted. And the sight of this formal costume was very bewildering to the young man as he started up in his bed. But next moment he seemed to know exactly how it was, and, more than that, to have known it all his life. Explanation seemed unnecessary. At any other moment, in any other place, a man would be startled to be suddenly woke up in the middle of the night. But Lindores had no such feeling; he did not even ask a question, but sprang up, and fixed his eyes, taking in all the strange circumstances, on his father's face.

"Get up, my boy," said Lord Gowrie, "and dress as quickly as you can; it is full time. I have lighted your candles, and your things are all ready. You have had a good long sleep."

Even now he did not ask, What is it? as under any other circumstances he would have done. He got up without a word, with an impulse of nervous speed and rapidity of movement such as only excitement can give, and dressed himself, his father helping him silently. It was a curious scene: the room gleaming with lights, the silence, the hurried toilet, the stillness of deep night all around. The house, though so full, and with the echoes of festivity but just over, was quiet as if there was not a creature within it—more quiet, indeed, for the stillness of vacancy is not half so impressive as the stillness of hushed and slumbering life.

Lord Gowrie went to the table when this first step was over, and poured out a glass of wine from a bottle which stood there,—a rich, golden-coloured, perfumy wine, which sent its scent through the room. "You will want all your strength," he said; "take this before you go. It is the famous Imperial Tokay; there is only a little left, and you will want all your strength."

Lindores took the wine; he had never drunk any like it before, and the peculiar fragrance remained in his mind, as perfumes so often do, with a whole world of association in them. His father's eyes dwelt upon him with a melancholy sympathy. "You are going to encounter the greatest trial of your life," he said; and taking the young man's hand into his, felt his pulse. "It is quick, but it is quite firm, and you have had a good long sleep." Then he did what it needs a great deal of pressure to induce an Englishman to do,—he kissed his son on the cheek. "God bless you!" he said, faltering. "Come, now, everything is ready, Lindores."

He took up in his hand a small lamp, which he had apparently brought with him, and led the way. By this time Lindores began to feel himself again, and to wake to the consciousness of all his own superiorities and enlightenments. The simple sense that he was one of the members of a family with a mystery, and that the moment of his personal encounter with this special power of darkness had come, had been the first thrilling, overwhelming thought. But now as he followed his father, Lindores began to remember that he himself was not altogether like other men; that there was that in him which would make it natural that he should throw some light, hitherto unthought of, upon this carefully-preserved darkness. What secret even there might be in it—secret of hereditary tendency, of psychic force, of mental conformation, or of some curious combination of circumstances at once more and less potent than these—it was for him to find out. He gathered all his forces about him, reminded himself of modern enlightenment, and bade his nerves be steel to all vulgar horrors. He, too, felt his own pulse as he followed his father. To spend the night perhaps amongst the skeletons of that old-world massacre, and to repent the sins of his ancestors—to be brought within the range of some optical illusion believed in hitherto by all the generations, and which, no doubt, was of a startling kind, or his father would not look so serious,—any of these he felt himself quite strong to encounter. His heart and spirit rose. A young man has but seldom the opportunity of distinguishing himself so early in his career; and his was such a chance as occurs to very few. No doubt it was something that would be extremely trying to the nerves and imagination. He called up all his powers to vanquish both. And along with this call upon himself to exertion, there was the less serious impulse of curiosity: he would see at last what the Secret Chamber was, where it was, how it fitted into the labyrinths of the old house. This he tried to put in its due place as a most interesting object. He said to himself that he would willingly have gone a long journey at any time to be present at such an exploration; and there is no doubt that in other circumstances a secret chamber, with probably some unthought-of historical interest in it, would have been a very fascinating discovery. He tried very hard to excite himself about this; but it was curious how fictitious he felt the interest, and how conscious he was that it was an effort to feel any curiosity at all on the subject. The fact was, that the Secret Chamber was entirely secondary—thrown back, as all accessories are, by a more pressing interest. The overpowering thought of what was in it drove aside all healthy, natural curiosity about itself.

It must not be supposed, however, that the father and son had a long way to go to have time for all these thoughts. Thoughts travel at lightning speed, and there was abundant leisure for this between the time they had left the door of Lindores' room and gone down the corridor, no further off than to Lord Gowrie's own chamber, naturally one of the chief rooms of the house. Nearly opposite this, a few steps further on, was a little neglected room devoted to lumber, with which Lindores had been familiar all his life. Why this nest of old rubbish, dust, and cobwebs should be so near the bedroom of the head of the house had been a matter of surprise to many people—to the guests who saw it while exploring, and to each new servant in succession who planned an attack upon its ancient stores, scandalised by finding it to have been neglected by their predecessors. All their attempts to clear it out had, however, been resisted, nobody could tell how, or indeed thought it worth while to inquire. As for Lindores, he had been used to the place from his childhood, and therefore accepted it as the most natural thing in the world. He had been in and out a hundred times in his play. And it was here, he remembered suddenly, that he had seen the bad picture of Earl Robert which had so curiously come into his eyes on his journeying here, by a mental movement which he had identified at once as unconscious cerebration. The first feeling in his mind, as his father went to the open door of this lumber-room, was a mixture of amusement and surprise. What was he going to pick up there? some old pentacle, some amulet or scrap of antiquated magic to act as armour against the evil one? But Lord Gowrie, going on and setting down the lamp on the table, turned round upon his son with a face of agitation and pain which barred all farther amusement: he grasped him by the hand, crushing it between his own. "Now my boy, my dear son," he said, in tones that were scarcely audible. His countenance was full of the dreary pain of a looker-on—one who has no share in the excitement of personal danger, but has the more terrible part of watching those who are in deadliest peril. He was a powerful man, and his large form shook with emotion; great beads of moisture stood upon his forehead. An old sword with a cross handle lay upon a dusty chair among other dusty and battered relics. "Take this with you," he said, in the same inaudible, breathless way—whether as a weapon, whether as a religious symbol, Lindores could not guess. The young man took it mechanically. His father pushed open a door which it seemed to him he had never seen before, and led him into another vaulted chamber. Here even the limited powers of speech Lord Gowrie had retained seemed to forsake him, and his voice became a mere hoarse murmur in his throat For want of speech he pointed to another door in the further corner of this small vacant room, gave him to understand by a gesture that he was to knock there, and then went back into the lumber-room. The door into this was left open, and a faint glimmer of the lamp shed light into this little intermediate place—this debatable land between the seen and the unseen. In spite of himself, Lindores' heart began to beat. He made a breathless pause, feeling his head go round. He held the old sword in his hand, not knowing what it was. Then, summoning all his courage, he went forward and knocked at the closed door. His knock was not loud, but it seemed to echo all over the silent house. Would everybody hear and wake, and rush to see what had happened? This caprice of imagination seized upon him, ousting all the firmer thoughts, the steadfast calm of mind with which he ought to have encountered the mystery. Would they all rush in, in wild *déshabille*, in terror and dismay, before the door opened? How long it was of opening! He touched the panel with his hand again.—This time there was no delay. In a moment, as if thrown suddenly open by some one within, the door moved. It opened just wide enough to let him enter, stopping half-way as if some one invisible held it, wide enough for welcome, but no more. Lindores stepped across the threshold with a beating heart. What was he about to see? the skeletons of the murdered victims? a ghostly charnel-house full of bloody traces of crime? He seemed to be hurried and pushed in as he made that step. What was this world of mystery into which he was plunged—what was it he saw?

He saw—nothing—except what was agreeable enough to behold,—an antiquated room hung with tapestry, very old tapestry of rude design, its colours faded into softness and harmony; between its folds here and there a panel of carved wood, rude too in design, with traces of half-worn gilding; a table covered with strange instruments, parchments, chemical tubes, and curious machinery, all with a quaintness of form and dimness of material that spoke of age. A heavy old velvet cover, thick with embroidery faded almost out of all colour, was on the table; on the wall above it, something that looked like a very old Venetian mirror, the glass so dim and crusted that it scarcely reflected at all; on the floor an old soft Persian carpet, worn into a vague blending of all colours. This was all that he thought he saw. His heart, which had been thumping so loud as almost to choke him, stopped that tremendous upward and downward motion like a steam piston; and he grew calm. Perfectly still, dim, unoccupied: yet not so dim either; there was no apparent source of light, no windows, curtains of tapestry drawn everywhere—no lamp visible, no fire—and yet a kind of strange light which made everything quite clear. He looked round, trying to smile at his terrors, trying to say to himself that it was the most curious place he had ever seen—that he must show Ffarrington some of that tapestry—that he must really bring away a panel of that carving,—when he suddenly saw that the door was shut by which he had entered—nay, more than shut, undiscernible, covered like all the rest of the walls by that strange tapestry. At this his heart began to beat again in spite of him. He looked round once more, and woke up to more vivid being with a sudden start. Had his eyes been incapable of vision on his first entrance? Unoccupied? Who was that in the great chair?

It seemed to Lindores that he had seen neither the chair nor the man when he came in. There they were, however, solid and unmistakable; the chair carved like the panels, the man seated in front of the table. He looked at Lindores with a calm and open gaze, inspecting him. The young man's heart seemed in his throat fluttering like a bird, but he was brave, and his mind made one final effort to break this spell. He tried to speak, labouring with a voice that would not sound, and with lips too parched to form a word. "I see how it is," was what he wanted to say. It was Earl Robert's face that was looking at him; and startled as he was, he dragged forth his philosophy to support him. What could it be but optical delusions, unconscious cerebration, occult seizure by the impressed and struggling mind of this one countenance? But he could not hear himself speak any word as he stood convulsed, struggling with dry lips and choking voice.

The Appearance smiled, as if knowing his thoughts—not unkindly, not malignly—with a certain amusement mingled with scorn. Then he spoke, and the sound seemed to breathe through the room not like any voice that Lindores had ever heard, a kind of utterance of the place, like the rustle of the air or the ripple of the sea. "You will learn better tonight: this is no phantom of your brain; it is I."

"In God's name," cried the young man in his soul; he did not know whether the words ever got into the air or not, if there was any air;—"in God's name, who are you?"

The figure rose as if coming to him to reply; and Lindores, overcome by the apparent approach, struggled into utterance. A cry came from him—he heard it this time—and even in his extremity felt a pang the more to hear the terror in his own voice. But he did not flinch, he stood desperate, all his strength concentrated in the act; he neither turned nor recoiled. Vaguely gleaming through his mind came the thought that to be thus brought in contact with the unseen was the experiment to be most desired on earth, the final settlement of a hundred questions; but his faculties were not sufficiently under command to entertain it. He only stood firm, that was all.

And the figure did not approach him; after a moment it subsided back again into the chair—subsided, for no sound, not the faintest, accompanied its movements. It was the form of a man of middle age, the hair white, but the beard only crisped with grey, the features those of the picture—a familiar face, more or less like all the Randolphs, but with an air of domination and power altogether unlike that of the race. He was dressed in a long robe of dark colour, embroidered with strange lines and angles. There was nothing repellent or terrible in his air—nothing except the noiselessness, the calm, the absolute stillness, which was as much in the place as in him, to keep up the involuntary trembling of the beholder. His expression was full of dignity and thoughtfulness, and not malignant or unkind. He might have been the kindly patriarch of the house, watching over its fortunes in a seclusion he had chosen. The pulses that had been beating in Lindores were stilled. What was his panic for? a gleam even of self-ridicule took possession of him, to be standing there like an absurd hero of antiquated romance with the rusty, dusty sword—good for nothing, surely not adapted for use against this noble old magician—in his hand—

"You are right," said the voice, once more answering his thoughts; "what could you do with that sword against me, young Lindores? Put it by. Why should my children meet me like an enemy? You are my flesh and blood. Give me your hand."

A shiver ran through the young man's frame. The hand that was held out to him was large and shapely and white, with a straight line across the palm—a family token upon which the Randolphs prided themselves—a friendly hand; and the face smiled upon him, fixing him with those calm, profound, blue eyes. "Come," said the voice. The word seemed to fill the place, melting upon him from every corner, whispering round him with softest persuasion. He was lulled and calmed in spite of himself. Spirit or no spirit, why should not he accept this proffered courtesy? What harm could come of it? The chief thing that retained him was the dragging of the old sword, heavy and useless, which he held mechanically, but which some internal feeling—he could not tell what—prevented him from putting down. Superstition, was it?

"Yes, that is superstition," said his ancestor, serenely; "put it down and come."

"You know my thoughts," said Lindores; "I did not speak."

"Your mind spoke, and spoke justly. Put down that emblem of brute force and superstition together. Here it is the intelligence that is supreme. Come."

Lindores stood doubtful. He was calm; the power of thought was restored to him. If this benevolent venerable patriarch was all he seemed, why his father's terror? why the secrecy in which his being was involved? His own mind, though calm, did not seem to act in the usual way. Thoughts seemed to be driven across it as by a wind. One of these came to him suddenly now—

> "How there looked him in the face,
>   An angel beautiful and bright,
>   And how he knew it was a fiend."

The words were not ended, when Earl Robert replied suddenly with impatience in his voice, "Fiends are of the fancy of men; like angels and other follies. I am your father. You know me; and you are mine, Lindores. I have power beyond what you can understand; but I want flesh and blood to reign and to enjoy. Come, Lindores!"

He put out his other hand. The action, the look, were those of kindness, almost of longing, and the face was familiar, the voice was that of the race. Supernatural! was it supernatural that this man should live here shut up for ages? and why? and how? Was there any explanation of it? The young man's brain began to reel. He could not tell which was real—the life he had left half an hour ago, or this. He tried to look round him, but could not; his eyes were caught by those other kindred eyes, which seemed to dilate and deepen as he looked at them, and drew him with a strange compulsion. He felt himself yielding, swaying towards the strange being who thus invited him. What might happen if he yielded? And he could not turn away, he could not tear himself from the fascination of those eyes. With a sudden strange impulse which was half despair and half a bewildering half-conscious desire to try one potency against another, he thrust forward the cross of the old sword between him and those appealing hands. "In the name of God!" he said.

Lindores never could tell whether it was that he himself grew faint, and that the dimness of swooning came into his eyes after this violence and strain of emotion, or if it was his spell that worked. But there was an instantaneous change. Everything swam around him for the moment, a giddiness and blindness seized him, and he saw nothing but the vague outlines of the room, empty as when he entered it. But gradually his consciousness came back, and he found himself standing on the same spot as before, clutching the old sword, and gradually, as though a dream, recognised the same figure emerging out of the mist which—was it solely in his own eyes?—had enveloped everything. But it was no longer in the same attitude. The hands which had been stretched out to him were busy now with some of the strange instruments on the table, moving about, now in the action of writing, now as if managing the keys of a telegraph. Lindores felt that his brain was all atwist and set wrong; but he was still a human being of his century. He thought of the telegraph with a keen thrill of curiosity in the midst of his reviving sensations. What communication was this which was going on before his eyes? The magician worked on. He had his face turned towards his victim, but his hands moved with unceasing activity. And Lindores, as he grew accustomed to the position, began to weary—to feel like a neglected suitor waiting for an audience. To be wound up to such a strain of feeling, then left to wait, was intolerable; impatience seized upon him. What circumstances can exist, however horrible, in which a human being will not feel impatience? He made a great many efforts to speak before he could succeed. It seemed to him that his body felt more fear than he did—that his muscles were contracted, his throat parched, his tongue refusing its office, although his mind was unaffected and undismayed. At last he found an utterance in spite of all resistance of his flesh and blood.

"Who are you?" he said hoarsely. "You that live here and oppress this house?"

The vision raised its eyes full upon him, with again that strange shadow of a smile, mocking yet not unkind. "Do you remember me," he said, "on your journey here?"

"That was—a delusion." The young man gasped for breath.

"More like that you are a delusion. You have lasted but one-and-twenty years, and I—for centuries."

"How? For centuries—and why! Answer me—are you man or demon?" cried Lindores, tearing the words, as he felt, out of his own throat. "Are you living or dead?"

The magician looked at him with the same intense gaze as before. "Be on my side, and you shall know everything, Lindores. I want one of my own race. Others I could have in plenty; but I want *you*. A Randolph, a

Randolph! and *you*. Dead! do I seem dead? You shall have everything—more than dreams can give—if you will be on my side."

Can he give what he has not? was the thought that ran through the mind of Lindores. But he could not speak it. Something that choked and stifled him was in his throat.

"Can I give what I have not? have everything—power, the one thing worth having; and you shall have more than power, for you are young—my son! Lindores!"

To argue was natural, and gave the young man strength. "Is this life," he said, "here? What is all your power worth—here? To sit for ages, and make a race unhappy?"

A momentary convulsion came across the still face. "You scorn me," he cried, with an appearance of emotion, "because you do not understand how I move the world. Power! 'Tis more than fancy can grasp. And you shall have it!" said the wizard, with what looked like a show of enthusiasm. He seemed to come nearer, to grow larger. He put forth his hand again, this time so close that it seemed impossible to escape. And a crowd of wishes seemed to rush upon the mind of Lindores. What harm to try if this might be true! To try what it meant—perhaps nothing, delusions, vain show, and then there could be no harm; or perhaps there was knowledge to be had, which was power. Try, try, try! the air buzzed about him. The room seemed full of voices urging him. His bodily frame rose into a tremendous whirl of excitement, his veins seemed to swell to bursting, his lips seemed to force a yes, in spite of him, quivering as they came apart. The hiss of the *s* seemed in his ears. He changed it into the name which was a spell too, and cried "Help me, God!" not knowing why.

Then there came another pause—he felt as if he had been dropped from something that had held him, and had fallen, and was faint. The excitement had been more than he could bear. Once more everything swam around him, and he did not know where he was. Had he escaped altogether? was the first waking wonder of consciousness in his mind.

But when he could think and see again, he was still in the same spot, surrounded by the old curtains and the carved panels—but alone. He felt, too, that he was able to move, but the strangest dual consciousness was in him throughout all the rest of his trial. His body felt to him as a frightened horse feels to a traveller at night—a thing separate from him, more frightened than he was—starting aside at every step, seeing more than its master. His limbs shook with fear and weakness, almost refusing to obey the action of his will, trembling under him with jerks aside when he compelled himself to move. The hair stood upright on his head—every finger trembled as with palsy—his lips, his eyelids, quivered with nervous agitation. But his mind was strong, stimulated to a desperate calm. He dragged himself round the room, he crossed the very spot where the magician had been—all was vacant, silent, clear. Had he vanquished the enemy? This thought came into his mind with an involuntary triumph. The old strain of feeling came back. Such efforts might be produced, perhaps, only by imagination, by excitement, by delusion—

Lindores looked up, by a sudden attraction he could not tell what: and the blood suddenly froze in his veins that had been so boiling and fermenting. Some one was looking at him from the old mirror on the wall. A face not human and life-like, like that of the inhabitant of this place, but ghostly and terrible, like one of the dead; and while he looked, a crowd of other faces came behind, all looking at him, some mournfully, some with a menace in their terrible eyes. The mirror did not change, but within its small dim space seemed to contain an innumerable company, crowded above and below, all with one gaze at him. His lips dropped apart with a gasp of horror. More and more and more! He was standing close by the table when this crowd came. Then all at once there was laid upon him a cold hand. He turned; close to his side, brushing him with his robe, holding him fast by the arm, sat Earl Robert in his great chair. A shriek came from the young man's lips. He seemed to hear it echoing away into unfathomable distance. The cold touch penetrated to his very soul.

"Do you try spells upon me, Lindores? That is a tool of the past. You shall have something better to work with. And are you so sure of whom you call upon? If there is such a one, why should He help you who never called on Him before?"

Lindores could not tell if these words were spoken; it was a communication rapid as the thoughts in the mind. And he felt as if something answered that was not all himself. He seemed to stand passive and hear the argument. "Does God reckon with a man in trouble, whether he has ever called to Him before? I call now" (now he felt it was himself that said): "go, evil spirit!—go, dead and cursed!—go, in the name of God!"

He felt himself flung violently against the wall. A faint laugh, stifled in the throat, and followed by a groan, rolled round the room; the old curtains seemed to open here and there, and flutter, as if with comings and goings. Lindores leaned with his back against the wall, and all his senses restored to him. He felt blood trickle down his neck; and in this contact once more with the physical, his body, in its madness of fright, grew manageable. For the first time he felt wholly master of himself. Though the magician was standing in his place, a great, majestic, appalling figure, he did not shrink. "Liar!" he cried, in a voice that rang and echoed as in natural air—"clinging to miserable life like a worm—like a reptile; promising all things, having nothing, but this den, unvisited by the light of day. Is this your power—your superiority to men who die? is it for this that you oppress a race, and make a house unhappy! I vow, in God's name, your reign is over! You and your secret shall last no more."

There was no reply. But Lindores felt his terrible ancestor's eyes getting once more that mesmeric mastery over him which had already almost overcome his powers. He must withdraw his own, or perish. He had a human horror of turning his back upon that watchful adversary:

to face him seemed the only safety; but to face him was to be conquered. Slowly, with a pang indescribable, he tore himself from that gaze: it seemed to drag his eyes out of their sockets, his heart out of his bosom. Resolutely, with the daring of desperation, he turned round to the spot where he entered—the spot where no door was,—hearing already in anticipation the step after him—feeling the grip that would crush and smother his exhausted life—but too desperate to care.

CHAPTER III

How wonderful is the blue dawning of the new day before the sun! not rosy-fingered, like that Aurora of the Greeks who comes later with all her wealth; but still, dreamy, wonderful, stealing out of the unseen, abashed by the solemnity of the new birth. When anxious watchers see that first brightness come stealing upon the waiting skies, what mingled relief and renewal of misery is in it! another long day to toil through—yet another sad night over! Lord Gowrie sat among the dust and cobwebs, his lamp flaring idly into the blue morning. He had heard his son's human voice, though nothing more; and he expected to have him brought out by invisible hands, as had happened to himself, and left lying in long deathly swoon outside that mystic door. This was how it had happened to heir after heir, as told from father to son, one after another, as the secret came down. One or two bearers of the name of Lindores had never recovered; most of them had been saddened and subdued for life. He remembered sadly the freshness of existence which had never come back to himself; the hopes that had never blossomed again; the assurance with which never more he had been able to go about the world. And now his son would be as himself—the glory gone out of his living—his ambitions, his aspirations wrecked. He had not been endowed as his boy was—he had been a plain, honest man, and nothing more; but experience and life had given him wisdom enough to smile by times at the coquetries of mind in which Lindores indulged. Were they all over now, those freaks of young intelligence, those enthusiasms of the soul? The curse of the house had come upon him—the magnetism of that strange presence, ever living, ever watchful, present in all the family history. His heart was sore for his son; and yet along with this there was a certain consolation to him in having henceforward a partner in the secret—some one to whom he could talk of it as he had not been able to talk since his own father died. Almost all the mental struggles which Gowrie had known had been connected with this mystery; and he had been obliged to hide them in his bosom—to conceal them even when they rent him in two. Now he had a partner in his trouble. This was what he was thinking as he sat through the night. How slowly the moments passed! He was not aware of the daylight coming in. After a while even thought got suspended in listening. Was not the time nearly over? He rose and began to pace about the encumbered space, which was but a step or two in extent. There was an old cupboard in the wall, in which there were restoratives—pungent essences and cordials, and fresh water which he had himself brought—everything was ready; presently the ghastly body of his boy, half dead, would be thrust forth into his care.

But this was not how it happened. While he waited, so intent that his whole frame seemed to be capable of hearing, he heard the closing of the door, boldly shut with a sound that rose in muffled echoes through the house, and Lindores himself appeared, ghastly indeed as a dead man, but walking upright and firmly, the lines of his face drawn, and his eyes staring. Lord Gowrie uttered a cry. He was more alarmed by this unexpected return than by the helpless prostration of the swoon which he had expected. He recoiled from his son as if he too had been a spirit. "Lindores!" he cried; was it Lindores, or some one else in his place? The boy seemed as if he did not see him. He went straight forward to where the water stood on the dusty table, and took a great draught, then turned to the door. "Lindores!" said his father, in miserable anxiety; "don't you know me?" Even then the young man only half looked at him, and put out a hand almost as cold as the hand that had clutched himself in the Secret Chamber; a faint smile came upon his face. "Don't stay here," he whispered; "come! come!"

Lord Gowrie drew his son's arm within his own, and felt the thrill through and through him of nerves strained beyond mortal strength. He could scarcely keep up with him as he stalked along the corridor to his room, stumbling as if he could not see, yet swift as an arrow. When they reached his room he turned and closed and locked the door, then laughed as he staggered to the bed. "That will not keep him out, will it?" he said.

"Lindores," said his father, "I expected to find you unconscious. I am almost more frightened to find you like this. I need not ask if you have seen him—"

"Oh, I have seen him. The old liar! Father, promise to expose him, to turn him out—promise to clear out that accursed old nest! It is our own fault. Why have we left such a place shut out from the eye of day? Isn't there something in the Bible about those who do evil hating the light?"

"Lindores! you don't often quote the Bible."

"No, I suppose not; but there is more truth in—many things than we thought."

"Lie down," said the anxious father. "Take some of this wine—try to sleep."

"Take it away; give me no more of that devil's drink. Talk to me—that's better. Did you go through it all the same, poor papa?—and hold me fast. You are warm—you are honest!" he cried. He put forth his hands over his father's, warming them with the contact. He put his cheek like a child against his father's arm. He gave a faint laugh, with the tears in his eyes. "Warm and honest," he repeated. "Kind flesh and blood! and did you go through it all the same?"

"My boy!" cried the father, feeling his heart glow and swell over the son who had been parted from him for years by that development of young manhood and ripening intellect which so often severs and loosens the ties of home. Lord Gowrie had felt that Lindores half despised his simple mind and duller imagination; but this childlike clinging overcame him, and tears stood in his eyes. "I fainted, I suppose. I never knew how it ended. They made what they liked of me. But you, my brave boy, you came out of your own will."

Lindores shivered. "I fled!" he said. "No honour in that. I had not courage to face him longer. I will tell you by-and-by. But I want to know about you."

What an ease it was to the father to speak! For years and years this had been shut up in his breast. It had made him lonely in the midst of his friends.

"Thank God," he said, "that I can speak to you, Lindores. Often and often I have been tempted to tell your mother. But why should I make her miserable? She knows there is something; she knows when I see him, but she knows no more."

"When you see him?" Lindores raised himself, with a return of his first ghastly look, in his bed. Then he raised his clenched fist wildly, and shook it in the air. "Vile devil, coward, deceiver!"

"Oh hush, hush, hush, Lindores! God help us! what troubles you may bring!"

"And God help me, whatever troubles I bring," said the young man. "I defy him, father. An accursed being like that must be less, not more powerful, than we are—with God to back us. Only stand by me: stand by me—"

"Hush, Lindores! You don't feel it yet—never to get out of hearing of him all your life! He will make you pay for it—if not now, after; when you remember he is there, whatever happens, knowing everything! But I hope it will not be so bad with you as with me, my poor boy.

God help you indeed if it is, for you have more imagination and more mind. I am able to forget him sometimes when I am occupied—when in the hunting-field, going across country. But you are not a hunting man, my poor boy," said Lord Gowrie, with a curious mixture of a regret, which was less serious than the other. Then he lowered his voice. "Lindores, this is what has happened to me since the moment I gave him my hand."

"I did not give him my hand."

"You did not give him your hand? God bless you, my boy! You stood out?" he cried, with tears again rushing to his eyes; "and they say—they say—but I don't know if there is any truth in it." Lord Gowrie got up from his son's side, and walked up and down with excited steps. "If there should be truth in it! Many people think the whole thing is a fancy. If there should be truth in it, Lindores!"

"In what, father?"

"They say, if he is once resisted his power is broken—once refused. *You* could stand against him—you! Forgive me, my boy, as I hope God will forgive me, to have thought so little of His best gifts," cried Lord Gowrie, coming back with wet eyes; and stooping, he kissed his son's hand. "I thought you would be more shaken by being more mind than body," he said, humbly. "I thought if I could but have saved you from the trial; and *you* are the conqueror!"

"Am I the conqueror? I think all my bones are broken, father—out of their sockets," said the young man, in a low voice. "I think I shall go to sleep."

"Yes, rest, my boy. It is the best thing for you," said the father, though with a pang of momentary disappointment. Lindores fell back upon the pillow. He was so pale that there were moments when the anxious watcher thought him not sleeping but dead. He put his hand out feebly, and grasped his father's hand. "Warm—honest," he said, with a feeble smile about his lips, and fell asleep.

The daylight was full in the room, breaking through shutters and curtains, and mocking at the lamp that still flared on the table. It seemed an emblem of the disorders, mental and material, of this strange night; and, as such, it affected the plain imagination of Lord Gowrie, who would have fain got up to extinguish it, and whose mind returned again and again, in spite of him, to this symptom of disturbance. By-and-by, when Lindores' grasp relaxed, and he got his hand free, he got up from his son's bedside, and put out the lamp, putting it carefully out of the way. With equal care he put away the wine from the table, and gave the room its ordinary aspect, softly opening a window to let in the fresh air of the morning. The park lay fresh in the early sunshine, still, except for the twittering of the birds, refreshed with dews, and shining in that soft radiance of the morning which is over before mortal cares are stirring. Never, perhaps, had Gowrie looked out upon the beautiful world around his house without a thought of the weird existence which was going on so near to him, which had gone on for centuries, shut up out of sight of the sunshine. The Secret Chamber had been present with him since ever he saw it. He had never been able to get free of the spell of it. He had felt himself watched, surrounded, spied upon, day after day, since he was of the age of Lindores, and that was thirty years ago. He turned it all over in his mind, as he stood there and his son slept. It had been on his lips to tell it all to his boy, who had now come to inherit the enlightenment of his race. And it was a disappointment to him to have it all forced back again, and silence imposed upon him once more. Would he care to hear it when he woke? would he not rather, as Lord Gowrie remembered to have done himself, thrust the thought as far as he could away from him, and endeavour to forget for the moment—until the time came when he would not be permitted to forget? He had been like that himself, he recollected now. He had not wished to hear his own father's tale. "I remember," he said to himself; "I remember"—turning over everything in his mind—if Lindores might only be willing to hear the story when he woke! But then he himself had not been willing when he was Lindores, and he could understand his son, and could not blame him; but it would be a disappointment. He was thinking this when he heard Lindores' voice calling him. He went back hastily to his bedside. It was strange to see him in his evening dress with his worn face, in the fresh light of the morning, which poured in at every crevice. "Does my mother know?" said Lindores; "what will she think?"

"She knows something; she knows you have some trial to go through. Most likely she will be praying for us both; that's the way of women," said Lord Gowrie, with the tremulous tenderness which comes into a man's voice sometimes when he speaks of a good wife. "I'll go and ease her mind, and tell her all is well over—"

"Not yet. Tell me first," said the young man, putting his hand upon his father's arm.

What an ease it was! "I was not so good to my father," he thought to himself, with sudden penitence for the long-past, long-forgotten fault, which, indeed, he had never realised as a fault before. And then he told his son what had been the story of his life—how he had scarcely ever sat alone without feeling, from some corner of the room, from behind some curtain, those eyes upon him; and how, in the difficulties of his life, that secret inhabitant of the house had been present, sitting by him and advising him. "Whenever there has been anything to do: when there has been a question between two ways, all in a moment I have seen him by me: I feel when he is coming. It does not matter where I am—here or anywhere—as soon as ever there is a question of family business; and always he persuades me to the wrong way, Lindores. Sometimes I yield to him, how can I help it? He makes everything so clear; he makes wrong seem right. If I have done unjust things in my day—"

"You have not, father."

"I have: there were these Highland people I turned out. I did not mean to do it, Lindores; but he showed me that it would be better

29

for the family. And my poor sister that married Tweedside and was wretched all her life. It was his doing, that marriage; he said she would be rich, and so she was, poor thing, poor thing! and died of it. And old Macalister's lease—Lindores, Lindores! when there is any business it makes my heart sick. I know he will come, and advise wrong, and tell me—something I will repent after."

"The thing to do is to decide beforehand, that, good or bad, you will not take his advice."

Lord Gowrie shivered. "I am not strong like you, or clever; I cannot resist. Sometimes I repent in time and don't do it; and then! But for your mother and you children, there is many a day I would not have given a farthing for my life."

"Father," said Lindores, springing from his bed, "two of us together can do many things. Give me your word to clear out this cursed den of darkness this very day."

"Lindores, hush, hush, for the sake of heaven!"

"I will not, for the sake of heaven! Throw it open—let everybody who likes see it—make an end of the secret—pull down everything, curtains, walls. What do you say?—sprinkle holy water? Are you laughing at me?"

"I did not speak," said Earl Gowrie, growing very pale, and grasping his son's arm with both his hands. "Hush, boy; do you think he does not hear?"

And then there was a low laugh close to them—so close that both shrank; a laugh no louder than a breath.

"Did you laugh—father?"

"No, Lindores." Lord Gowrie had his eyes fixed. He was as pale as the dead. He held his son tight for a moment; then his gaze and his grasp relaxed, and he fell back feebly in a chair.

"You see!" he said; "whatever we do it will be the same; we are under his power."

And then there ensued the blank pause with which baffled men confront a hopeless situation. But at that moment the first faint stirrings of the house—a window being opened, a bar undone, a movement of feet, and subdued voices—became audible in the stillness of the morning. Lord Gowrie roused himself at once. "We must not be found like this," he said; "we must not show how we have spent the night. It is over, thank God! and oh, my boy, forgive me! I am thankful there are two of us to bear it; it makes the burden lighter—though I ask your pardon humbly for saying so. I would have saved you if I could, Lindores."

"I don't wish to have been saved; but *I* will not bear it. I will end it," the young man said, with an oath out of which his emotion took all profanity. His father said, "Hush, hush." With a look of terror and pain, he left him; and yet there was a thrill of tender pride in his mind. How brave the boy was! even after he had been *there*. Could it be that this would all come to nothing, as every other attempt to resist had done before?

"I suppose you know all about it now, Lindores," said his friend Ffarrington, after breakfast; "luckily for us who are going over the house. What a glorious old place it is!"

"I don't think that Lindores enjoys the glorious old place today," said another of the guests under his breath. "How pale he is! He doesn't look as if he had slept."

"I will take you over every nook where I have ever been," said Lindores. He looked at his father with almost command in his eyes. "Come with me, all of you. We shall have no more secrets here."

"Are you mad?" said his father in his ear.

"Never mind," cried the young man. "Oh, trust me; I will do it with judgment. Is everybody ready?" There was an excitement about him that half frightened, half roused the party. They all rose, eager, yet doubtful. His mother came to him and took his arm.

"Lindores! you will do nothing to vex your father; don't make him unhappy. I don't know your secrets, you two; but look, he has enough to bear."

"I want you to know our secrets, mother. Why should we have secrets from you?"

"Why, indeed?" she said, with tears in her eyes. "But, Lindores, my dearest boy, don't make it worse for *him.*"

"I give you my word, I will be wary," he said; and she left him to go to his father, who followed the party, with an anxious look upon his face.

"Are you coming, too?" he asked.

"I? No; I will not go: but trust him—trust the boy, John."

"He can do nothing; he will not be able to do anything," he said.

And thus the guests set out on their round—the son in advance, excited and tremulous, the father anxious and watchful behind. They began in the usual way, with the old state-rooms and picture-gallery; and in a short time the party had half forgotten that there was anything unusual in the inspection. When, however, they were half-way down the gallery, Lindores stopped short with an air of wonder. "You have had it put back then?" he said. He was standing in front of the vacant space where Earl Robert's portrait ought to have been. "What is it?" they all cried, crowding upon him, ready for any marvel. But as there was nothing to be seen, the strangers smiled among themselves. "Yes, to be sure, there is nothing so suggestive as a vacant place," said a lady who was of the party. "Whose portrait ought to be there, Lord Lindores?"

He looked at his father, who made a slight assenting gesture, then shook his head drearily.

"Who put it there?" Lindores said, in a whisper.

"It is not there; but you and I see it," said Lord Gowrie, with a sigh.

Then the strangers perceived that something had moved the father and the son, and, notwithstanding their eager curiosity, obeyed the dictates of politeness, and dispersed into groups looking at the other

pictures. Lindores set his teeth and clenched his hands. Fury was growing upon him—not the awe that filled his father's mind. "We will leave
the rest of this to another time," he cried, turning to the others, almost
fiercely. "Come, I will show you something more striking now." He made
no further pretence of going systematically over the house. He turned
and went straight upstairs, and along the corridor. "Are we going over
the bedrooms?" some one said. Lindores led the way straight to the old
lumber-room, a strange place for such a gay party. The ladies drew their
dresses about them. There was not room for half of them. Those who
could get in began to handle the strange things that lay about, touching
them with dainty fingers, exclaiming how dusty they were. The window
was half blocked up by old armour and rusty weapons; but this did not
hinder the full summer daylight from penetrating in a flood of light.
Lindores went in with fiery determination on his face. He went straight
to the wall, as if he would go through, then paused with a blank gaze.
"Where is the door?" he said.

"You are forgetting yourself," said Lord Gowrie, speaking over the
heads of the others. "Lindores! you know very well there never was
any door there; the wall is very thick; you can see by the depth of the
window. There is no door there."

The young man felt it over with his hand. The wall was smooth, and
covered with the dust of ages. With a groan he turned away. At this
moment a suppressed laugh, low, yet distinct, sounded close by him.
"You laughed?" he said, fiercely, to Ffarrington, striking his hand upon
his shoulder.

"I—laughed! Nothing was farther from my thoughts," said his friend,
who was curiously examining something that lay upon an old carved
chair. "Look here! what a wonderful sword, cross-hilted! Is it an Andrea?
What's the matter, Lindores?"

Lindores had seized it from his hands; he dashed it against the wall
with a suppressed oath. The two or three people in the room stood aghast.

"Lindores!" his father said, in a tone of warning. The young man dropped the useless weapon with a groan. "Then God help us!" he said; "but I will find another way."

"There is a very interesting room close by," said Lord Gowrie, hastily—"this way! Lindores has been put out by—some changes that have been made without his knowledge," he said, calmly. "You must not mind him. He is disappointed. He is perhaps too much accustomed to have his own way."

But Lord Gowrie knew that no one believed him. He took them to the adjoining room, and told them some easy story of an apparition that was supposed to haunt it. "Have you ever seen it?" the guests said, pretending interest. "Not I; but we don't mind ghosts in this house," he answered, with a smile. And then they resumed their round of the old noble mystic house.

I cannot tell the reader what young Lindores has done to carry out his pledged word and redeem his family. It may not be known, perhaps, for another generation, and it will not be for me to write that concluding chapter: but when, in the ripeness of time, it can be narrated, no one will say that the mystery of Gowrie Castle has been a vulgar horror, though there are some who are disposed to think so now.

EARTHBOUND

CHAPTER I

THERE was but a small party for Christmas at Daintrey. The family were in mourning, which meant more than it usually means, and the whole life of the place was subdued. Nevertheless, the brothers and sisters were young, and were beginning to rise above the impression of the grief which had come upon them. The gloom had lightened a little; they began to forget the details of death, and regard the image of their brother in an aspect more familiar. It was not long since the news had come, and yet already this change had taken place, as was inevitable. The father and mother were less easily cheered; but life must go on even though death interrupts. The girls and boys could not be made to sit like mutes around a grave. They had to rise up again, and go on with their individual existence. Lady Beresford, who was a wise mother, felt and acknowledged this, though her heart was still bleeding. Christmas was coming; and though there could be no Christmas festivities in the ordinary sense of the word, one or two old friends and connections were invited. Sir Robert, for his part, was opposed to the appearance of strangers. He was never very fond of visitors. "What do you want with people here?" he said, with a kind of growl, in which he disguised his grief. "Surely once in a way the girls might get through Christmas without visitors. Christmas! the very idea of these horrible merry Christmases that we shall have to go through makes me ill!"

"I should do without them only too gladly, Robert: but the girls and the boys are too young to be cooped up. Grief is so monotonous, and they are so young. It is not that they love *him* the less; but they must live—for that matter, we must all go on living," she said, keeping with an effort the tears in her eyes. A mother who cannot give herself over to her sorrow, who must work through all her little daily round of duties all the same, and think of the girls' bonnets, and the boots and flannels of the boys at school, and only now and then in a spare moment can shut her door or turn her face to the wall and weep a little over her dead, the tears that have been gathering slowly while she has smiled and talked and kept everything going through the long day—has a hard task when her troubles come; but Lady Beresford bore her burden as sweetly as a woman could, holding up as long as was possible, then stopping to have her cry out, and rising and going on again. Sir Robert became morose with his grief; but she had no time for self-indulgence. And naturally she had her way, and the few were invited whom it had seemed to her good to invite. One of them was Edmund Coventry, who had been a ward of Sir Robert, and now in his manhood calculated upon being a member of the Daintrey party at all those periods which are specially dedicated to home. He was a young man of excellent character and very fair fortune; and, if the truth must be told, the heads of the house at Daintrey had concluded that he would be a very convenient match for Maud, who was the second girl. Perhaps it would be better to say that one of the heads of the house had already perceived and accepted this view. A matchmaking mother is a thing that is supposed on English soil to be extremely objectionable; and yet if she does not think of the welfare of her girls, who is to do it? The French mother considers it her first duty. Lady Beresford was a high-minded Englishwoman, and not a scheming mamma; but she could not shut her eyes to the fact that Edmund Coventry was exactly suited to Maud. And so, among the few who came to spend a very quiet Christmas at Daintrey, and "cheer a sad house," which was what she said in her invitations, Edmund was one of the first of whom she thought.

"Poor boy!" she said, "he has always come here. He has no other place where he will care to go. Of course he will know that it will not be lively. But he is a good boy. I do not think he will mind."

"I am sure, mamma, he will not mind," said Susan, who was the eldest. Susan was going to make a by no means brilliant marriage. She was to marry a young man who was in the diplomatic service, but had no money, and was scarcely the sort of man to be a diplomat; so that the prizes of that profession seemed improbable to him. And she thought it very desirable that Maud and Edmund Coventry should see a good deal of each other. "He will be glad to be with us in our trouble," she said; "he was always fond of Willie." Thus the invitation was given half in love and tender certainty of sympathy, yet half with a certain calculation too.

The other guests were of a very quiet kind—a brother of Sir Robert's, a lonely bachelor; a widowed sister of Lady Beresford's with her little boy and girl; the former clergyman of the parish, who had been Willie's tutor once upon a time; a nephew who was an orphan, and had no home to spend his Christmas in; and Edmund. "He will be the only little bit of liveliness. He will help to cheer us up," Susan said. Her attaché was to come too, but only for a few days. He was one of those to whom social duties were important, and he had a great many visits to pay. But for this mourning they would have been married before now.

Edmund Coventry was a young man who was very well off, and very greatly esteemed. He was twenty-seven—no longer a boy. He had a very nice estate, and a house in town, and no relations to speak of. He was very well-looking, without being handsome, which is perhaps the sort of compromise with nature which is most approved in England. There are a great many people who do not care for unusually handsome men. Beauty is an extravagance, they feel, in the male portion of the world. But Edmund's good looks did not go the length of beauty. He was not a tall, muscular, well-developed hero, but slight, and not more than of middle stature. With all he was an ingratiating, lovable young man, very gentle in manners, very tender in his friendships; no doubt he would make an excellent husband. There was no need to explain to him the position of affairs in the house. He knew all about it, and he sympathised with them in every point. "Mamma hesitated to ask you," said Maud, "because we were to be so quiet." "Could I wish to be anything but quiet?" he said, with a tender half-reproach. "Do you think, after all the happy times here, that I have no feeling." But, indeed, no one had thought that, as Maud made haste to say.

The carols were sung, but with tears in them. The house was dressed as usual with holly and all the decorations of the time; and there was at least a great deal of conversation which lengthened the gloom and silence of the previous period. Even Sir Robert was glad to talk to Mr Lightfoot, who had been the rector in former times. On Christmas night the attempt at games was somewhat doleful as it will be, alas! this Christmas in many a sorrowing and many an anxious house; but the talk and the little bustle of renewed movement did everybody good. The commonplace ghost-stories which are among the ordinary foolishnesses of Christmas did not suit with the more serious tone in which their thoughts flowed; but there was some talk among the older people about those sensations and presentiments that seem sometimes to convey a kind of prophecy, only understood after the event, of sorrow on the way; and the young ones amused themselves after a sort with discussions of those new-fangled fancies which have replaced that old favourite lore. They talked about what is called spiritualism, and of many things, both in that fantastic faith and in the older ghostly traditions, which we are all half glad to think cannot be explained. The older people, indeed, unhesitatingly rejected all mediums and supernatural operators of every kind as impostors; but even on this point various members of the party had things to tell which they did not know how to explain. "Is not there some tradition of a ghost about Daintrey?" Mr Lightfoot, the old rector, said, as they all sat in a wide circle round the great glowing fire just before the moment should arrive for bed-candles and general good-nights. There was not very much light in the room, but, large as it was, it was all ruddy and brilliant with the blaze of the great cheerful fire.

"Nothing of the sort," said Sir Robert emphatically. It was he who was most strong as to the whole thing being an imposition, and who "did not believe a word" of the stories he was told.

"I believe there is something—very vague," said Lady Beresford. But there was a meaning look exchanged between them, and the talk suddenly came to an end.

And by and by the ladies went all flocking out of the room, carrying their lights, like a procession of the wise virgins in the parable. But their black dresses made that procession a sad one, though the soft bloom of the young faces came out with even more effect when the light found nothing else to dwell upon. The young men found a little relief from the gravity of the conversation in the smoking-room, where Mr Beresford the elder, the uncle of the party, discoursed upon town and its charms, and congratulated himself that he was not like his brother Robert, the head of the family, and compelled to pass his winters in the middle of those damp acres of park. "It would kill me in a year," Mr Beresford said. On the whole they were all glad that the worst was over, and Christmas got safely done with for that year.

CHAPTER II

Edmund showed no inclination to cut his visit short; he stayed on after Uncle Reginald had returned to his dear club and his rooms in St James's Street, and the attaché had gone on upon his round of visits, and young Beresford, the cousin, had returned to his work. The eldest of the sons at home was over twenty; the other two were boys at school. And Susan and Maud and little Edie were the girls. It could not be a very sad house, after all, with all that youth in it; and on the whole Daintrey began to turn round as it were, like the earth when a new day is breaking, turning itself to meet the light. Edmund was very much at home and very comfortable, and he was pleased to think that he was doing them good, as Lady Beresford told him with a smile of tender gratitude. It had not yet occurred to him that of all people in the world Maud was the one who would suit him most exactly for a wife. But he was in a very promising way for making that discovery, which had already faintly gleamed upon the consciousness of Maud herself as neither unlikely nor unpleasant. They saw a great deal of each other, though not a bit too much. They were like brother and sister, Lady Beresford said; which was quite true: and yet there was always a possibility of something more.

Daintrey was a handsome house of no particular period, built almost due east and west like a church. The front entrance was by a square court shut in by a screen-wall built between the two wings. At the back the wings were very shallow projecting but slightly from the *corps de logis*. On the south side of the house was a green terrace, as high as the windows of the sitting-rooms, ascended by handsome marble steps ornamented with vases as in an Italian garden and separated by the brilliant parterres of the flower-garden from the house. Running along the upper end of the garden and connecting it with the west end of the house was the lime-tree walk, a noble bit of avenue at right angles with the terrace. Both of these were beautiful—but the little square corner which connected them was not beautiful. Here, for no apparent reason at all, a wall had been built, of the date of some hundred years back, a high brick wall, quite out of place, screening in a square and rather gloomy angle of grass, in the midst of which stood a high pedestal surmounted by a large stone vase. Whether this was meant to commemorate anything, or whether it was merely supposed to be ornamental, in the days of George III, nobody could tell; but that it was very funereal and ugly was certain. In the side of this wall farthest from the house was a door which opened into the byway through the park. Perhaps the wall had been built to stop some right of way; perhaps—but there is little use in multiplying peradventures. There stood the wall built to shut out no one knew what; there loomed aloft the funeral urn upon its pedestal raised to commemorate no one knew what. Sometimes the door would be locked by a sulky gardener, and the key had to be hunted for in the house and out of it, high and low. At such moments Sir Robert, especially if he had himself to wait, would vow that he would throw down the wall and abolish both urn and door. But Sir Robert was an absolute Tory in action, though something of a Liberal in politics; and threatened walls live long, especially when there is no reason why they should live.

Edmund had gone out with the intention of walking to the village one of these wintry afternoons. There had been talk of skating, but the ice was not quite solid enough for skating, and his errands to the village were manifold. He were going to see about Maud's skates, which wanted something done to them. He was going to the Rectory to tell the new rector, who was young and a great athlete, to join the party at the pond tomorrow if the frost "held"; and he had other little commissions to do. When there is nothing better to be done it is something for a man to have commissions in the village—it gives him a reason for his walk; it makes him feel that he is not absolutely without an occupation. The boys were all about the pond, helping it to freeze, as the keeper said—watching, at least, with the most anxious eyes, how this process went on. Edmund came out at the western door of the house facing a low red sun, which shone into his eyes, casting long level gleams of light across the grass and dying it orange. He was very lighthearted today, with a feeling that poor Willie Beresford had died long ago, and that life had begun again, and that the prospects of existence were opening out. Perhaps it was Maud, whose sweetness and pleasant society had suggested to him long stretches of happy life to come. He went out, glad even of the sharpness of the air, pleased to hear the crackling under his feet which betokened the frost, and admiring the fairy whiteness in which the great trees had robed themselves. All lit up with those red rays, with warm and gorgeous belts of colour upon the sky, and every prospect of cold and fine weather, the things most desirable when there is a frost and it is Christmas, the prospect round him was of itself exhilarating. How foolish, he thought, of the girls not to come out, to get the benefit of the smart walk through the park, and the keen fresh air which made his countenance glow. Talk of summer! The park at Daintrey was lovely always, but it never was more beautiful than it was now, with that red sunshine lighting up all those stately white giants in their robes of rime. He started lightly, closing the door after him with a cheerful bang, and turning his steps towards the lime-tree walk, through which one great beam of sunshine like red gold had pierced in the opening between the two greatest trees. This looked like a golden bridge cutting the little avenue in two; beyond it there was the shadow of the wall already described which thrust itself straight in front of the low sun.

While Edmund admired this great broad blaze of light he was startled by seeing something move beyond it in the darker part—something white, which he could not make out so long as he was himself in the sun. But when he had crossed that bridge of light he was still more surprised to see in front of him, at the end of the avenue, a woman, a lady, walking along with the most composed and gentle tread. The road was not exactly a private road—all the people from the village, almost everybody who came to Daintrey on foot, used it. But Edmund thought he knew all the people about, and he certainly did not know anyone whose appearance was at all like that of the lady who preceded him to the door in the wall—unless it were one of the girls masquerading; but he had just left the girls with their mother round the fire, and he could not entertain this idea. The dress, too, struck him with great surprise. It was a white dress, with a black mantle round the shoulders, and a large hat: not unlike the kind of costume which people in æsthetic circles begin to affect, but far more real and natural, it seemed to him—though how he could judge at this distance and with only the lady's back visible it would be difficult to tell. The curious thing was that the moment Edmund saw this pretty figure in front of him his heart began to beat. He had the same feeling which a man sometimes has when he suddenly meets a lovely face and says to himself that, please God, this woman is the one woman for him. But such a thing would be absurd when you consider that it was only her back he saw. Yet it made his heart beat; he was seized with a great desire to follow, to "get a good look" at her, to know what she could be doing here and who she was. What had she been doing there? Surely a creature of so much grace, moving like that, dressed like that, could not possibly have been visiting the servants' hall; and that she had not been in the drawing-room he was sure. If she only would turn round at the sound of his step:—but she did not turn round. She moved on as if she heard nothing—across the curious little square, straight to the door in the wall. Come, Edmund said to himself, if she is going to the village I must over-take her. And he did not hurry, feeling sure she could not escape him. He was pleased by the little mystery—Who could it be? But he must find out before he returned, for unknown ladies do not walk about in a park in the country, or go to and fro between the village and the great house, without being easily traceable. What a pretty walk she had! so light that her step was not audible—no creaking and crunching upon fallen twigs and stones and frostbound sod as with him. He was charmed with the pretty graceful figure—certainly a little like Maud, slimmer and not quite so straight, with a pretty droop in it of fragility and dependence, but yet certainly like—younger perhaps, though Maud was but nineteen. He followed her softly, promising to himself to quicken his steps as soon as she should have passed the door in the wall to which she was leading the way. Presently, about two minutes before him, she reached the door; he was so near that he could see her half turn round as if to look who was behind: but, though she must have perceived him, she closed the door upon him as she passed through—not very civil, he thought; but perhaps she was *espiègle*, and could not resist a little merry affront to him, innocently provocative, as is the fashion of girls. He hurried along the few intervening steps of the way, and opened the door. Perhaps after all she knew him; perhaps it *was* Maud, who was very fond of fun in the old days. The smile was almost a laugh on his mouth when he stepped out of the park and let the door swing carelessly behind him—not shutting it elaborately, as she had taken the trouble to do.

Strange, very strange! There was nobody to be seen on the other side of the door; certainly it must be Maud or one of the girls. She had slipped behind a bush, no doubt, to bewilder him. There were several byways running in different directions—one towards the deserted cricket-ground, another towards the keeper's cottage, beside the straight road which led to the village. Probably she had tucked up her dress and made a dart among the brushwood out of sight. He stood for a moment looking after her, now one way, now another, but he could see no one. "I know you," he cried, "I know you; where are you, Maud?" But there was no answer from among the brushwood. Finally, he had to make up his mind that her trick had been successful, that she had got away, and that if he was to execute his commissions in the village he must not lose any time. But he went along with only half the spirit with which he had started, his mind quite absorbed in this adventure. As he resumed his way he met one of the keepers coming in the opposite direction, whom he stopped to ask if he had met a lady on his way. The man looked at him as if he thought him mad, but answered No, he had met no one. "A lady in a white dress and a black mantle," said Edmund. "Lord bless you, sir," said the keeper, "a white dress!"—and then it occurred to Edmund for the first time how entirely inappropriate such a garb was to the season. It must have been one of the girls who had "dressed up," as they used to be so fond of doing in the old days, to give him a fright. And yet in his heart he did not in the least believe this explanation he had given to himself. Even Maud, though he liked her so much, had never excited that sudden and causeless emotion in his heart. It was someone new—someone who had never crossed his path before, and who was destined to work he knew not what commotion in it. But then, who could it be?

"Did you go out after I went out?" he asked when he went back to Daintrey. "Tell me, did you or anyone take a run into the park?"

"Oh, no; mother would not let us go. She said we could not go to skate tomorrow if we went out so late today."

"Or has anyone been here? Did you have any visitors?" Edmund asked, though he knew very well that this could not explain the presence of the lady who must have left the house before he did. Maud looked up at him with her soft blue eyes.

"We have had no one," she said. "We did not stir all the afternoon. Mother had a headache, and we did not wish to leave her. After you went out we sat and talked till the dressing-bell rang. That was all; but why do you suppose we must have had visitors?" Edmund felt—he could scarcely tell why—a little shyness and unwillingness to explain himself.

"Because I met a lady in the park," he said, "and could not make out who she was. Have you any new neighbours since I have been gone?"

Maud shook her head. "Nobody," she said. Nobody had been calling. Nobody had intruded into the neighbourhood. She looked earnestly at the young man, who, for his part, was a little excited by his own questions, but not at all unpleasantly excited.

"I thought for a moment you were playing me a trick. She looked a little like you—that is, her figure looked like you. I did not see her face."

"Like me?" Maud was half pleased, but more surprised. "I play you a trick? I don't think," she said, with a sad look, "that I shall ever do that again."

"But I hope you will a hundred times," said the young man; and this pleased her, though she could not have told why. "But help me to find out who it is," he went on. "I feel annoyed that I don't know everybody, as I used to do. She was dressed in white with a—"

"In white! You must have been dreaming," said Maud, in amazement.

He stopped short again. "That's why I thought it must be you," he said, yet with a little conscious jesuitry, for he had not thought so—indeed, had assured himself that the little stir of his being which he had experienced could only mean that this was some one of a different kind from any he had met before: a new woman, a creature born to influence him. "But it is quite true, and I was not dreaming. She had on a white gown. Something black over her shoulders like, the thing ladies have been wearing lately: I forget how you call it—not a cloak nor a scarf—something put round and knotted behind like this," said Edmund, doing his best to show how, upon himself with his hands.

"A fichu, you mean," said Maud, suffering herself to be betrayed into a smile.

"A fichu, that's the thing; and a large broad hat. But she did not look like art-needlework—she looked quite natural."

"What an interest you must have taken in this lady! When did you meet her? It could not have been anyone coming here, for no one has been here all day."

"I met her—but I did not meet her—I followed her along the lime-tree walk and out by the little corner door."

"How very strange! I cannot think who it can have been. And where did she go after?"

"That is the strangest of all," said Edmund. "She disappeared some-where. That was another reason why I thought it must have been you. I cannot tell where she went. Down by the keeper's cottage, I suppose; but I saw her no more."

"I'll tell you who it was," said Maud, just a little piqued—"it must have been the keeper's niece, who has come for a little change. She is in a dressmaker's in London. Of course she will dress nicely—though to wear *white* on a winter afternoon, trailing across the damp grass—" She laughed again but not so sweetly as before. "This must have been your lady, Edmund, I fear."

"I do not believe it. I cannot believe it," he said, much vexed; but after a good deal of resistance he was brought to allow that as he had only seen her back, and that at a little distance, he could not have any such certainty as he had supposed that she was a lady.

"Besides," said Maud, with a little gentle triumph, "a girl like that may walk like a lady and dress like a lady. She has got to be among ladies most of her time, and to see the best people. Unless you talked to her and found she dropped her h's, or had vulgar ideas, how could you tell? Indeed, sometimes they talk even, just as nicely as we do," said the young lady, more just than many of her kind. This seemed to make an end of the question. At least Edmund could find no more to say; and Lady Beresford, who had observed the long and interesting conversation in which he had been engaged with Maud, gave him a still kinder smile than usual when she bade him good night.

CHAPTER III

Next day the frost held; the pond was bearing, and the whole house turned out to skate—even Sir Robert. Lady Beresford looked on with that indulgent wonder with which a woman regards a man's delight in outdoor amusements, and the charm they exercise over him. She was unfeignedly glad that her husband should be roused from that growling seclusion in the library, which looked like temper and meant grief—glad to the bottom of her heart; and yet there was a wondering in her mind, a sensation of half-grieved, half-smiling surprise. She was glad to get them all out of the house, and said "Thank God!" fervently, that here was something which would take off the strain, which would bring in a little amusement, and help the convalescence of grief which was working itself so quickly in these young people; and then she went up to her own room and shut her door, feeling as if she, who had the best right to it, had got that faithful sorrow all to herself, and uncovered his picture, and read his last letter, and wept out all the tears that had been gathering and gathering. Meanwhile, the rest had got out of the shadow for the moment, and the pond was a merry scene. Sir Robert skated about very solemnly at first, taking long turns round the island that lay at one end of the long piece of water; but by and by he began to help little Edie and give directions to Tom. This diversion filled up the whole day and the next. Edmund had been half vexed, half irritated by the supposed discovery that his white lady was the keeper's niece, especially as Maud had already given him several little playful reminders and he determined, accordingly, that he would not allow himself to think any more of the little figure which had so charmed him. Of course it was mere imagination, nothing else—a girl's back, in a black fichu and white gown. What could anyone make of that? There was in his mind a lurking purpose of coming home from the ice some evening by the keeper's cottage, just to see; but even that he did not carry out for those two days. On the third afternoon, however, by some chance, he was left to come home alone. The others had set out before he was ready. He heard their voices sounding cheerily through the frosty night air, a good way on, upon the path before him, when he completed his last long whirl round the island, during which Sir Robert had got impatient, and summoned all his flock about him. They had all lingered to the last moment possible, as there were signs of the frost breaking. It was dark, so dark that Edmund could scarcely see to take his skates off, and all the hollows of the park were full of mist, and the sky overspread and blurred, and covered with clouds. It was clearer in the east, however, and there an early pale-eyed young moon, with a certain eagerness about her, as though full of impatience to see what was going on in the earth, had got up hastily in a bit of blue. She touched the mists, and made them poetical, gradually lightening over the milky expanse of the park, in which the trees stood up like bands of shadows.

Suddenly it came into Edmund's head that this was the very moment to carry out his intention. He took up his skates hastily, and walked round by the other end of the pond towards the cottage of Ferney the keeper. The moon, getting brighter every moment, threw the whole little settlement of this small habitation in the midst of the park and woods, into brilliant relief. There was a sound of dogs and human voices populating the stillness, and the cluster of low red roofs, the smoke from the chimneys, the cheerful blaze of firelight out of the uncovered windows, seemed to cheer and warm the whole landscape. Half ashamed of his own artifice, Edmund stopped at the door to give some message to the keeper. In the room beyond he saw a young woman seated at a table sewing, the light of a candle throwing a full light upon her. She was dressed in black, with the usual white collar and little locket—a handsome, pale girl: and as Edmund stared in, forgetful of politeness in his curiosity, she got up, with a reserve that was in itself coquettish, and walked to the other end of the room. When he saw this movement he had almost laughed aloud. That the lady of the lime-walk! They might as well have told him that good Mrs Ferney, with her stout, matronly bulk, and white apron, was the lady he had met. He went off, pleased with his own discrimination, pleased that he had not been mistaken, wondering if he should ever meet her again anywhere. He felt sure that he would know her, wherever he might see her, by her figure and by her walk.

He asked the keeper some trivial question to justify his pause at the house, then walked on, whistling, with cheerful speed, till he came to the little corner door, as it was called; but he had scarcely got within, when he checked himself abruptly. The moon was shining full across the green terrace and the empty beds of the flower-garden, streaming upon this little forlorn angle and its big ugly urn. Full in its light, softly crossing in front of the big pedestal, her pretty figure relieved against it, within half a dozen paces of him, coming towards him, was the lady he had seen before. Her dress was the same, dead white, with the black fichu, all frills and fringe, tied behind; a broad hat, thrown back a little from her face. His heart gave a great jump when he saw that in a moment he must pass close, and that she could not in any way conceal herself from him. He almost stopped short, but she came on softly without embarrassment, without alarm. Certainly she was like Maud: a tender little pensive face, with soft, very large eyes—which must be blue, Edmund felt—a pensive half-smile about the mouth. She was neither startled by the sight of him nor did she take a single step out of his way, but went on at the same composed pace. She had almost passed him, when he bethought himself to pull off his hat. This seemed to give her a little movement of surprise. She half turned her head to look at him, and the half-smile on her delicate lips brightened a little. It was too slight, too evanescent, to be called pleasure; and yet it was something like pleasure that lighted up the gentle face. Then she passed on, and in another moment had gone out by the door. He had not opened it for her, as politeness required. He had been too much taken by surprise—bewildered by the sudden appearance. Even now he stood still, dazed, not knowing what to do, puzzled how to address a lady whom he did not know, to intrude into an acquaintance whether she wished it or not, but yet feeling it impossible to let her go like this. He stood—was it for a moment, or longer?—hesitating, wondering: then rushed after her, meaning to say that she could not possibly cross the park at this hour alone, that she must permit him to accompany her. In his haste he made a dash at the door, threw it open, plunged out into the wide white desert where she had gone. The moon shone full upon all the breadth of the park. The ground was higher here, and there was less mist; the pathway wound along for a hundred yards or so fully visible; but no one was there. "Again!" he cried, speaking the word aloud in his confusion and annoyance. The bushes indeed clustered thick upon the way to the keeper's cottage. Could this be a second niece, a daughter, another young woman living there? He was so vexed, so disappointed, so tantalised, that he did not know what to do or say.

"Has Ferney a daughter as well as a niece?" he said to Maud, singling her out again, her mother remarked, from all the rest.

"A daughter? Oh, no; nobody but Jane. They brought her up; but that is all. Why do you take so much interest in the Ferneys, Edmund? You have always known them, ever since you first came here."

Then Edmund told his story. How once more he had seen the strange lady: how she had passed through the door, and once more gone down the keeper's way; or, at least, so he supposed. Had she gone to the village he must have seen her. This time Maud became excited, too. She took her mother into council. "Mother, do you know anyone who has lately come to the village, or to any of the houses about? I should think she must be a crazy person. Edmund has met her twice in the Lime-tree Walk, in a white dress—"

"Edmund must have been dreaming," Lady Beresford said.

"Not any more than I am now. I saw her quite plain tonight. There is something in her air, generally, that reminds me of Maud. I thought it was Maud herself playing me a trick the first time I saw her."

"And dressed in white. Such an extraordinary thing!" said Maud. "Who can it be?"

This incident of the dress moved the ladies more than it did the man. He had to explain to them exactly what kind of a dress it was that she wore. "Though I daresay he has not a notion," said Lady Beresford. "Probably it is only some light colour. Men never know—"

A slight look of uneasiness got into her face. She listened as the dress was described with reluctance, trying to change the subject; but the others were very much interested. "A dress not like anything you ladies wear now," Edmund said.

"A dress, I should say, very like what the art people wear. It must be some artistic person who has taken lodgings in the village," said Mrs Cole, who was Lady Beresford's sister. "Depend upon it that is what she is, an art-student, not rich, living in some little rooms, studying the effects of a winter landscape, or something of that sort. Perhaps Ferney has let her his parlour. Hasn't he got a parlour? That is what this strange visitor must be."

This was not quite so objectionable to Edmund's feelings as the other guess, and the talk got quite animated about his lady. Only Lady Beresford did not quite like it. "Please not to say anything about her to Sir Robert," she said; "he is not fond of strangers about." And she was visibly uneasy. But no one could tell why.

As for Edmund himself, his mind was very much occupied with this pretty vision. He thought, with a thrill all through him, of the soft look of surprised pleasure that had come over her face as he took off his hat. Why should she be surprised? It was a thing any gentleman ought to have done, meeting her there, all alone, a stranger in the place, where he was himself at home. The thing he regretted was that he had not been a little quicker, that he had not followed her out, and asked her to let him see her safely across the park. Perhaps she would not have liked that. Perhaps the suggestion that it was not safe to walk about alone might have offended her. But she did not look at all like one of those women who assert a right to walk alone, and to do whatever pleases them. Anyhow, he would not let her escape him so another time; and no doubt he would meet her again. After this he was continually haunting the Lime-tree Walk. The last day of the skating he made an excuse to return early, but she was not there; and, indeed, he did not see her again till his heart had been sick with disappointment on two or three occasions. The frost broke up; then came a day or two of rain, and all the bondage of the ice melted, and the paths ran in little torrents, and a few feeble spikes of snowdrops began to come up in the empty flower-beds. The weather grew mild all of a sudden. And one day the hounds met near Daintrey, and all the party went out. They came back in the afternoon, tired, and damp, and soiled with the mud; but when the others went in to be warmed and dried, and made comfortable, having had enough of air and exercise for the day, Edmund lingered outside, as he now always did, as long as he could get any excuse for doing so. And this time he was rewarded. In the middle of the Lime-tree Walk he saw her suddenly coming towards him. One moment there had seemed to be nobody about. He turned his head to see what was meant by some little stir behind him; and when he turned again she was there, walking towards him, with her soft, gentle, composed tread. Her hands were clasped before her. Her white dress trailed a little behind her, but seemed to have no stain upon it, or mark of the wet. Her head was a little thrown back. Ah, yes! surely they were blue, those eyes; they could not have been anything but blue. And she had very little colour in her face, just enough to make it lifelike, and give an appearance of health and perfection; no sickliness, no incompleteness, was in the hue. The soft little half-smile was still upon the lips—lips that were like rose-coral, not very red, but warm and soft. She came on without paying any attention to Edmund, as if, indeed, she did not see him. And this piqued him a little. But his heart leaped so at the sight of her that he was not capable of cool judgment or criticism. This time his mind was made up. If it was rude, he was very sorry, but he must speak to her, whatever happened. He stopped suddenly when they met, and once more took off his hat. And then, in a moment, like the sun rising, that expression of pleasure came to her face. The smile grew brighter. She stopped, too, and looked at him with such satisfaction, such a tender interest in her eyes, that he was utterly confounded, and stood gazing at her, the words that he had meant to say failing him. Rude! no, evidently she did not think him rude. A gentle delight seemed to spread over her—affectionate pleasure, as if of a happiness she had vainly expected, and for which she was thankful beyond words. After all, it was she who spoke first. She said, in the softest little musical voice, a little thin, but sweet, like the cooing of a dove; and what she said was as remarkable in its simplicity as the fact that she was the first to begin the acquaintance. "So you see me!" was, in tones of gentle pleasure, what she said.

"See you!—indeed this is now the third time that I have the pleasure of seeing you," said Edmund eagerly. "The last night I could not forgive myself for not asking if I might walk home with you. It was very late for you to walk alone across the park."

To this she answered nothing, but looked at him with the softest, caressing looks, as if it were a pleasure to her to hear his voice; and yet the perfect modesty, simplicity, and innocence of the virginal countenance uplifted to him, made every thought but those of respect and even reverence impossible to Edmund. At the same time he was slightly abashed by this steadfast look, which might have made a vain man complacent, but for something in it of unapproachable purity and isolation which gave the beholder a sense of awe. Edmund did not know how to go on. It was more difficult than could be told to proceed in the conversation. Phrases about the happiness of making her acquaintance—about the desire of the ladies at Daintrey to know if, they could be of service to the stranger, which he had (though totally without authority) conned and prepared, no longer seemed within his power of utterance. He stammered forth something about "Lady Beresford—would be glad to see you—to be of use." To which she shook her head half sadly, half with a kind of shadowy amusement. "You have come to the neighbourhood lately?" he said at last.

"No; oh, no; I have been here—about Daintrey—a long, long time." These strange words were interrupted by a little faint laugh like an echo, like a laugh in music, the most spiritual liquid roll of soft words. "I have been a long time here."

Edmund grew more and more confused. "If that was so I must have seen you," he said; "but perhaps you think a little time long. It would be natural, you are so young."

"Nineteen," she said; "I never was any more than nineteen; but it is a long, long time ago."

Then it began to dawn upon Edmund, though it was an idea he received with the greatest reluctance, that this tender, beautiful creature must be, not mad—that was too harsh a word—but like Ophelia, distraught. "Do you come out alone?" he said, gently. "Is there no one with you in these winter nights? it is dreary and cold in the park. I don't think you ought to be alone."

She smiled upon him, again not saying anything for a moment. Then she said suddenly and very low, "I am always about here."

"You mean you are fond of this walk," Edmund said.

Again she smiled. "I go all about," she said, very softly, "sometimes into the house; but no one sees me. That is what made me so glad when you spoke. I have seen you often, but you are confused with the other ones. So many, so many I have seen. Now that you have spoken to me I will always remember which is you."

Certainly she must be distraught. He was very sorry for her, very much touched by her, but also, though why he could not tell, a little alarmed, his heart beating very unsteadily and plunging in his breast.

"I hope," he said, "not out of any intrusive or impertinent feeling, but for safety, I hope you will let me see you home."

Again he heard the little roll of the laugh, so utterly soft and distant; but she made no reply. "I have seen a great many, a great many," she said; "they all come and go, but they do not see me. That is the punishment I have. The house is altered. But I take a great interest in it: I was always fond of it." Then the innocent little laugh was succeeded by a gentle, scarcely audible sigh.

All this time the evening had been darkening, the sun had set, the mists were creeping up once more in all the hollows. Edmund felt a chill run through him. "It is getting late," he said, "and cold. If you are going to the village it is a long walk. Forgive me, but I think you should let me take you home."

She looked at him almost mocking, but with such a tender version of mockery; then turned and went towards the door in the wall. Her movements were so gentle and light that Edmund felt himself noisy, stumbling, awkward in every step he took. Her little feet seemed scarcely to touch the earth. He walked on beside her confused, trembling, afraid, yet full of a strange happiness; and the moon, which had been rising all the time, came shining upon them through the lofty, slender lime branches. It seemed to him in his bewildered condition, that it was like some poem he had read, or some dream he had dreamt, to walk thus in this measured soft cadence, with the moon upon their heads all broken and chequered by the anatomy of the great trees, like dark lines traced upon the sky. Then they came into the full moonlight, in the corner where the urn stood upon its pedestal. It seemed to Edward that she went more slowly, as if lingering. "This is a gloomy corner," he said, forcing himself to speak. For the charm of the silence had come over him, and words seemed hard things to disturb those soft moments as they flowed away.

"Not gloomy to me. I was always fond of it. When it was put up we were all pleased. That was what was wrong in me. You know," she said, with her little soft laugh, "I was so fond of the house and the trees, and everything that was our own. I thought there was nothing better, nothing so good. I was all for the earth, and nothing more. That is why I am here so much." She paused, and gave a little sigh: but then added, brightening, "It is not hard: when you are used to it, when now and then you meet with someone who sees you, it is not so hard. I am a little sad sometimes, but very happy now."

And again she looked at him with that look of tender pleasure—enough to turn any man's head. Edmund's went round and round—he could say nothing more, but stammer, repeating himself, "It is a long walk; you must let me see you safely home across the park."

She answered him only by that low laugh, but even softer, sweeter, than before. Then he opened the door for her. As she passed through she smiled upon him with a little wave of her hand. For his part he had put his foot on a soft piece of turf sodden with the rain, and it took him a minute to extricate the heel of his boot which had sunk into it. A minute, scarcely so much as a minute, but when he stepped out eagerly after her, his head full of that walk across the park, she was nowhere to be seen. One minute, not so much. Where was she? How had she managed to elude him? He was wild with disappointment and anger. Once more he made a hurried search behind all the bushes, in every little clump of brushwood. There was not a trace of her; though he thought once he heard her low melodious laugh. Was it a trick she was playing him? What was the meaning of it? But when he had walked about for nearly an hour, Edmund had to go back to the house disappointed. Once more she had escaped him; his head was giddy, his heart beating loud, his whole being full of agitation and excitement. What did it mean? and who was she, this mysterious girl?

Edmund felt like a man in a dream as he came downstairs, and sat among the party at table, where the meal went on amid cheerful conversation. For himself he seemed quite incapable of taking any share in it. It flowed round him like something in which he had no voice. Afterwards the ladies asked him in the drawing-room, their voices coming to him faintly as out of a cloud, whether he had seen the white lady again. But it was impossible to him to speak of her tonight. He answered briefly, saying no, though it was not true; and pretended to have letters to write, that universal excuse for pre-occupation. But when he escaped from the circle on this pretence, he did not write any letters. He sat in his room, opening his window, though the night was not so balmy as to make this desirable; and with his head supported by his hands, gazed out upon the great darkness round. The moon set early, and the skies were veiled with clouds, and nothing was discernible but the dark outlines of the trees, and a great dimness of space and air. Now and then he thought he saw her below, a flicker of white moving about, as if it might have been her dress; and it was only by strenuous resolution that he kept himself from rushing wildly into the night, with a kind of mad hope of meeting her. Then he gathered together in his mind all that she had said, which was so sweet, so tender, and yet, God help him, so wild. "When you meet with someone who sees you"—"I was nineteen—but it is long, long ago." What could it mean? Was it, indeed, the sweet bells jangled out of tune, of some lovely nature? Edmund's eyes filled with tears. He said to himself that if it was so, he would take more care of her than anyone; he would be her tender protector, her keeper to preserve her from everything that could hurt her innocence. What a strange fatal charm was it that had fallen upon him thus unawares? He could think of nothing else. Ophelia—but far more sweet in her madness—pure as a vision, with that dear look of happiness in her face. Could anything be more sweet than that she should be happy when he spoke to her, her face full of pleasure at the sound of his voice? Edmund's heart melted altogether at this thought. But those sweet fairy-tricks should not suffice her another day. He would find her, whatever might happen; he would secure her beyond all possibility of escape. Her reason, what did it matter about her reason. Love would supply the place. And thus he spent the evening in a kind of soft delirium, able to think of nothing, to see and hear nothing, but his new-born yet all-absorbing love.

CHAPTER IV

Edmund did not sleep all night. He rose excited and restless, in the dim cold dawn of the winter morning; he was silent as a ghost at the cheerful breakfast table; he excused himself from all the occupations of the day. He had "things to do," he said; and in fact he was impatient and unhappy until he found an opportunity to steal out unseen by anyone. He went hastily through the Lime-tree Walk, following exactly the course he had taken the previous evening with *her*. There he contemplated the park in the clear daylight with wondering and anxious scrutiny. The little road down by the back of the green terrace, which led to the keeper's cottage, was the only one by which she could possibly have gone. A little plantation of young trees was at the corner, and as it wound downwards, though the declivity was slight, there were various scattered bushes, furze and broom, and a few old knotted hawthorn thickets, darned out and in with pendants of brambles, showing here and there a red leaf still. There any mischievous girl could have played hide-and-seek with a petulant lover for hours together. Edmund felt a little lightening of the anxiety which possessed him as he saw these interruptions of the way. But if it was indeed by this way she had gone, she could not have afterwards emerged into the park without passing at least by Ferney's cottage. Perhaps, as someone had suggested, she was a lodger there after all. He went slowly towards it, examining every corner of the way, and every bit of cover. His search was so slow and minute that it took him a long time. He emerged upon Ferney's little enclosure almost before he was aware.

When his step was heard on the gravel, someone came to the window to see who it was, and Edmund heard a little exclamation. "Aunt! here's that gentleman again." Was he, then, coming to some real elucidation of all his wonderings? Mrs Ferney came to the half-open door in answer to his summons. He thought she looked a little disturbed. He spoke peremptorily, to leave her no room for thought, or settling beforehand what she was to say. "I want to know if you have a lodger—a lady living in your house?"

Mrs Ferney's countenance grew more disturbed than ever. "Well, sir—, no, Mr Edmund, I've got no lodger. There's Ferney's niece staying on a visit."

"Is that your niece sitting in the room on the right hand?" When Edmund said this, a chair was hastily drawn back out of his range of vision, and a voice said, "La!"

"I mean a totally different person," he cried, with a little impatience; "a lady; very young; very slight; with blue eyes; in a white dress, and something black round her shoulders."

Mrs Ferney was gazing at him with wide open eyes, but a visible air of relief. "No, indeed, sir; nothing of the sort. Not a soul lives here but Ferney and me, and, for the present, Ada Jane."

"Where, then, can she live?" he said half to himself. Mrs Ferney thought he had taken leave of his senses. She stood and gazed at him with bewildered looks, making a curtsey, and much relieved to see that he was not "after" Ada Jane. Edmund walked away without so much as a glance at the window where Ada Jane was lurking expectant. He went to the village, where he walked about not knowing what to do, looking in at every window. He could not stop everybody he met there to ask them did they know where he could find a lady with blue eyes and in a white gown? He did the only other thing that was practicable in the circumstances. He went to see the Rector, whom he asked that question, and to whom he told his little story. The Rector was a young man, and he was sympathetic. He thought of all the ladies within twenty miles, and described them, without finding any one who at all resembled the lady whom Edmund sought. "Besides," the young enquirer had still so much reason left in him as to say, "what would it advantage me if Miss Ingestre, who lives fifteen miles off, were like her? Miss Ingestre would not come here and wander about the Lime-tree Walk." So that nothing was to be made of it in any direction. When he left the Rectory the short afternoon was beginning to wane. He saw nobody along all the length of the way, and when he came to the door in the wall found it locked; evidently she had not passed that way today.

It was again a misty afternoon; the sun veiled in clouds. Edmund went down by the path that led towards Ferney's, and got across the brook and round by the corner of the house, which was a way practicable to one who had been a boy there, and knew all about the surroundings and by-ways of the place. What he meant was to hurry round to the conservatories, in which he was likely to find the head gardener, and get the key from him. What if she should come to her favourite walk and find it closed against her? He was breathless with haste scrambling up the bank, rushing along at his most rapid pace, lest this foolish obstacle should prevent their meeting: when suddenly, in the midst of his excitement, all at once his heart stood still. In spite of the locked door, she was standing there. It was earlier than he had ever seen her before. His heart stopped short, then leapt into wilder beating than ever. He did not ask himself how she got through. Why should he think of any such trivial obstacle? She was there, that was all he thought of; and this time it was evident that she was looking for him. She waved her hand to him with the prettiest gesture. She was standing against the pedestal, her white dress standing out from that background. He noticed for the first time how white and pure was the fullness of the flounce where it fell upon the grass, without a mark on it of the wetness around. This seemed to him quite natural, an exquisite quality, somehow, in herself, which kept everything about her white and pure.

"I was going," he said, flushed and eager, "to get the key. I thought you would wonder to find it shut. But you came through before it was shut, I suppose."

She smiled. It seemed to be a rule with her to answer none of his questions. She looked at him with a sort of innocent admiration, mixed with the pleasure in her face. "It is so long since I have spoken to anyone—since I have seen anyone run to meet me," she said. "I wonder how it is that you, out of them all—"

"Yes," he said, taking up her words, "that is what I cannot understand, how I, of all the people in Daintrey, should have been so happy as to meet you. We are like old friends now, are we not? we have seen each other so often. I am Edmund Coventry, once Sir Robert's ward, and free of the house. Might I ask your name?"

There was no embarrassment in her face. From first to last she was never embarrassed, but always full of sweet composure: and her smile seemed to express a hundred different feelings. There was amusement in it, and a little regret, and always that affectionate pleasure. "I was Maud," she said, quite simply. Edmund could not understand why she should put her name in the past tense, and it gave him a subtle, little thrill of pain, he could scarcely tell why.

"Maud—it is the very sweetest name," he said, with a half-adoring passion; "but what else? You will not let me say Maud. Tell me your other name."

What a strange smile it was! It seemed to go on like an accompaniment in music, confusing the listener who was so anxious to gather every word that came from her lips. He did not seem to know that she had not said anything, so full was the air of that sweet influence. A little while after he began again to speak himself.

"These meetings have made a change in my life," he said. "I was taking the future quite easily, not thinking what it was to bring forth; but now I see that one ought to select one's path, to settle, to take up the more serious part of life. All this I have learned since I have known you; since I have loved you," he added, very low, looking earnestly in her face.

She took the confession quite calmly; not a tinge of additional colour, not the slightest shyness or confusion appeared in her. She kept her quiet, sweet, ease of manner undisturbed. And what was Edmund to say more? He felt somehow baffled, helpless, before this invulnerable calm.

"Won't you say anything to me?" he cried; "I don't know who you are, or where you are living, but I love you, Maud. Do not be angry."

"Oh, no! Not angry," she said, in her soft voice; "only you cannot understand. I am not here to make friends, though I have always wished that someone might see me and speak. And before you spoke I had noticed you; I thought to myself, This one surely—this one surely! There was something about you; but there had been so many, so many before," she said, with an innocent, wistful look, like the unconscious protest against neglect, yet acquiescence of a child.

"But you will give me an answer, Maud? I love you, sweet. I do not know," said Edmund, with passion, "what has happened to you; what it is that makes you wander like this; but I will not mind, whatever it is. I will take care of you; I will watch over you; it will make no difference to me. Do you not understand me, dear?" He put out his hand to take hers, to secure her attention, to show her how serious he was. And then Edmund felt as if the whole misty heaven and earth were going round about him. He could not find the hand he sought. It was as if some spell prevented him from touching her. He felt again more baffled, more confounded, and hopelessly kept back, than words could say.

"You must not ask me questions," she made answer, softly, after a pause. "It is not permitted to answer questions. I am here—for a time. I have been here no one could tell how long. We do not count as you do. If I told you more than this you would not understand."

"I will understand if it is about you. But, Maud, Maud, answer me first. Give me your hand. Won't you give me your hand?"

A look of trouble came into her face; yet so soft, so shadowy, that it did not seem pain. The smile did not go out of her eyes. She shook her head gently, standing so near him, her hands crossed, clasping each other. He had only to put out his arms and take her into them, but he could not. She was close, close to him, and yet—what was it that stood between? Not the mild refusal with which she shook her head; something that chilled his blood in its ardour, and made his heart contract with awe. He put out his hands beseeching, but seemed to come no nearer; and yet she did not draw back, nor move away from him. Edmund did not seem to himself to know what he was saying, what was happening, and yet he heard and meant every word that rushed to his lips. "Sweet! I will understand anything; I know there must be something strange. Whatever it is I accept it, I accept it! Say you will love me, Maud! Say you will—marry me!"

What happened? One of the Beresford boys, as Edmund dimly perceived, had been approaching, rushing along towards the door; but somehow the intruder had made no difference to him, and had not stopped him in his impassioned suit. At this moment, however, the boy rushed headlong past, dashing against her, touching Edmund's coat as he plunged along. The lovely, gentle figure was straight in his way. Edmund caught him by the throat with a fury beyond words.

"The lady!" he stammered out; "you brute, do you not see the lady?" and flung him wildly to a distance upon the wet ground.

Fred Beresford was altogether taken by surprise. He was not a boy of a patient temper, and he was in a hurry; but the wildness of the other bewildered him. He picked himself up, and came forward wondering, to where Edmund stood, pale as death, and gazing wildly about him. Fred's wrath was entirely quailed at this sight. "What is it?" he asked, quite timidly and softly laying his hand on Edmund's arm.

The young man was trembling in every limb; he did not seem able to move. His eyes were staring wildly here and there. There was no softening dusk as yet to conceal anything; all was white daylight, cold and pale and clear. When he felt Fred's touch he turned upon him for one second, furious, violently thrusting him away. "You have killed her!" he said; and then clutching the boy again, "Where is she? where is she? where is she?" Edmund cried. Fred felt the whole trembling weight of his companion upon him. His boyish strength swayed under the burden.

"Are you ill, old fellow?" he said, alarmed. "What is the matter? I thought you were saying poetry. I don't know what you mean about a lady."

"You have killed her," he said, wildly clutching the boy's throat; then, all in a moment, he softened, and burst into a transport of cries. "Where is she? where is she? Maud! Maud! come back to me," cried the young man, with a voice of despair. There was nothing to be seen, Fred swore afterwards, nothing, except the big stone pedestal with the urn upon it, and behind, the mossy old wall.

"I say—you are ill," said the boy. "Come in, that's the best thing to do; come in to mother. Maud's there with her, if it's Maud you want. Edmund, come along."

Edmund broke from him, pushing him away. He went all round the pedestal, wandering about it, feeling it with his hands. Then he held out those hands piteously, appealing, into the empty air. "Maud! Maud!" he cried. "Don't laugh at me; don't play with me," as if he were talking to somebody, the astonished boy described. Fred at last ran in alarmed to the library where Sir Robert was sitting. "I wish you'd come out, father, into the Lime-tree Walk to Edmund—he's gone mad," the boy cried.

When Sir Robert went out, Edmund was standing leaning against one of the lime trees, gazing at the green space which contained the pedestal and the urn. When he was entreated to come in, he answered quite gently, that if he only waited patiently she would be sure to come back. "This is where she always comes. She is fond of this place," he said. "There are things I don't understand about her, but she will come. I am sure she will come if you will only let me wait." "Tell me, my good fellow, all about it," Sir Robert said. He was a kind man when his attention was fully roused, and now he remembered that his wife had told him something of a strange lady whom Edmund had seen in the park. Edmund told him the whole story, standing there with his back against the tree. He asked Sir Robert first to stand close to him, almost behind him, that nothing might interfere with his clear vision round. And then he told him all. "She always tricks me," he said, with an attempt at a laugh. "She is so innocent—like a child. How she got away this time I cannot tell. There seems nothing to hide behind here. But she always does it. I confess, sir," he added, with great candour and gravity, "there are many things about her I do not understand; but whatever they are, I am ready to accept them all."

"Have you ever seen her more than once in the same day?" asked Sir Robert. "No?" "Then come with me, Edmund, it is of no use waiting. I think I can tell you something about her." Sir Robert put his arm into that of the young man. He scarcely knew himself what he meant; but it was clear that something must be done. And Edmund yielded to the mingled reason and temptation. No, he had never seen her twice the same day; and to know about her, was not that what he wanted most in the world? He suffered himself, after one long glance around, to be led away.

Sir Robert took him upstairs to an old gallery which he remembered very well as a child, which had been given up to the children's romps on wet days, a place full of pictures, the accumulations of an old house—all kinds of grim portraits of early Beresfords. There were some good pictures among them, he had always remembered to have heard said, and so long as Edmund could recollect there had been an intention expressed of disinterring these treasures. "I don't know where it is exactly; I don't know if it is still here. It was by a pupil of Sir Joshua's, and with something of his feeling. I have always intended to bring it downstairs," Sir Robert said, rummaging as he spoke among old dusty canvasses. Edmund stood by listless, in the lull of reaction after his great excitement. It was not here, he thought, that anything would be told him about *her*. He did not understand what his companion meant. He was only waiting, feeling hazily that he had some further trial of patience to go through, not very anxious now for anything but the end of the day, and that another might dawn, on which, perhaps, he might see her again.

"Was she like this?" said Sir Robert, at last. Edmund went after him slowly, languidly, to the square of light in front of the great window whither he was dragging a picture in an old-fashioned black frame. Then the young man gave a great cry.

There she stood looking out of the old canvas with the smile he knew so well—her blue eyes looking upwards, the soft curves about her mouth, her hands clasped before her, and every detail exactly as he had seen her an hour ago; the white dress with its flounce, the black scarf with all its little frills. Then he fell down on his knees before the beautiful little figure, with a cry which was half alarm and half joy.

Sir Robert drew his breath quick; in fact, he had not been prepared for such success to his experiment. He was confounded by the explanation he had himself suggested. "Do you mean that this is—the person," he said, in a husky voice, and glanced round him with a certain shrinking. His ruddy countenance paled. "I should prefer," he said, with a little difficulty, "to tell you the story in my own room. But turn first to the back of the picture and look at the date. Now come along. I don't like this vacant old place."

Edmund looked at the date; it did not convey any particular idea to his mind.

"Seven, seven, seven," he said to himself; seven is one of the numbers of perfection. It must be that the painter had meant. Otherwise it made no impression upon him. He went down to the library, having first placed the picture carefully in the light where he could come and worship it again. Sir Robert sat down in his usual chair, looking pale. "Sit down, Edmund," he said, "my poor boy. I am afraid you are not in your usual health. You must see the doctor; you must try change of scene."

"What has that to do with it?" said Edmund, astonished. "You were to tell me who she is—that is of far more importance to me than my health, which is excellent, all the same. Who is she? You gave me your promise—"

"Is—?" said Sir Robert. "Edmund, my dear fellow, you must have heard the story, though you don't remember it. It must have excited your imagination. Did you notice the date on the picture? I told you to look at it."

"The date! What has that to do with it? Seven, seven, I forget what it was."

"Seventeen hundred and seventy-seven," said Sir Robert, solemnly. "Seventeen hundred and seventy-seven—nearly a hundred years ago."

There was no intelligence in Edmund's eyes. "I knew there must be something strange about her," he said; "it would be vain to conceal that from one's self. There are many things I don't understand—but I am willing to accept—anything, Sir Robert—"

"Edmund!" cried Sir Robert, almost wildly, "command yourself. You don't seem to see. My dear fellow, this is all a delusion. You have seen no lady. It has been your imagination working. How in the name of all that is reasonable could you see a woman who has been dead for a hundred years?"

The young man looked up startled. Confusion seemed to envelop everything round him. "A hundred years," he said to himself, wondering; then laughed, and repeated, "I saw no lady? I am going to marry her, Sir Robert."

"God bless us all!" said Sir Robert, with a voice of terror. "Edmund, my dear fellow—Edmund, see a doctor, see a clergyman. I'll send for old Parkins and for the Rector. You can't, you can't go on like this, you know."

Edmund's brain was still too much confused to take in any impression from what was said. "A hundred years," he repeated to himself, with a smile. "It is strange; but I always felt there was something strange. I told you there were many things I did not understand. But what may be the meaning—this hundred years? Is this all you have to tell me, sir?" he continued, trying to wake up from the confused sense of mystery, yet almost of pleasure, which the picture brought him. He did not understand it—but then in the whole matter there was so little that he could understand.

"All," Sir Robert said. He was in great excitement and distress. "I don't want the ladies to know if we can help it. Don't say anything to them, I entreat of you. And, my dear boy, if you would go and lie down, I will send for Parkins to come directly. I'll have the Rector up in half an hour. It will yield to remedies—it will yield to remedies," Sir Robert said.

"I am quite well," said Edmund. To him it seemed that Sir Robert was going out of his senses. "But I will not keep you longer, and I will say nothing to the ladies. In the meantime," he added, in his confusion, "I have got—some letters to write."

"The very best thing you can do; occupy yourself—occupy yourself, my dear fellow," said Sir Robert, patting him on the shoulder. Edmund felt that his guardian was glad to be rid of him. Perhaps it was not wonderful that Sir Robert did not understand him; he did not understand himself. His head was confused as if the fog had got into it. To some things he seemed to attach no importance at all, while others were quite clear to him, and had all their natural weight. "Seventeen, seven, seven." He repeated this over to himself with a smile, but whether it was a charm, or a fact, or what it was, he could not tell; on the other hand, he thought the precaution about the ladies was quite right. And he could not appear without betraying that something had happened to him. He sent word downstairs by his servant that he had caught a cold and was going to keep to his room; and there he received the visit of old Dr Parkins with much conscious amusement, but would not say a word to him of what had befallen him, and utterly confounded the old doctor, who could say nothing but that his pulse was excited, and that it would be necessary for him to keep quiet for a day or two. Then the Rector came, much abashed, as a man called upon to minister to a mind diseased, and knowing nothing about it, was likely to be. When they were gone Edmund spent the night alone. He wrote a long letter to—he did not know whom—giving an account of the whole, so little as there was of it, and so much. "I know there is something strange," he wrote, "but nothing to prevent me taking the charge of her, taking care of her. An hour a day of her will be more to me than twenty-four of any other. I know there are things which I can't understand." When he had done this it was late, and all the family had gone to bed. He heard them going one by one—a sound of steps in the long passages, mounting the stairs, a little gleam of the passing lights under his door. By and by silence fell upon everything. There was no sound or stir anywhere—all silent, all dark, the doors shut fast, soft waves of quiet breathing going through the house. He came out with his light in his hand and stood for a moment on the threshold of his door—an adventurer bound upon a last voyage, a sailor setting out into unknown seas. Then he went up, up to the upper part of the house, past all the closed doors, moving quietly through lines of unseen sleepers on every side. The great house was as silent as the grave.

The moon was shining full from the west, just about to set, as she had risen, early. There was a large west window in the gallery, and this was full of silvery light pouring in, making all white and dazzling. The portrait, which had been drawn towards this window to get the evening light, stood there still, receiving the white illumination of the moonlight. Edmund walked up—holding in his hand a candle, which flamed yellow and earthly in that radiance from heaven—through the whiteness, a sort of milky way, with the annals of the past on every side of him. He came to the picture of his love, and threw himself down beside it on the floor. There she stood before him, shadowed in the moonlight—the same, and yet not the same. Something disappointing, narrower, smaller, was in the pictured countenance. As he gazed at it the confusion grew in his mind; all that was real seemed to die away from him. In the vehemence of this sense of loss, he began to speak to her, tears filling his eyes, and her face shining more and more like life through that tremulous medium. "Maud! Maud! I do not understand you; I do not know you; but I love you," he said in a rapture, not knowing that he said it. Then he came to himself with a gasp. There, close to the frame of the picture, her shoulder touching it, stood the original. He held up his candle, like a yellow flaming torch. For the moment, in the silent moonlight, with all the world asleep around, alone with these two—were they two?—his reason went from him. He raised himself to his knees, and knelt like a devotee before a shrine—his arms widely opened, his face raised, wild with worship: were they two, standing side by side, comparing themselves each to each, or were they one?

"You have come to me at last—you have come to me—Maud!"

She looked at him as before with her soft smile. There was no reply in her to his passion. "I did wrong to speak to you," she said; "you do not understand. I was so pleased that you saw me. No one sees me. I come and go, sometimes out, sometimes in. I go to their rooms and they do not see me. Then when I find one that will speak—that will smile, I am glad." There came from her, mingled together, the soft laugh and the sigh, that made his heart stand still. "But no more—but no more," she said.

And there seemed to creep about him a chill. He had never felt it before. When he had seen her first all had been soft as her looks, delightful as the bloom on her face. The bloom was still on her face, but shaded as by a mist. Nor could he see as he did before. The moonlight confused the soft features—or perhaps it was his yellow flaming human candle, not everlasting like the other light, ready to burn out and extinguish itself. His strength and his senses seemed to fail.

"I do not understand," he cried; "I do not understand! but whatever it is, I accept—I accept. Dead or living, Maud, Maud, come with me—let us be together! Come!" he said, stretching his arms wildly.

She did not draw back nor move, but neither did he touch her with his longing arms. Did fear seize them half-way extended? He could not tell. They dropped down by his side, and his heart dropped, sinking within him. She stood before him unmoved—always the same calm, the half smile on her lips, her blue eyes pleased and tender. Then she shook her head slowly, gently.

"It is not permitted. I told you I had loved the earth and all that was on it: and now I am earthbound. I could not go if I would, and I would not if I could. What we have to do, that is what we love best. But I never thought that you would mistake so much—that you would not understand. Now I know why there are so few that see us. It is to keep them from harm," she said with a soft sigh. "Ah me! when the only thing we long for, it is sometimes to speak—but I will never wish for it more—"

"Maud!" He threw himself at her feet again with a great cry. "Touch me—mark me, that I may be yours always. If not in life, yet in death. Say we shall meet when I die."

Once more she shook her head. "How can I tell? I do not know you in the soul. You will do what is appointed; but do not be sorry, you will like to do it,"* she said, with her sweet look of tender pleasure. "Good-bye, brother—good-bye!"

"I will not let you go!" he cried: "I will not let you go!" and seized her in his arms.

Then in Edmund's head was a roaring of echoes, a clanging of noises, a blast as of great trumpets and music; and he knew no more.

"Edmund is not in his room; his bed has not been slept in," said Lady Beresford, coming hastily upstairs next morning immediately after she had gone down. Sir Robert had not yet left his dressing-room. She was pale and full of alarm. "His door was open; there is no trace of him. I have sent out over all the park. He must have left the house last night. And Fred tells me the strangest story. What is it, Robert?" Sir Robert was very much disturbed himself, but he would make no certain reply.

"I daresay he will be found wandering about somewhere. He has got some nonsense in his head." Then he hurried down to the Lime-tree

---

* Prima vuol ben; ma non lascia il talento
Che divina giustizia contra voglia,
Come fù al peccar, pone al tormento.
    PURGATORIO, Cant. xxi.

Walk, and out to the park, looking under the bushes and trees. If he had found Edmund there lying white and stark, Sir Robert would not have been surprised. They searched for him all the morning, but found no trace anywhere. Later in the day, Sir Robert suddenly bethought himself of another possibility. He hurried up to the old gallery, calling his eldest son to go with him. And there, indeed, they found Edmund—lying on the floor. But not dead, nor raving; pale enough, pale as a ghost, but asleep; his candle long ago burnt out to the socket, and the soft little face he had loved, placidly watching over him from the picture, as unmoved, though not so sweet, as the vision he had seen.

It cannot be said that Edmund Coventry was well enough to leave Daintrey that day, nor for several days. But he went away as soon as it was possible, going off from the great door, and by the drive, not approaching the Lime-tree Walk. He had no brain-fever, nor any other kind of fever. Various changes were perceptible, the Beresfords thought, in his life; but other people were unconscious of them. He had always been a gentle soul, friendly, and charitable, and true. More than a year after, when he met his former guardian and family in town, the old intercourse was renewed, and that came to pass which Lady Beresford had always thought would be so very suitable. He married Maud, and made her a very good husband. But he would never go to Daintrey again. And though there have been a great many versions of the story scattered abroad, and the Beresfords, once so silent on the subject, have become in their hearts a little proud of it—though it is supposed against their will that it should be known—no one else, so far as we have ever heard, has been again accosted by the gentle little lady who was earthbound. Perhaps her time of willing punishment is over, and she is earthbound no more.

THE OPEN DOOR

I TOOK the house of Brentwood on my return from India in 18—, for the temporary accommodation of my family, until I could find a permanent home for them. It had many advantages which made it peculiarly appropriate. It was within reach of Edinburgh, and my boy Roland, whose education had been considerably neglected, could go in and out to school, which was thought to be better for him than either leaving home altogether or staying there always with a tutor. The first of these expedients would have seemed preferable to me, the second commended itself to his mother. The doctor, like a judicious man, took the midway between. "Put him on his pony, and let him ride into the High School every morning; it will do him all the good in the world," Dr Simson said; "and when it is bad weather there is the train." His mother accepted this solution of the difficulty more easily than I could have hoped; and our pale-faced boy, who had never known anything more invigorating than Simla, began to encounter the brisk breezes of the North in the subdued severity of the month of May. Before the time of the vacation in July we had the satisfaction of seeing him begin to acquire something of the brown and ruddy complexion of his schoolfellows. The English system did not commend itself to Scotland in these days. There was no little Eton at Fettes; nor do I think, if there had been, that a genteel exotic of that class would have tempted either my wife or me. The lad was doubly precious to us, being the only one left us of many; and he was fragile in body, we believed, and deeply sensitive in mind. To keep him at home, and yet to send him to school—to combine the advantages of the two systems—seemed to be everything that could be desired. The two girls also found at Brentwood everything they wanted. They were near enough to Edinburgh to have masters and lessons as many as they required for completing that never-ending education which the young people seem to require nowadays. Their mother married me when she was younger than Agatha, and I should like to see them improve upon their mother! I myself was then no more than twenty-five—an age at which I see the young fellows now groping about them, with no notion what they are going to do with their lives. However, I suppose every generation has a conceit of itself which elevates it, in its own opinion, above that which comes after it.

Brentwood stands on that fine and wealthy slope of country, one of the richest in Scotland, which lies between the Pentland Hills and the Firth. In clear weather you could see the blue gleam—like a bent bow, embracing the wealthy fields and scattered houses—of the great estuary on one side of you; and on the other the blue heights, not gigantic like those we had been used to, but just high enough for all the glories of the atmosphere, the play of clouds, and sweet reflections, which give to a hilly country an interest and a charm which nothing else can emulate. Edinburgh, with its two lesser heights—the Castle and the Calton Hill—its spires and towers piercing through the smoke, and Arthur's Seat, lying crouched behind, like a guardian no longer very needful, taking his repose beside the well-beloved charge, which is now, so to speak, able to take care of itself without him—lay at our right hand. From the lawn and drawing-room windows we could see all these varieties of landscape. The colour was sometimes a little chilly, but sometimes, also, as animated and full of vicissitude as a drama. I was never tired of it. Its colour and freshness revived the eyes which had grown weary of arid plains and blazing skies. It was always cheery, and fresh, and full of repose.

The village of Brentwood lay almost under the house, on the other side of the deep little ravine, down which a stream—which ought to have been a lovely, wild, and frolicsome little river—flowed between its rocks and trees. The river, like so many in that district, had, however, in its earlier life been sacrificed to trade, and was grimy with paper-making. But this did not affect our pleasure in it so much as I have known it to affect other streams. Perhaps our water was more rapid—perhaps less clogged with dirt and refuse. Our side of the dell was charmingly *accidenté*, and clothed with fine trees, through which various paths wound down to the river-side and to the village bridge which crossed the stream. The village lay in the hollow, and climbed, with very prosaic houses, the other side. Village architecture does not flourish in Scotland. The blue slates and the grey stone are sworn foes to the picturesque; and though I do not, for my own part, dislike the interior of an old-fashioned pewed and galleried church, with its little family settlements on all sides, the square box outside, with its bit of a spire like a handle to lift it by, is not an improvement to the landscape. Still a cluster of houses on differing elevations—with scraps of garden coming in between, a hedgerow with clothes laid out to dry, the opening of a street with its rural sociability, the women at their doors, the slow waggon lumbering along—gives a centre to the landscape It was cheerful to look at, and convenient in a hundred ways. Within ourselves we had walks in plenty, the glen being always beautiful in all its phases, whether the woods were green in the spring or ruddy in the autumn. In the park which surrounded the house were the ruins of the former mansion of Brentwood, a much smaller and less important house than the solid Georgian edifice which we inhabited. The ruins were picturesque, however, and gave importance to the place. Even we, who were but temporary tenants, felt a vague pride in them, as if they somehow reflected a certain consequence upon ourselves. The old building had the remains of a tower, an indistinguishable mass of mason-work, overgrown with ivy, and the shells of walls attached to this were half filled up with soil. I had never examined it closely, I am ashamed to say. There was a large room, or what had been a large room, with the lower part of the windows still existing, on the principal floor, and underneath other windows, which were perfect, though half filled up with fallen soil, and waving with a wild growth of brambles and chance growths of all kinds. This was the oldest part of all. At a little distance were some very commonplace and disjointed fragments of building, one of them suggesting a certain pathos by its very commonness and the complete wreck which it showed. This was the end of a low gable, a bit of grey wall, all encrusted with lichens, in which was a common doorway. Probably it had been a servants' entrance, a back-door, or opening into what are called "the offices" in Scotland. No offices remained to be entered—pantry and kitchen had all been swept out of being; but there stood the doorway open and vacant, free to all the winds, to the rabbits, and every wild creature. It struck my eye, the first time I went to Brentwood, like a melancholy comment upon a life that was over. A door that led to nothing—closed once, perhaps, with anxious care, bolted and guarded, now void of any meaning. It impressed me, I remember, from the first; so perhaps it may be said that my mind was prepared to attach to it an importance which nothing justified.

The summer was a very happy period of repose for us all. The warmth of Indian suns was still in our veins. It seemed to us that we could never have enough of the greenness, the dewiness, the freshness of the northern landscape. Even its mists were pleasant to us, taking all the fever out of us, and pouring in vigour and refreshment. In autumn we followed the fashion of the time, and went away for change which we did not in the least require. It was when the family had settled down for the winter, when the days were short and dark, and the rigorous reign of frost upon us, that the incidents occurred which alone could justify me in intruding upon the world my private affairs. These incidents were, however, of so curious a character, that I hope my inevitable references to my own family and pressing personal interests will meet with a general pardon.

I was absent in London when these events began. In London an old Indian plunges back into the interests with which all his previous life has been associated, and meets old friends at every step. I had been circulating among some half-dozen of these—enjoying the return to my former life in shadow, though I had been so thankful in substance to throw it aside—and had missed some of my home letters, what with going down from Friday to Monday to old Benbow's place in the country, and stopping on the way back to dine and sleep at Sellar's and to take a look into Cross's stables, which occupied another day. It is never safe to miss one's letters. In this transitory life, as the Prayer-book says, how can one ever be certain what is going to happen? All was well at home. I knew exactly (I thought) what they would have to say to me: "The weather has been so fine, that Roland has not once gone by train, and he enjoys the ride beyond anything." "Dear papa, be sure that you don't forget anything, but bring us so-and-so, and so-and-so"—a list as long as my arm. Dear girls and dearer mother! I would not for the world have forgotten their commissions, or lost their little letters, for all the Benbows and Crosses in the world.

But I was confident in my home-comfort and peacefulness. When I got back to my club, however, three or four letters were lying for me, upon some of which I noticed the "immediate," "urgent," which old-fashioned people and anxious people still believe will influence the post-office and quicken the speed of the mails. I was about to open one of these, when the club porter brought me two telegrams, one of which, he said, had arrived the night before. I opened, as was to be expected, the last first, and this was what I read: "Why don't you come or answer? For God's sake, come. He is much worse." This was a thunderbolt to fall upon a man's head who had one only son, and he the light of his eyes! The other telegram, which I opened with hands trembling so much that I lost time by my haste, was to much the same purport: "No better; doctor afraid of brain-fever. Calls for you day and night. Let nothing detain you." The first thing I did was to look up the time-tables to see if there was any way of getting off sooner than by the night train, though I knew well enough there was not; and then I read the letters, which furnished, alas! too clearly, all the details. They told me that the boy had been pale for some time, with a scared look. His mother had noticed it before I left home, but would not say anything to alarm me. This look had increased day by day; and soon it was observed that Roland came home at a wild gallop through the park, his pony panting and in foam, himself "as white as a sheet," but with the perspiration streaming from his forehead. For a long time he had resisted all questioning, but at length had developed such strange changes of mood, showing a reluctance to go to school, a desire to be fetched in the carriage at night—which was a ridiculous piece of luxury—an unwillingness to go out into the grounds, and nervous start at every sound, that his mother had insisted upon an explanation. When the boy—our boy Roland, who had never known what fear was—began to talk to her of voices he had heard in the park, and shadows that had appeared to him among the ruins, my wife promptly put him to bed and sent for Dr Simson—which, of course, was the only thing to do.

I hurried off that evening, as may be supposed, with an anxious heart. How I got through the hours before the starting of the train, I cannot tell. We must all be thankful for the quickness of the railway when in anxiety; but to have thrown myself into a post-chaise as soon as horses could be put to, would have been a relief. I got to Edinburgh very early in the blackness of the winter morning, and scarcely dared look the man in the face, at whom I gasped "What news?" My wife had sent the brougham for me, which I concluded, before the man spoke, was a bad sign. His answer was that stereotyped answer which leaves the imagination so wildly free—"Just the same." Just the same! What might that mean? The horses seemed to me to creep along the long dark country road. As we dashed through the park, I thought I heard some one moaning among the trees, and clenched my fist at him (whoever he might be) with fury. Why had the fool of a woman at the gate allowed any one to come in to disturb the quiet of the place? If I had not been in such hot haste to get home, I think I should have stopped the carriage and got out to see what tramp it was that had made an entrance, and chosen my grounds, of all places in the world,—when my boy was ill!—to grumble and groan in. But I had no reason to complain of our slow pace here. The horses flew like lightning along the intervening path, and drew up at the door all panting, as if they had run a race. My wife stood waiting to receive me with a pale face, and a candle in her hand, which made her look paler still as the wind blew the flame about. "He is sleeping," she said in a whisper, as if her voice might wake him. And I replied, when I could find my voice, also in a whisper, as though the jingling of the horses' furniture and the sound of their hoofs must not have been more dangerous. I stood on the steps with her a moment, almost afraid to go in, now that I was here; and it seemed to me that I saw without observing, if I may say so, that the horses were unwilling to turn round, though their stables lay that way, or that the men were unwilling. These things occurred to me afterwards, though at the moment I was not capable of anything but to ask questions and to hear of the condition of the boy.

I looked at him from the door of his room, for we were afraid to go near, lest we should disturb that blessed sleep. It looked like actual sleep—not the lethargy into which my wife told me he would sometimes fall. She told me everything in the next room, which communicated with his, rising now and then and going to the door of communication; and in this there was much that was very startling and confusing to the mind. It appeared that ever since the winter began, since it was early dark, and night had fallen before his return from school, he had been hearing voices among the ruins—at first only a groaning, he said, at which his pony was as much alarmed as he was, but by degrees a voice. The tears ran down my wife's cheeks as she described to me how he would start up in the night and cry out, "Oh, mother, let me in! oh, mother, let me in!" with a pathos which rent her heart. And she sitting there all the time, only longing to do everything his heart could desire! But though she would try to soothe him, crying, "You are at home, my darling. I am here. Don't you know me? Your mother is here!" he would only stare at her, and after a while spring up again with the same cry. At other times he would be quite reasonable, she said, asking eagerly when I was coming, but declaring that he must go with me as soon as I did so, "to let them in." "The doctor thinks his nervous system must have received a shock," my wife said. "Oh, Henry, can it be that we have pushed him on too much with his work—a delicate boy like Roland?—and what is his work in comparison with his health? Even you would think little of honours or prizes if it hurt the boy's health." Even I! as if I were an inhuman father sacrificing my child to my ambition. But I would not increase her trouble by taking any notice. After a while they persuaded me to lie down, to rest, and to eat—none of which things had been possible since I received their letters. The mere fact of being on the spot, of course, in itself was a great thing; and when I knew that I could be called in a moment, as soon as he was awake and wanted me, I felt capable, even in the dark, chill morning twilight, to snatch an hour or two's sleep. As it happened, I was so worn out with the strain of anxiety, and he so quieted and consoled by knowing I had come, that I was not disturbed till the afternoon, when the twilight had again settled down. There was just daylight enough to see his face when I went to him; and what a change in a fortnight! He was paler and more worn, I thought, than even in those dreadful days in the plains before we left India. His hair seemed to me to have grown long and lank; his eyes were like blazing lights projecting out of his white face. He got hold of my hand in a cold and tremulous clutch, and waved to everybody to go away. "Go away—even mother," he said,—"go away." This went to her heart, for she did not like that even I should have more of the boy's confidence than herself; but my wife has never been a woman to think of herself, and she left us alone. "Are they all gone?" he said, eagerly. "They would not let me speak. The doctor treated me as if I were a fool. You know I am not a fool, papa."

"Yes, yes, my boy, I know; but you are ill, and quiet is so necessary. You are not only not a fool, Roland, but you are reasonable and understand. When you are ill you must deny yourself; you must not do everything that you might do being well."

He waved his thin hand with a sort of indignation. "Then, father, I am not ill," he cried. "Oh, I thought when you came you would not stop me,—you would see the sense of it! What do you think is the matter with me, all of you? Simson is well enough, but he is only a doctor. What do you think is the matter with me? I am no more ill than you are. A doctor, of course, he thinks you are ill the moment he looks at you— that's what he's there for—and claps you into bed."

"Which is the best place for you at present, my dear boy."

"I made up my mind," cried the little fellow, "that I would stand it till you came home. I said to myself, I won't frighten mother and the girls. But now, father," he cried, half jumping out of bed, "it's not illness,—it's a secret."

His eyes shone so wildly, his face was so swept with strong feeling, that my heart sank within me. It could be nothing but fever that did it, and fever had been so fatal. I got him into my arms to put him back into bed. "Roland," I said, humouring the poor child, which I knew was the only way, "if you are going to tell me this secret to do any good, you know you must be quite quiet, and not excite yourself. If you excite yourself, I must not let you speak."

"Yes, father," said the boy. He was quiet directly, like a man, as if he quite understood. When I had laid him back on his pillow, he looked up at me with that grateful sweet look with which children, when they are ill, break one's heart, the water coming into his eyes in his weakness. "I was sure as soon as you were here you would know what to do," he said.

"To be sure, my boy. Now keep quiet, and tell it all out like a man." To think I was telling lies to my own child! for I did it only to humour him, thinking, poor little fellow, his brain was wrong.

"Yes, father. Father, there is some one in the park,—some one that has been badly used."

"Hush, my dear; you remember, there is to be no excitement. Well, who is this somebody, and who has been ill-using him? We will soon put a stop to that."

"Ah," cried Roland, "but it is not so easy as you think. I don't know who it is. It is just a cry. Oh, if you could hear it! It gets into my head in my sleep. I heard it as clear—as clear;—and they think that I am dreaming—or raving perhaps," the boy said, with a sort of disdainful smile.

This look of his perplexed me; it was less like fever than I thought "Are you quite sure you have not dreamt it, Roland?" I said.

"Dreamt?—that!" He was springing up again when he suddenly bethought himself, and lay down flat with the same sort of smile on his face. "The pony heard it too," he said. "She jumped as if she had been shot. If I had not grasped at the reins,—for I was frightened, father—"

"No shame to you, my boy," said I, though I scarcely knew why.

"If I hadn't held to her like a leech, she'd have pitched me over her head, and never drew breath till we were at the door. Did the pony dream it?" he said, with a soft disdain, yet indulgence for my foolishness. Then he added slowly: "It was only a cry the first time, and all the time before you went away. I wouldn't tell you, for it was so wretched to be frightened. I thought it might be a hare or a rabbit snared, and I went in the morning and looked, but there was nothing. It was after you went I heard it really first, and this is what he says." He raised himself on his elbow close to me, and looked me in the face. "'Oh, mother, let me in! oh, mother, let me in!'" As he said the words a mist came over his face, the mouth quivered, the soft features all melted and changed, and when he had ended these pitiful words, dissolved in a shower of heavy tears.

Was it a hallucination? Was it the fever of the brain? Was it the disordered fancy caused by great bodily weakness? How could I tell? I thought it wisest to accept it as if it were all true.

"This is very touching, Roland," I said.

"Oh, if you had just heard it, father! I said to myself; if father heard it he would do something; but mamma, you know, she's given over to Simson, and that fellow's a doctor, and never thinks of anything but clapping you into bed."

"We must not blame Simson for being a doctor, Roland."

"No, no," said my boy, with delightful toleration and indulgence; "oh no; that's the good of him—that's what he's for; I know that. But you—you are different; you are just father: and you'll do something,—directly, papa, directly,—this very night."

"Surely," I said. "No doubt it is some little lost child."

He gave me a sudden, swift look, investigating my face as though to see whether, after all, this was everything my eminence as "father" came to,—no more than that? Then he got hold of my shoulder, clutching it with his thin hand: "Look here," he said, with a quiver in his voice; "suppose it wasn't—living at all!"

"My dear boy, how then could you have heard it?" I said.

He turned away from me with a pettish exclamation—"As if you didn't know better than that!"

"Do you want to tell me it is a ghost?" I said.

Roland withdrew his hand; his countenance assumed an aspect of great dignity and gravity; a slight quiver remained about his lips. "Whatever it was—you always said we were not to call names. It was something—in trouble. Oh, father, in terrible trouble!"

"But, my boy," I said—I was at my wits' end—"if it was a child that was lost, or any poor human creature—but, Roland, what do you want me to do?"

"I should know if I was you," said the child, eagerly. "That is what I always said to myself—Father will know. Oh, papa, papa, to have to face it night after night, in such terrible, terrible trouble! and never to be able to do it any good. I don't want to cry; it's like a baby, I know; but what can I do else?—out there all by itself in the ruin, and nobody to help it. I can't bear it, I can't bear it!" cried my generous boy. And in his weakness he burst out, after many attempts to restrain it, into a great childish fit of sobbing and tears.

I do not know that I ever was in a greater perplexity in my life; and afterwards, when I thought of it, there was something comic in it too. It is bad enough to find your child's mind possessed with the conviction that he has seen—or heard—a ghost. But that he should require you to go instantly and help that ghost, was the most bewildering experience that had ever come my way. I am a sober man myself, and not superstitious—at least any more than everybody is superstitious. Of course I do not believe in ghosts; but I don't deny, any more than other people, that there are stories, which I cannot pretend to understand. My blood got a sort of chill in my veins at the idea that Roland should be a ghost-seer; for that generally means a hysterical temperament and weak health, and all that men most hate and fear for their children. But that I should take up his ghost and right its wrongs, and save it from its trouble, was such a mission as was enough to confuse any man. I did my best to console my boy without giving any promise of this astonishing kind; but he was too sharp for me. He would have none of my caresses. With sobs breaking in at intervals upon his voice, and the rain-drops hanging on his eyelids, he yet returned to the charge.

"It will be there now—it will be there all the night. Oh think, papa, think, if it was me! I can't rest for thinking of it. Don't!" he cried, putting away my hand—"don't! You go and help it, and mother can take care of me."

"But, Roland, what can I do?"

My boy opened his eyes, which were large with weakness and fever, and gave me a smile such, I think, as sick children only know the secret of. "I was sure you would know as soon as you came. I always said—Father will know: and mother," he cried, with a softening of repose upon his face, his limbs relaxing, his form sinking with a luxurious ease in his bed—"mother can come and take care of me."

I called her, and saw him turn to her with the complete dependence of a child, and then I went away and left them, as perplexed a man as any in Scotland. I must say, however, I had this consolation, that my mind was greatly eased about Roland. He might be under a hallucination, but his head was clear enough, and I did not think him so ill as everybody else did. The girls were astonished even at the ease with which I took it. "How do you think he is?" they said in a breath, coming round me, laying hold of me. "Not half so ill as I expected," I said; "not very bad at all." "Oh, papa, you are a darling!" cried Agatha, kissing me, and crying upon my shoulder; while little Jeanie, who was as pale as Roland, clasped both her arms round mine, and could not speak at all. I knew nothing about it, not half so much as Simson: but they believed in me; they had a feeling that all would go right now. God is very good to you when your children look to you like that. It makes one humble, not proud. I was not worthy of it; and then I recollected that I had to act the part of a father to Roland's ghost, which made me almost laugh, though I might just as well have cried. It was the strangest mission that ever was entrusted to mortal man.

It was then I remembered suddenly the looks of the men when they turned to take the brougham to the stables in the dark that morning: they had not liked it, and the horses had not liked it. I remembered that even in my anxiety about Roland I had heard them tearing along the avenue back to the stables, and had made a memorandum mentally that I must speak of it. It seemed to me that the best thing I could do was to go to the stables now and make a few inquiries. It is impossible to fathom the minds of rustics; there might be some devilry of practical joking, for anything I knew; or they might have some interest in getting up a bad reputation for the Brentwood avenue. It was getting dark by the time I went out, and nobody who knows the country will need to be told how black is the darkness of a November night under high laurel-bushes and yew-trees. I walked into the heart of the shrubberies two or three times, not seeing a step before me, till I came out upon the broader carriage-road, where the trees opened a little, and there was a faint grey glimmer of sky visible; under which the great limes and elms stood darkling like ghosts; but it grew black again as I approached the corner where the ruins lay. Both eyes and ears were on the alert, as may be supposed; but I could see nothing in the absolute gloom, and, so far as I can recollect, I heard nothing. Nevertheless there came a strong impression upon me that somebody was there. It is a sensation which most people have felt. I have seen when it has been strong enough to awake me out of sleep, the sense of some one looking at me. I suppose my imagination had been affected by Roland's story; and the mystery of the darkness is always full of suggestions. I stamped my feet violently on the gravel to arouse myself, and called out sharply, "Who's there?" Nobody answered, nor did I expect any one to answer, but the impression had been made. I was so foolish that I did not like to look back, but went sideways, keeping an eye on the gloom behind. It was with great relief that I spied the light in the stables, making a sort of oasis in the darkness. I walked very quickly into the midst of that lighted and cheerful place, and thought the clank of the groom's pail one of the pleasantest sounds I had ever heard. The coachman was the head of this little colony, and it was to his house I went to pursue my investigations. He was a native of the district, and had taken care of the place in the absence of the family for years; it was impossible but that he must know everything that was going on, and all the traditions of the place. The men, I could see, eyed me anxiously when I thus appeared at such an hour among them, and followed me with their eyes to Jarvis's house, where he lived alone with his old wife, their children being all married and out in the world. Mrs Jarvis met me with anxious questions. How was the poor young gentleman? but the others knew, I could see by their faces, that not even this was the foremost thing in my mind.

"Noises?—ou ay, there'll be noises—the wind in the trees, and the water soughing down the glen. As for tramps, Cornel, no, there's little o' that kind o' cattle about here and Merran at the gate's a careful body." Jarvis moved about with some embarrassment from one leg to another as he spoke. He kept in the shade, and did not look at me more than he could help. Evidently his mind was perturbed, and he had reasons for keeping his own counsel. His wife sat by, giving him a quick look now and then, but saying nothing. The kitchen was very snug, and warm, and bright—as different as could be from the drill and mystery of the night outside.

"I think you are trifling with me, Jarvis," I said.

"Triflin', Cornel? no me. What would I trifle for? If the deevil himsel was in the auld hoose, I have no interest in't one way or another—"

"Sandy, hold your peace!" cried his wife, imperatively.

"And what am I to hold my peace for, wi' the Cornel standing there asking a' thae questions? I'm saying, if the deevil himsel—"

"And I'm telling ye hold your peace!" cried the woman, in great excitement. "Dark November weather and lang nichts, and us that ken a' we ken. How daur ye name—a name that shouldna be spoken?" She threw down her stocking and got up, also in great agitation. "I tell't ye you never could keep it. It's no a thing that will hide; and the haill toun kens as weel as you or me. Tell the Cornel straight out—or see, I'll do it. I dinna hold wi' your secrets: and a secret that the haill toun kens!" She snapped her fingers with an air of large disdain. As for Jarvis, ruddy and big as he was, he shrank to nothing before this decided woman. He repeated to her two or three times her own adjuration, "Hold your peace!" then, suddenly changing his tone, cried out, "Tell him then, confound ye! I'll wash my hands o't. If a' the ghosts in Scotland were in the auld hoose, is that ony concern o' mine?"

After this I elicited without much difficulty the whole story. In the opinion of the Jarvises, and of everybody about, the certainty that the place was haunted was beyond all doubt. As Sandy and his wife warmed to the tale, one tripping up another in their eagerness to tell everything, it gradually developed as distinct a superstition as I ever heard, and not without poetry and pathos. How long it was since the voice had been heard first, nobody could tell with certainty. Jarvis's opinion was that his father, who had been coachman at Brentwood before him, had never heard anything about it, and that the whole thing had arisen within the last ten years, since the complete dismantling of the old house: which was a wonderfully modern date for a tale so well authenticated. According to these witnesses, and to several whom I questioned afterwards, and who were all in perfect agreement, it was only in the months of November and December that "the visitation" occurred. During these months, the darkest of the year, scarcely a night passed without the recurrence of these inexplicable cries. Nothing, it was said, had ever been seen—at least nothing that could be identified. Some people, bolder or more imaginative than the others, had seen the darkness moving, Mrs Jarvis said, with unconscious poetry. It began when night fell, and continued, at intervals, till day broke. Very often it was only an inarticulate cry and moaning, but sometimes the words which had taken possession of my poor boy's fancy had been distinctly audible—"Oh, mother, let me in!" The Jarvises were not aware that there had ever been any investigation into it. The estate of Brentwood had lapsed into the hands of a distant branch of the family, who had lived but little there; and of the many people who had taken it, as I had done, few had remained through two Decembers. And nobody had taken the trouble to make a very close examination into the facts. "No, no," Jarvis said, shaking his head, "No, no, Cornel. Wha wad set themsels up for a laughin'-stock to a' the country-side, making a wark about a ghost? Naebody believes in ghosts. It bid to be the wind in the trees, the last gentleman said, or some effec' o' the water wrastlin' among the rocks. He said it was a' quite easy explained: but he gave up the hoose. And when you cam, Cornel, we were awfu' anxious you should never hear. What for should I have spoiled the bargain and hairmed the property for no-thing?"

"Do you call my child's life nothing?" I said in the trouble of the moment, unable to restrain myself. "And instead of telling this all to me, you have told it to him—to a delicate boy, a child unable to sift evidence, or judge for himself, a tender-hearted young creature—"

I was walking about the room with an anger all the hotter that I felt it to be most likely quite unjust. My heart was full of bitterness against the stolid retainers of a family who were content to risk other people's children and comfort rather than let a house lie empty. If I had been warned I might have taken precautions, or left the place, or sent Roland away, a hundred things which now I could not do; and here I was with my boy in a brain-fever, and his life, the most precious life on earth, hanging in the balance, dependent on whether or not I could get to the reason of a commonplace ghost-story! I paced about in high wrath, not seeing what I was to do; for, to take Roland away, even if he were able to travel, would not settle his agitated mind; and I feared even that a scientific explanation of refracted sound, or reverberation, or any other of the easy certainties with which we elder men are silenced, would have very little effect upon the boy.

"Cornel," said Jarvis, solemnly, "and *she'll* bear me witness—the young gentleman never heard a word from me—no, nor from either groom or gardener; I'll gie ye my word for that. In the first place, he's no a lad that invites ye to talk. There are some that are, and some that arena. Some will draw ye on, till ye've tellt them a' the clatter of the toun, and a' ye ken, and whiles mair. But Maister Roland, his mind's fu' of his books. He's aye civil and kind, and a fine lad; but no that sort. And ye see it's for a' our interest, Cornel, that you should stay at Brentwood. I took it upon me mysel to pass the word—'No a syllable to Maister Roland, nor to the young leddies—no a syllable.' The women-servants, that have little reason to be out at night, ken little or nothing about it. And some think it grand to have a ghost so long as they're no in the way of coming across it. If you had been tellt the story to begin with maybe ye would have thought so yourself."

This was true enough, though it did not throw any light upon my perplexity. If we had heard of it to start with, it is possible that all the family would have considered the possession of a ghost a distinct advantage. It is the fashion of the times. We never think what a risk it is to play with young imaginations, but cry out, in the fashionable jargon, "A ghost!—nothing else was wanted to make it perfect." I should not have been above this myself. I should have smiled, of course, at the idea of the ghost at all, but then to feel that it was mine would have pleased my vanity. Oh yes, I claim no exemption. The girls would have been delighted. I could fancy their eagerness, their interest, and excitement. No; if we had been told, it would have done no good—we should have made the bargain all the more eagerly, the fools that we are. "And there has been no attempt to investigate it," I said, "to see what it really is?"

"Eh, Cornel," said the coachman's wife, "wha would investigate, as ye call it, a thing that nobody believes in? Ye would be the laughin'-stock of a' the country-side, as my man says."

"But you believe in it," I said, turning upon her hastily. The woman was taken by surprise. She made a step backward out of my way.

"Lord, Cornel, how ye frichten a body! Me!—there's awfu' strange things in this world. An unlearned person doesna ken what to think. But the minister and the gentry they just laugh in your face. Inquire into the thing that is not! Na, na, we just let it be."

"Come with me, Jarvis," I said, hastily, "and we'll make an attempt at least. Say nothing to the men or to anybody. I'll come back after dinner, and we'll make a serious attempt to see what it is, if it is anything. If I hear it—which I doubt—you may be sure I shall never rest till I make it out. Be ready for me about ten o'clock."

"Me, Cornel!" Jarvis said, in a faint voice. I had not been looking at him in my own preoccupation, but when I did so, I found that the greatest change had come over the fat and ruddy coachman. "Me, Cornel!" he repeated, wiping the perspiration from his brow. His ruddy face hung in flabby folds, his knees knocked together, his voice seemed half extinguished in his throat. Then he began to rub his hands and smile upon me in a deprecating imbecile way. "There's nothing I wouldna do to pleasure ye, Cornel," taking a step further back. "I'm sure, *she* kens I've aye said I never had to do with a mair fair, weel-spoken gentleman—" Here Jarvis came to a pause, again looking at me, rubbing his hands.

"Well?" I said.

"But eh, sir!" he went on, with the same imbecile yet insinuating smile, "if ye'll reflect that I am no used to my feet. With a horse atween my legs, or the reins in my hand, I'm maybe nae worse than other men; but on fit, Cornel—It's no the—bogles;—but I've been cavalry, ye see," with a little hoarse laugh, "a' my life. To face a thing ye didna understan'—on your feet, Cornel."

"Well, sir, if *I* do it," said I tartly, "why shouldn't you?"

"Eh, Cornel, there's an awfu' difference. In the first place, ye tramp about the haill country-side, and think naething of it; but a walk tires the mair than a hunard miles' drive: and then ye're a gentleman, and do your ain pleasure; and you're no so auld as me; and it's for your ain bairn, ye see, Cornel; and then—"

"He believes in it, Cornel, and you dinna believe in it," the woman said.

"Will you come with me?" I said, turning to her.

She jumped back, upsetting her chair in her bewilderment. "Me!" with a scream, and then fell into a sort of hysterical laugh. "I wouldna say but what I would go; but what would the folk say to hear of Cornel Mortimer with an auld silly woman at his heels?"

The suggestion made me laugh too, though I had little inclination for it. "I'm sorry you have so little spirit, Jarvis," I said. "I must find some one else, I suppose."

Jarvis, touched by this, began to remonstrate, but I cut him short. My butler was a soldier who had been with me in India, and was not supposed to fear anything—man or devil,—certainly not the former; and I felt that I was losing time. The Jarvises were too thankful to get rid of me. They attended me to the door with the most anxious courtesies. Outside, the two grooms stood close by, a little confused by my sudden exit. I don't know if perhaps they had been listening—at least standing as near as possible, to catch any scrap of the conversation. I waved my hand to them as I went past, in answer to their salutations, and it was very apparent to me that they also were glad to see me go.

And it will be thought very strange, but it would be weak not to add, that I myself, though bent on the investigation I have spoken of, pledged to Roland to carry it out, and feeling that my boy's health, perhaps his life, depended on the result of my inquiry,—I felt the most unaccountable reluctance to pass these ruins on my way home. My curiosity was intense; and yet it was all my mind could do to pull my body along. I daresay the scientific people would describe it the other way, and attribute my cowardice to the state of my stomach. I went on; but if I had followed my impulse, I should have turned and bolted. Everything in me seemed to cry out against it; my heart thumped, my pulses all began, like sledge-hammers, beating against my ears and every sensitive part. It was very dark, as I have said; the old house, with its shapeless tower, loomed a heavy mass through the darkness, which was only not entirely so solid as itself. On the other hand, the great dark cedars of which we were so proud seemed to fill up the night. My foot strayed out of the path in my confusion and the gloom together, and I brought myself up with a cry as I felt myself knock against something solid. What was it? The contact with hard stone and lime and prickly bramble-bushes restored me a little to myself. "Oh, it's only the old gable," I said aloud, with a little laugh to reassure myself. The rough feeling of the stones reconciled me. As I groped about thus, I shook off my visionary folly. What so easily explained as that I should have strayed from the path in the darkness? This brought me back to common existence, as if I had been shaken by a wise hand out of all the silliness of superstition. How silly it was, after all! What did it matter which path I took? I laughed again, this time with better heart—when suddenly, in a moment, the blood was chilled in my veins, a shiver stole along my spine, my faculties seemed to forsake me. Close by me at my side, at my feet, there was a sigh. No, not a groan, not a moaning, not anything so tangible—a perfectly soft, faint, inarticulate sigh. I sprang back, and my heart stopped beating. Mistaken! no, mistake was impossible. I heard it as clearly as I hear myself speak; a long, soft, weary sigh, as if drawn to the utmost, and emptying out a load of sadness that filled the breast. To hear this in the solitude, in the dark, in the night (though it was still early), had an effect which I cannot describe. I feel it now—something cold creeping over me, up into my hair, and down to my feet, which refused to move. I cried out, with a trembling voice, "Who is there?" as I had done before—but there was no reply.

I got home I don't quite know how; but in my mind there was no longer any indifference as to the thing, whatever it was, that haunted these ruins. My scepticism disappeared like a mist. I was as firmly determined that there was something as Roland was. I did not for a moment pretend to myself that it was possible I could be deceived; there were movements and noises which I understood all about, cracklings of small branches in the frost, and little rolls of gravel on the path, such as have a very eerie sound sometimes, and perplex you with wonder as to who has done it, *when there is no real mystery*; but I assure you all these little movements of nature don't affect you one bit *when there is something*. I understood *them*. I did not understand the sigh. That was not simple nature; there was meaning in it—feeling, the soul of a creature invisible. This is the thing that human nature trembles at—a creature invisible, yet with sensations, feelings, a power somehow of expressing itself. I had not the same sense of unwillingness to turn my back upon the scene of the mystery which I had experienced in going to the stables; but I almost ran home, impelled by eagerness to get everything done that had to be done, in order to apply myself to finding it out. Bagley was in the hall as usual when I went in. He was always there in the afternoon, always with the appearance of perfect occupation, yet, so far as I know, never doing anything. The door was open, so that I hurried in without any pause, breathless; but the sight of his calm regard, as he came to help me off with my overcoat, subdued me in a moment. Anything out of the way, anything incomprehensible, faded to nothing in the presence of Bagley. You saw and wondered how *he* was made: the parting of his hair, the tie of his white neckcloth, the fit of his trousers, all perfect as works of art; but you could see how they were done, which makes all the difference. I flung myself upon him, so to speak, without waiting to note the extreme unlikeness of the man to anything of the kind I meant. "Bagley," I said, "I want you to come out with me tonight to watch for—"

"Poachers, Colonel," he said, a gleam of pleasure running all over him.

"No, Bagley; a great deal worse," I cried.

"Yes, Colonel; at what hour, sir?" the man said; but then I had not told him what it was.

It was ten o'clock when we set out. All was perfectly quiet indoors. My wife was with Roland, who had been quite calm, she said, and who (though, no doubt, the fever must run its course) had been better ever since I came. I told Bagley to put on a thick greatcoat over his evening coat, and did the same myself—with strong boots; for the soil was like a sponge, or worse. Talking to him, I almost forgot what we were going to do. It was darker even than it had been before, and Bagley kept very close to me as we went along. I had a small lantern in my hand, which gave us a partial guidance. We had come to the corner where the path turns. On one side was the bowling-green, which the girls had taken possession of for their croquet-ground—a wonderful enclosure surrounded by high hedges of holly, three hundred years old and more; on the other, the ruins. Both were black as night; but before we got so far, there was a little opening in which we could just discern the trees and the lighter line of the road. I thought it best to pause there and take breath. "Bagley," I said, "there is something about these ruins I don't understand. It is there I am going. Keep your eyes open and your wits about you. Be ready to pounce upon any stranger you see—anything, man or woman. Don't hurt, but seize—anything you see." "Colonel," said Bagley, with a little tremor in his breath, "they do say there's things there—as is neither man nor woman." There was no time for words. "Are you game to follow me, my man? that's the question," I said. Bagley fell in without a word, and saluted. I knew then I had nothing to fear.

We went, so far as I could guess, exactly as I had come, when I heard that sigh. The darkness, however, was so complete that all marks, as of trees or paths, disappeared. One moment we felt our feet on the gravel, another sinking noiselessly into the slippery grass, that was all. I had shut up my lantern, not wishing to scare any one, whoever it might be. Bagley followed, it seemed to me, exactly in my footsteps as I made my way, as I supposed, towards the mass of the ruined house. We seemed to take a long time groping along seeking this; the squash of the wet soil under our feet was the only thing that marked our progress. After a while I stood still to see, or rather feel, where we were. The darkness was very still, but no stiller than is usual in a winter's night. The sounds I have mentioned—the crackling of twigs, the roll of a pebble, the sound of some rustle in the dead leaves, or creeping creature on the grass—were audible when you listened, all mysterious enough when your mind is disengaged, but to me cheering now as signs of the livingness of nature, even in the death of the frost. As we stood still there came up from the trees in the glen the prolonged hoot of an owl. Bagley started with alarm, being in a state of general nervousness, and not knowing what he was afraid of. But to me the sound was encouraging and pleasant, being so comprehensible. "An owl," I said, under my breath. "Y—es, Colonel," said Bagley, his teeth chattering. We stood still about five minutes, while it broke into the still brooding of the air, the sound widening out in circles, dying upon the darkness. This sound, which is not a cheerful one, made me almost gay. It was natural, and relieved the tension of the mind. I moved on with new courage, my nervous excitement calming down.

When all at once, quite suddenly, close to us, at our feet, there broke out a cry. I made a spring backwards in the first moment of surprise and horror, and in doing so came sharply against the same rough masonry and brambles that had struck me before. This new sound came upwards from the ground—a low, moaning, wailing voice, full of suffering and pain. The contrast between it and the hoot of the owl was indescribable; the one with a wholesome wildness and naturalness that hurt nobody— the other, a sound that made one's blood curdle, full of human misery. With a great deal of fumbling—for in spite of everything I could do to keep up my courage my hands shook—I managed to remove the slide of my lantern. The light leaped out like something living, and made the place visible in a moment. We were what would have been inside the ruined building had anything remained but the gable-wall which I have described. It was close to us, the vacant doorway in it going out straight into the blackness outside. The light showed the bit of wall, the ivy glistening upon it in clouds of dark green, the bramble-branches waving, and below, the open door—a door that led to nothing. It was from this the voice came which died out just as the light flashed upon this strange scene. There was a moment's silence, and then it broke forth again. The sound was so near, so penetrating, so pitiful, that, in the nervous start I gave, the light fell out of my hand. As I groped for it in the dark my hand was clutched by Bagley, who I think must have dropped upon his knees; but I was too much perturbed myself to think much of this. He clutched at me in the confusion of his terror, forgetting all his usual decorum. "For God's sake, what is it, sir?" he gasped. If I yielded, there was evidently an end of both of us. "I can't tell," I said, "any more than you; that's what we've got to find out: up, man, up!" I pulled him to his feet. "Will you go round and examine the other side, or will you stay here with the lantern?" Bagley gasped at me with a face of horror. "Can't we stay together, Colonel?" he said—his knees were trembling under him. I pushed him against the corner of the wall, and put the light into his hands. "Stand fast till I come back; shake yourself together, man; let nothing pass you," I said. The voice was within two or three feet of us, of that there could be no doubt.

I went myself to the other side of the wall, keeping close to it. The light shook in Bagley's hand, but, tremulous though it was, shone out through the vacant door, one oblong block of light marking all the crumbling corners and hanging masses of foliage. Was that something dark huddled in a heap by the side of it? I pushed forward across the light in the doorway, and fell upon it with my hands; but it was only a juniper-bush growing close against the wall. Meanwhile, the sight of my figure crossing the doorway had brought Bagley's nervous excitement to a height: he flew at me, gripping my shoulder. "I've got him, Colonel! I've got him!" he cried, with a voice of sudden exultation. He thought it was a man, and was at once relieved. But at that moment the voice burst forth again between us, at our feet—more close to us than any separate being could be. He dropped off from me, and fell against the wall, his jaw dropping as if he were dying. I suppose, at the same moment, he saw that it was me whom he had clutched. I, for my part, had scarcely more command of myself. I snatched the light out of his hand, and flashed it all about me wildly. Nothing,—the juniper-bush which I thought I had never seen before, the heavy growth of the glistening ivy, the brambles waving. It was close to my ears now, crying, crying, pleading as if for life. Either I heard the same words Roland had heard, or else, in my excitement, his imagination got possession of mine. The voice went on, growing into distinct articulation, but wavering about, now from one point, now from another, as if the owner of it were moving slowly back and forward. "Mother! mother!" and then an outburst of wailing. As my mind steadied, getting accustomed (as one's mind gets accustomed to anything), it seemed to me as if some uneasy, miserable creature was pacing up and down before a closed door. Sometimes—but that must have been excitement—I thought I heard a sound like knocking, and then another burst, "Oh, mother! mother!" All this close, close to the space where I was standing with my lantern—now before me, now behind me: a creature restless, unhappy, moaning, crying, before the vacant doorway, which no one could either shut or open more.

"Do you hear it, Bagley? do you hear what it is saying?" I cried, stepping in through the doorway. He was lying against the wall—his eyes glazed, half dead with terror. He made a motion of his lips as if to answer me, but no sounds came; then lifted his hand with a curious imperative movement as if ordering me to be silent and listen. And how long I did so I cannot tell. It began to have an interest, an exciting hold upon me, which I could not describe. It seemed to call up visibly a scene any one could understand—a something shut out, restlessly wandering to and fro; sometimes the voice dropped, as if throwing itself down—sometimes wandered off a few paces, growing sharp and clear. "Oh, mother, let me in! oh, mother, mother, let me in! oh, let me in!" every word was clear to me. No wonder the boy had gone wild with pity. I tried to steady my mind upon Roland, upon his conviction that I could do something, but my head swam with the excitement, even when I partially overcame the terror. At last the words died away, and there was a sound of sobs and moaning. I cried out, "In the name of God who are you?" with a kind of feeling in my mind that to use the name of God was profane, seeing that I did not believe in ghosts or anything supernatural; but I did it all the same, and waited, my heart giving a leap of terror lest there should be a reply. Why this should have been I cannot tell, but I had a feeling that if there was an answer it would be more than I could bear. But there was no answer; the moaning went on, and then, as if it had been real, the voice rose a little higher again, the words recommenced, "Oh, mother, let me in! oh, mother, let me in!" with an expression that was heart-breaking to hear.

As if it had been real! What do I mean by that? I suppose I got less alarmed as the thing went on. I began to recover the use of my senses—I seemed to explain it all to myself by saying that this had once happened, that it was a recollection of a real scene. Why there should have seemed something quite satisfactory and composing in this explanation I cannot tell, but so it was. I began to listen almost as if it had been a play, forgetting Bagley, who, I almost think, had fainted, leaning against the wall. I was startled out of this strange spectatorship that had fallen upon me by the sudden rush of something which made my heart jump once more, a large black figure in the doorway waving its arms. "Come in! come in! come in!" it shouted out hoarsely at the top of a deep bass voice, and then poor Bagley fell down senseless across the threshold. He was less sophisticated than I,—he had not been able to bear it any longer. I took him for something supernatural, as he took me, and it was some time before I awoke to the necessities of the moment. I remembered only after, that from the time I began to give my attention to the man, I heard the other voice no more. It was some time before I brought him to. It must have been a strange scene: the lantern making a luminous spot in the darkness, the man's white face lying on the black earth, I over him, doing what I could for him. Probably I should have been thought to be murdering him had any one seen us. When at last I succeeded in pouring a little brandy down his throat, he sat up and looked about him wildly. "What's up?" he said; then recognising me, tried to struggle to his feet with a faint "Beg your pardon, Colonel." I got him home as best I could, making him lean upon my arm. The great fellow was as weak as a child. Fortunately he did not for some time remember what had happened. From the time Bagley fell the voice had stopped, and all was still.

"You've got an epidemic in your house, Colonel," Simson said to me next morning. "What's the meaning of it all? Here's your butler raving about a voice. This will never do, you know; and so far as I can make out, you are in it too."

"Yes, I am in it, doctor. I thought I had better speak to you. Of course you are treating Roland all right—but the boy is not raving, he is as sane as you or me. It's all true."

"As sane as—I—or you. I never thought the boy insane. He's got cerebral excitement, fever. I don't know what you've got. There's something very queer about the look of your eyes."

"Come," said I, "you can't put us all to bed, you know. You had better listen and hear the symptoms in full."

The doctor shrugged his shoulders, but he listened to me patiently. He did not believe a word of the story, that was clear; but he heard it all from beginning to end. "My dear fellow," he said, "the boy told me just the same. It's an epidemic. When one person falls a victim to this sort of thing, it's as safe as can be—there's always two or three."

"Then how do you account for it?" I said.

"Oh, account for it!—that's a different matter; there's no accounting for the freaks our brains are subject to. If it's delusion; if it's some trick of the echoes or the winds—some phonetic disturbance or other—"

"Come with me tonight, and judge for yourself," I said.

Upon this he laughed aloud, then said, "That's not such a bad idea; but it would ruin me for ever if it were known that John Simson was ghost-hunting."

"There it is," said I; "you dart down on us who are unlearned with your phonetic disturbances, but you daren't examine what the thing really is for fear of being laughed at. That's science!"

"It's not science—it's common-sense," said the doctor. "The thing has delusion on the front of it. It is encouraging an unwholesome tendency even to examine. What good could come of it? Even if I am convinced, I shouldn't believe."

"I should have said so yesterday; and I don't want you to be convinced or to believe," said I. "If you prove it to be a delusion, I shall be very much obliged to you for one. Come; somebody must go with me."

"You are cool," said the doctor. "You've disabled this poor fellow of yours, and made him—on that point—a lunatic for life; and now you want to disable me. But for once, I'll do it. To save appearance, if you'll give me a bed, I'll come over after my last rounds."

It was agreed that I should meet him at the gate, and that we should visit the scene of last night's occurrences before we came to the house, so that nobody might be the wiser. It was scarcely possible to hope that the cause of Bagley's sudden illness should not somehow steal into the knowledge of the servants at least, and it was better that all should be done as quietly as possible. The day seemed to me a very long one. I had to spend a certain part of it with Roland, which was a terrible ordeal for me—for what could I say to the boy? The improvement continued, but he was still in a very precarious state, and the trembling vehemence with which he turned to me when his mother left the room filled me with alarm. "Father?" he said, quietly. "Yes, my boy; I am giving my best attention to it—all is being done that I can do. I have not come to any conclusion—yet I am neglecting nothing you said," I cried. What I could not do was to give his active mind any encouragement to dwell upon the mystery. It was a hard predicament, for some satisfaction had to be given him. He looked at me very wistfully, with the great blue eyes which shone so large and brilliant out of his white and worn face. "You must trust me," I said. "Yes, father. Father understands," he said to himself, as if to soothe some inward doubt. I left him as soon as I could. He was about the most precious thing I had on earth, and his health my first thought; but yet somehow, in the excitement of this other subject, I put that aside, and preferred not to dwell upon Roland, which was the most curious part of it all.

That night at eleven I met Simson at the gate. He had come by train, and I let him in gently myself. I had been so much absorbed in the coming experiment that I passed the ruins in going to meet him, almost without thought, if you can understand that. I had my lantern; and he showed me a coil of taper which he had ready for use. "There is nothing like light," he said, in his scoffing tone. It was a very still night, scarcely a sound, but not so dark. We could keep the path without difficulty as we went along. As we approached the spot we could hear a low moaning, broken occasionally by a bitter cry. "Perhaps that is your voice," said the doctor; "I thought it must be something of the kind. That's a poor brute caught in some of these infernal traps of yours; you'll find it among the bushes somewhere." I said nothing. I felt no particular fear, but a triumphant satisfaction in what was to follow. I led him to the spot where Bagley and I had stood on the previous night. All was silent as a winter night could be—so silent that we heard far off the sound of the horses in the stables, the shutting of a window at the house. Simson lighted his taper and went peering about, poking into all the corners. We looked like two conspirators lying in wait for some unfortunate traveller; but not a sound broke the quiet. The moaning had stopped before we came up; a star or two shone over us in the sky, looking down as if surprised at our strange proceedings. Dr Simson did nothing but utter subdued laughs under his breath. "I thought as much," he said. "It is just the same with tables and all other kinds of ghostly apparatus; a sceptic's presence stops everything. When I am present nothing ever comes off. How long do you think it will be necessary to stay here? Oh, I don't complain; only, when *you* are satisfied, *I* am—quite."

I will not deny that I was disappointed beyond measure by this result. It made me look like a credulous fool. It gave the doctor such a pull over me as nothing else could. I should point all his morals for years to come, and his materialism, his scepticism, would be increased beyond endurance. "It seems, indeed," I said, "that there is to be no—""Manifestation," he said, laughing; "that is what all the mediums say. No manifestations, in consequence of the presence of an unbeliever." His laugh sounded very uncomfortable to me in the silence; and it was now near midnight. But that laugh seemed the signal; before it died away the moaning we had heard before was resumed. It started from some distance off, and came towards us, nearer and nearer, like some one walking along and moaning to himself. There could be no idea now that it was a hare caught in a trap. The approach was slow, like that of a weak person with little halts and pauses. We heard it coming along the grass straight towards the vacant doorway. Simson had been a little startled by the first sound. He said hastily, "That child has no business to be out so late." But he felt, as well as I, that this was no child's voice. As it came nearer, he grew silent, and, going to the doorway with his taper, stood looking out towards the sound. The taper being unprotected blew about in the night air, though there was scarcely any wind. I threw the light of my lantern steady and white across the same space. It was in a blaze of light in the midst of the blackness. A little icy thrill had gone over me at the first sound, but as it came close, I confess that my only feeling was satisfaction. The scoffer could scoff no more. The light touched his own face, and showed a very perplexed countenance. If he was afraid, he concealed it with great success, but he was perplexed. And then all that had happened on the previous night was enacted once more. It fell strangely upon me with a sense of repetition. Every cry, every sob seemed the same as before. I listened almost without any emotion at all in my own person, thinking of its effect upon Simson. He maintained a very bold front on the whole. All that coming and going of the voice was, if our ears could be trusted, exactly in front of the vacant, blank doorway, blazing full of light, which caught and shone in the glistening leaves of the great hollies at a little distance. Not a rabbit could have crossed the turf without being seen;— but there was nothing. After a time, Simson, with a certain caution and bodily reluctance, as it seemed to me, went out with his roll of taper into this space. His figure showed against the holly in full outline. Just at this moment the voice sank, as was its custom, and seemed to fling itself down at the door. Simson recoiled violently, as if some one had come up against him, then turned, and held his taper low as if examining something. "Do you see anybody?" I cried in a whisper, feeling the chill of nervous panic steal over me at this action. "It's nothing but a—confounded juniper-bush," he said. This I knew very well to be nonsense, for the juniper-bush was on the other side. He went about after this round and round, poking his taper everywhere, then returned to me on the inner side of the wall. He scoffed no longer; his face was contracted and pale. "How long does this go on?" he whispered to me, like a man who does not wish to interrupt some one who is speaking. I had become too much perturbed myself to remark whether the successions and changes of the voice were the same as last night. It suddenly went out in the air almost as he was speaking, with a soft reiterated sob dying away. If there had been anything to be seen, I should have said that the person was at that moment crouching on the ground close to the door.

We walked home very silent afterwards. It was only when we were in sight of the house that I said, "What do you think of it?" "I can't tell what to think of it," he said, quickly. He took—though he was a very temperate man—not the claret I was going to offer him, but some brandy from the tray, and swallowed it almost undiluted. "Mind you, I don't believe a word of it," he said, when he had lighted his candle; "but I can't tell what to think," he turned round to add, when he was half-way upstairs.

All of this, however, did me no good with the solution of my problem. I was to help this weeping, sobbing thing, which was already to me as distinct a personality as anything I knew—or what should I say to Roland? It was on my heart that my boy would die if I could not find some way of helping this creature. You may be surprised that I should speak of it in this way. I did not know if it was man or woman; but I no more doubted that it was a soul in pain than I doubted my own being; and it was my business to soothe this pain—to deliver it, if that was possible. Was ever such a task given to an anxious father trembling for his only boy? I felt in my heart, fantastic as it may appear, that I must fulfil this somehow, or part with my child; and you may conceive that rather than do that I was ready to die. But even my dying would not have advanced me—unless by bringing me into the same world with that seeker at the door.

Next morning Simson was out before breakfast, and came in with evident signs of the damp grass on his boots, and a look of worry and weariness, which did not say much for the night he had passed. He improved a little after breakfast, and visited his two patients, for Bagley was still an invalid. I went out with him on his way to the train, to hear what he had to say about the boy. "He is going on very well," he said; "there are no complications as yet. But mind you, that's not a boy to be trifled with, Mortimer. Not a word to him about last night." I had to tell him then of my last interview with Roland, and of the impossible demand he had made upon me—by which, though he tried to laugh, he was much discomposed, as I could see. "We must just perjure ourselves all round," he said, "and swear you exorcised it;" but the man was too kind-hearted to be satisfied with that. "It's frightfully serious for you, Mortimer. I can't laugh as I should like to. I wish I saw a way out of it, for your sake. By the way," he added shortly, "didn't you notice that juniper-bush on the left-hand side?" "There was one on the right hand of the door. I noticed you made that mistake last night." "Mistake!" he cried, with a curious low laugh, pulling up the collar of his coat as though he felt the cold,— "there's no juniper there this morning, left or right. Just go and see." As he stepped into the train a few minutes after, he looked back upon me and beckoned me for a parting word. "I'm coming back tonight," he said.

I don't think I had any feeling about this as I turned away from that common bustle of the railway which made my private preoccupations feel so strangely out of date. There had been a distinct satisfaction in my mind before that his scepticism had been so entirely defeated. But the more serious part of the matter pressed upon me now. I went straight from the railway to the manse, which stood on a little plateau on the side of the river opposite to the woods of Brentwood. The minister was one of a class which is not so common in Scotland as it used to be. He was a man of good family, well educated in the Scotch way, strong in philosophy, not so strong in Greek, strongest of all in experience,—a man who had "come across," in the course of his life, most people of note that had ever been in Scotland—and who was said to be very sound in doctrine, without infringing the toleration with which old men, who are good men, are generally endowed. He was old-fashioned; perhaps he did not think so much about the troublous problems of theology as many of the young men, nor ask himself any hard questions about the Confession of Faith—but he understood human nature, which is perhaps better. He received me with a cordial welcome. "Come away, Colonel Mortimer," he said; "I'm all the more glad to see you, that I feel it's a good sign for the boy. He's doing well?—God be praised—and the Lord bless him and keep him. He has many a poor body's prayers—and that can do nobody harm."

"He will need them all, Dr Moncrieff," I said, "and your counsel too." And I told him the story—more than I had told Simson. The old clergyman listened to me with many suppressed exclamations, and at the end the water stood in his eyes.

"That's just beautiful," he said. "I do not mind to have heard anything like it; it's as fine as Burns when he wished deliverance to one—that is prayed for in no kirk. Ay, ay! so he would have you console the poor lost spirit? God bless the boy! There's something more than common in that, Colonel Mortimer. And also the faith of him in his father!—I would like to put that into a sermon." Then the old gentleman gave me an alarmed look, and said, "No, no; I was not meaning a sermon; but I must write it down for the 'Children's Record.'" I saw the thought that passed through his mind. Either he thought, or he feared I would think, of a funeral sermon. You may believe this did not make me more cheerful.

I can scarcely say that Dr Moncrieff gave me any advice. How could any one advise on such a subject? But he said, "I think I'll come too. I'm an old man; I'm less liable to be frighted than those that are further off the world unseen. It behoves me to think of my own journey there. I've no cut-and-dry beliefs on the subject. I'll come too: and maybe at the moment the Lord will put into our heads what to do."

This gave me a little comfort—more than Simson had given me. To be clear about the cause of it was not my grand desire. It was another thing that was in my mind—my boy. As for the poor soul at the open door, I had no more doubt, as I have said, of its existence than I had of my own. It was no ghost to me. I knew the creature, and it was in trouble. That was my feeling about it, as it was Roland's. To hear it first was a great shock to my nerves, but not now; a man will get accustomed to anything. But to do something for it was the great problem; how was I to be serviceable to a being that was invisible, that was mortal no longer? "Maybe at the moment the Lord will put it into our heads." This is very old-fashioned phraseology, and a week before, most likely, I should have smiled (though always with kindness) at Dr Moncrieff's credulity; but there was a great comfort, whether rational or otherwise I cannot say, in the mere sound of the words.

The road to the station and the village lay through the glen—not by the ruins; but though the sunshine and the fresh air, and the beauty of the trees, and the sound of the water were all very soothing to the spirits, my mind was so full of my own subject that I could not refrain from turning to the right hand as I got to the top of the glen, and going straight to the place which I may call the scene of all my thoughts. It was lying full in the sunshine, like all the rest of the world. The ruined gable looked due east, and in the present aspect of the sun the light streamed down through the doorway as our lantern had done, throwing a flood of light upon the damp grass beyond. There was a strange suggestion in the open door—so futile, a kind of emblem of vanity—all free around, so that you could go where you pleased, and yet that semblance of an enclosure—that way of entrance, unnecessary, leading to nothing. And why any creature should pray and weep to get in—to nothing: or be kept out—by nothing! You could not dwell upon it, or it made your brain go round. I remembered, however, what Simson said about the juniper, with a little smile on my own mind as to the inaccuracy of rec-ollection, which even a scientific man will be guilty of. I could see now the light of my lantern gleaming upon the wet glistening surface of the spiky leaves at the right hand—and he ready to go to the stake for it that it was the left! I went round to make sure. And then I saw what he had said. Right or left there was no juniper at all. I was confounded by this, though it was entirely a matter of detail: nothing at all: a bush of brambles waving, the grass growing up to the very walls. But after all, though it gave me a shock for a moment, what did that matter? There were marks as if a number of footsteps had been up and down in front of the door; but these might have been our steps; and all was bright, and peaceful, and still. I poked about the other ruin—the larger ruins of the old house—for some time, as I had done before. There were marks upon the grass here and there, I could not call them footsteps, all about; but that told for nothing one way or another. I had examined the ruined rooms closely the first day. They were half filled up with soil and *débris*, withered brackens and bramble—no refuge for any one there. It vexed me that Jarvis should see me coming from that spot when he came up to me for his orders. I don't know whether my nocturnal expeditions had got wind among the servants. But there was a significant look in his face. Something in it I felt was like my own sensation when Simson in the midst of his scepticism was struck dumb. Jarvis felt satisfied that his veracity had been put beyond question. I never spoke to a servant of mine in such a peremptory tone before. I sent him away "with a flea in his lug," as the man described it afterwards. Interference of any kind was intolerable to me at such a moment.

But what was strangest of all was, that I could not face Roland. I did not go up to his room as I would have naturally done at once. This the girls could not understand. They saw there was some mystery in it. "Mother has gone to lie down," Agatha said; "he has had such a good night." "But he wants you so, papa!" cried little Jeanie, always with her two arms embracing mine in a pretty way she had. I was obliged to go at last—but what could I say? I could only kiss him, and tell him to keep still—that I was doing all I could. There is something mystical about the patience of a child. "It will come all right, won't it, father?" he said. "God grant it may! I hope so, Roland." "Oh yes, it will come all right." Perhaps he understood that in the midst of my anxiety I could not stay with him as I should have done otherwise. But the girls were more surprised than it is possible to describe. They looked at me with wondering eyes. "If I were ill, papa, and you only stayed with me a moment, I should break my heart," said Agatha. But the boy had a sympathetic feeling. He knew that of my own will I would not have done it. I shut myself up in the library, where I could not rest, but kept pacing up and down like a caged beast. What could I do? and if I could do nothing, what would become of my boy? These were the questions that, without ceasing, pursued each other through my mind.

Simson came out to dinner, and when the house was all still, and most of the servants in bed, we went out and met Dr Moncrieff, as we had appointed, at the head of the glen. Simson, for his part, was disposed to scoff at the Doctor. "If there are to be any spells, you know, I'll cut the whole concern," he said. I did not make him any reply. I had not invited him; he could go or come as he pleased. He was very talkative, far more so than suited my humour, as we went on. "One thing is certain, you know, there must be some human agency," he said. "It is all bosh about apparitions. I never have investigated the laws of sound to any great extent, and there's a great deal in ventriloquism that we don't know much about." "If it's the same to you," I said, "I wish you'd keep all that to yourself, Simson. It doesn't suit my state of mind." "Oh, I hope I know how to respect idiosyncrasy," he said. The very tone of his voice irritated me beyond measure. These scientific fellows, I wonder people put up with them as they do, when you have no mind for their cold-blooded confidence. Dr Moncrieff met us about eleven o'clock, the same time as on the previous night. He was a large man, with a venerable countenance and white hair—old, but in full vigour, and thinking less of a cold night walk than many a younger man. He had his lantern as I had. We were fully provided with means of lighting the place, and we were all of us resolute men. We had a rapid consultation as we went up, and the result was that we divided to different posts. Dr Moncrieff remained inside the wall—if you can call that inside where there was no wall but one. Simson placed himself on the side next the ruins, so as to intercept any communication with the old house, which was what his mind was fixed upon. I was posted on the other side. To say that nothing could come near without being seen was self-evident. It had been so also on the previous night. Now, with our three lights in the midst of the darkness, the whole place seemed illuminated. Dr Moncrieff's lantern, which was a large one, without any means of shutting up—an old-fashioned lantern with a pierced and ornamental top—shone steadily, the rays shooting out of it upward into the gloom. He placed it on the grass, where the middle of the room, if this had been a room, would have been. The usual effect of the light streaming out of the doorway was prevented by the illumination which Simson and I on either side supplied. With these differences, everything seemed as on the previous night.

And what occurred was exactly the same, with the same air of repetition, point for point, as I had formerly remarked. I declare that it seemed to me as if I were pushed against, put aside, by the owner of the voice as he paced up and down in his trouble,—though these are perfectly futile words, seeing that the stream of light from my lantern, and that from Simson's taper, lay broad and clear, without a shadow, without the smallest break, across the entire breadth of the grass. I had ceased even to be alarmed, for my part. My heart was rent with pity and trouble—pity for the poor suffering human creature that moaned and pleaded so, and trouble for myself and my boy. God! if I could not find any help—and what help could I find?—Roland would die.

We were all perfectly still till the first outburst was exhausted, as I knew (by experience) it would be. Dr Moncrieff, to whom it was new, was quite motionless on the other side of the wall, as we were in our places. My heart had remained almost at its usual beating during the voice. I was used to it; it did not rouse all my pulses as it did at first. But just as it threw itself sobbing at the door (I cannot use other words), there suddenly came something which sent the blood coursing through my veins and my heart into my mouth. It was a voice inside the wall— the minister's well-known voice. I would have been prepared for it in any kind of adjuration, but I was not prepared for what I heard. It came out with a sort of stammering, as if too much moved for utterance. "Willie, Willie! Oh, God preserve us! is it you?"

These simple words had an effect upon me that the voice of the invisible creature had ceased to have. I thought the old man, whom I had brought into this danger, had gone mad with terror. I made a dash round to the other side of the wall, half crazed myself with the thought. He was standing where I had left him, his shadow thrown vague and large upon the grass by the lantern which stood at his feet. I lifted my own light to see his face as I rushed forward. He was very pale, his eyes wet and glistening, his mouth quivering with parted lips. He neither saw nor heard me. We that had gone through this experience before, had crouched towards each other to get a little strength to bear it. But he was not even aware that I was there. His whole being seemed absorbed in anxiety and tenderness. He held out his hands, which trembled, but it seemed to me with eagerness, not fear. He went on speaking all the time. "Willie, if it is you—and it's you, if it is not a delusion of Satan,— Willie, lad! why come ye here frighting them that know you not? Why came ye not to me?"

He seemed to wait for an answer. When his voice ceased, his countenance, every line moving, continued to speak. Simson gave me another terrible shock, stealing into the open doorway with his light, as much awe-stricken, as wildly curious, as I. But the minister resumed, without seeing Simson, speaking to some one else. His voice took a tone of expostulation—

"Is this right to come here? Your mother's gone with your name on her lips. Do you think she would ever close her door on her own lad? Do ye think the Lord will close the door, ye faint-hearted creature? No!—I forbid ye! I forbid ye!" cried the old man. The sobbing voice had begun to resume its cries. He made a step forward, calling out the last words in a voice of command. "I forbid ye! Cry out no more to man. Go home, ye wandering spirit! go home! Do you hear me?—me that christened ye, that have struggled with ye, that have wrestled for ye with the Lord!" Here the loud tones of his voice sank into tenderness. "And her too, poor woman! poor woman! her you are calling upon. She's no here. You'll find her with the Lord. Go there and seek her, not here. Do you hear me, lad? go after her there. He'll let you in, though it's late. Man, take heart! if you will lie and sob and greet, let it be at heaven's gate, and no your poor mother's ruined door."

He stopped to get his breath: and the voice had stopped, not as it had done before, when its time was exhausted and all its repetitions said, but with a sobbing catch in the breath as if overruled. Then the minister spoke again, "Are you hearing me, Will? Oh, laddie, you've liked the beggarly elements all your days. Be done with them now. Go home to the Father—the Father! Are you hearing me?" Here the old man sank down upon his knees, his face raised upwards, his hands held up with a tremble in them, all white in the light in the midst of the darkness. I resisted as long as I could, though I cannot why,—then I, too, dropped upon my knees. Simson all the time stood in the doorway, with an expression in his face such as words could not tell, his under lip dropped, his eyes wild, staring. It seemed to be to him, that image of blank ignorance and wonder, that we were praying. All the time the voice, with a low arrested sobbing, lay just where he was standing, as I thought.

"Lord," the minister said—"Lord, take him into Thy everlasting habitations. The mother he cries to is with Thee. Who can open to him but Thee? Lord, when is it too late for Thee, or what is too hard for Thee? Lord, let that woman there draw him inower! Let her draw him inower!"

I sprang forward to catch something in my arms that flung itself wildly within the door. The illusion was so strong, that I never paused till I felt my forehead graze against the wall and my hands clutch the ground—for there was nobody there to save from falling, as in my foolishness I thought. Simson held out his hand to me to help me up. He was trembling and cold, his lower lip hanging, his speech almost inarticulate. "It's gone," he said, stammering,—"it's gone!" We leant upon each other for a moment, trembling so much both of us that the whole scene trembled as if it were going to dissolve and disappear; and yet as long as I live I will never forget it—the shining of the strange lights, the blackness all round, the kneeling figure with all the whiteness of the light concentrated on its white venerable head and uplifted hands. A strange solemn stillness seemed to close all round us. By intervals a single syllable, "Lord! Lord!" came from the old minister's lips. He saw none of us, nor thought of us. I never knew how long we stood, like sentinels guarding him at his prayers, holding our lights in a confused dazed way, not knowing what we did. But at last he rose from his knees, and standing up at his full height, raised his arms, as the Scotch manner is at the end of a religious service, and solemnly gave the apostolical benediction—to what? to the silent earth, the dark woods, the wide breathing atmosphere—for we were but spectators gasping an Amen!

It seemed to me that it must be the middle of the night, as we all walked back. It was in reality very late. Dr Moncrieff put his arm into mine. He walked slowly, with an air of exhaustion. It was as if we were coming from a deathbed. Something hushed and solemnised the very air. There was that sense of relief in it which there always is at the end of a death-struggle. And nature, persistent, never daunted, came back in all of us, as we returned into the ways of life. We said nothing to each other, indeed, for a time; but when we got clear of the trees and reached the opening near the house, where we could see the sky, Dr Moncrieff himself was the first to speak. "I must be going," he said; "it's very late, I'm afraid. I will go down the glen, as I came."

"But not alone. I am going with you, Doctor."

"Well, I will not oppose it. I am an old man, and agitation wearies more than work. Yes; I'll be thankful of your arm. Tonight, Colonel, you've done me more good turns than one."

I pressed his hand on my arm, not feeling able to speak. But Simson, who turned with us, and who had gone along all this time with his taper flaring, in entire unconsciousness, came to himself, apparently at the sound of our voices, and put out that wild little torch with a quick movement, as if of shame. "Let me carry your lantern," he said; "it is heavy." He recovered with a spring, and in a moment, from the awe-stricken spectator he had been, became himself, sceptical and cynical. "I should like to ask you a question," he said. "Do you believe in Purgatory, Doctor? It's not in the tenets of the Church, so far as I know."

"Sir," said Dr Moncrieff, "an old man like me is sometimes not very sure what he believes. There is just one thing I am certain of—and that is the loving-kindness of God."

"But I thought that was in this life. I am no theologian—"

"Sir," said the old man again, with a tremor in him which I could feel going over all his frame, "if I saw a friend of mine within the gates of hell, I would not despair but his Father would take him by the hand still—if he cried like *yon*."

"I allow it is very strange—very strange. I cannot see through it. That there must be human agency, I feel sure. Doctor, what made you decide upon the person and the name?"

The minister put out his hand with the impatience which a man might show if he were asked how he recognised his brother. "Tuts!" he said, in familiar speech—then more solemnly, "how should I not recognise a person that I know better—far better—than I know you?"

"Then you saw the man?"

Dr Moncrieff made no reply. He moved his hand again with a little impatient movement, and walked on, leaning heavily on my arm. And we went on for a long time without another word, threading the dark paths, which were steep and slippery with the damp of the winter. The air was very still—not more than enough to make a faint sighing in the branches, which mingled with the sound of the water to which we were descending. When we spoke again, it was about indifferent matters— about the height of the river, and the recent rains. We parted with the minister at his own door, where his old housekeeper appeared in great perturbation, waiting for him. "Eh me, minister! the young gentleman will be worse?" she cried.

"Far from that—better. God bless him!" Dr Moncrieff said.

I think if Simson had begun again to me with his questions, I should have pitched him over the rocks as we returned up the glen; but he was silent, by a good inspiration. And the sky was clearer than it had been for many nights, shining high over the trees, with here and there a star faintly gleaming through the wilderness of dark and bare branches. The air, as I have said, was very soft in them, with a subdued and peaceful cadence. It was real, like every natural sound, and came to us like a hush of peace and relief. I thought there was a sound in it as of the breath of a sleeper, and it seemed clear to me that Roland must be sleeping, satisfied and calm. We went up to his room when we went in. There we found the complete hush of rest. My wife looked up out of a doze, and gave me a smile: "I think he is a great deal better; but you are very late," she said in a whisper, shading the light with her hand that the doctor might see his patient. The boy had got back something like his own colour. He woke as we stood all round his bed. His eyes had the happy half-awakened look of childhood, glad to shut again, yet pleased with the interruption and glimmer of the light. I stooped over him and kissed his forehead, which was moist and cool. "All is well, Roland," I said. He looked up at me with a glance of pleasure, and took my hand and laid his cheek upon it, and so went to sleep.

For some nights after, I watched among the ruins, spending all the dark hours up to midnight patrolling about the bit of wall which was associated with so many emotions; but I heard nothing, and saw nothing beyond the quiet course of nature: nor so far as I am aware, has anything been heard again. Dr Moncrieff gave me the history of the youth, whom he never hesitated to name. I did not ask, as Simson did, how he recognised him. He had been a prodigal—weak, foolish, easily imposed upon, and "led away," as people say. All that we had heard had passed actually in life, the Doctor said. The young man had come home thus a day or two after his mother died—who was no more than the housekeeper in the old house—and distracted with the news, had thrown himself down at the door and called upon her to let him in. The old man could scarcely speak of it for tears. To me it seemed as if—heaven help us, how little do we know about anything!—a scene like that might impress itself somehow upon the hidden heart of nature. I do not pretend to know how, but the repetition had struck me at the time as, in its terrible strangeness and incomprehensibility, almost mechanical—as if the unseen actor could not exceed or vary, but was bound to re-enact the whole. One thing that struck me, however, greatly, was the likeness between the old minister and my boy in the manner of regarding these strange phenomena. Dr Moncrieff was not terrified, as I had been myself, and all the rest of us. It was no "ghost," as I fear we all vulgarly considered it, to him—but a poor creature whom he knew under these conditions, just as he had known him in the flesh, having no doubt of his identity. And to Roland it was the same. This spirit in pain—if it was a spirit—this voice out of the unseen—was a poor fellow-creature in misery, to be succoured and helped out of his trouble, to my boy. He spoke to me quite frankly about it when he got better. "I knew father would find out some way," he said. And this was when he was strong and well, and all idea that he would turn hysterical or become a seer of visions had happily passed away.

I must add one curious fact which does not seem to me to have any relation to the above, but which Simson made great use of, as the human agency which he was determined to find somehow. We had examined the ruins very closely at the time of these occurrences; but afterwards, when all was over, as we went casually about them one Sunday afternoon in the idleness of that unemployed day, Simson with his stick penetrated an old window which had been entirely blocked up with fallen soil. He jumped down into it in great excitement, and called me to follow. There we found a little hole—for it was more a hole than a room—entirely hidden under the ivy and ruins, in which there was a quantity of straw laid in a corner, as if some one had made a bed there, and some remains of crusts about the floor. Some one had lodged there, and not very long before, he made out; and that this unknown being was the author of all the mysterious sounds we heard he is convinced. "I told you it was human agency," he said, triumphantly. He forgets, I suppose, how he and I stood with our lights seeing nothing, while the space between us was audibly traversed by something that could speak, and sob, and suffer. There is no argument with men of this kind. He is ready to get up a laugh against me on this slender ground. "I was puzzled myself—I could not make it out—but I always felt convinced human agency was at the bottom of it. And here it is—and a clever fellow he must have been," the Doctor says.

Bagley left my service as soon as he got well. He assured me it was no want of respect; but he could not stand "them kind of things," and the man was so shaken and ghastly that I was glad to give him a present and let him go. For my own part, I made a point of staying out the time, two years, for which I had taken Brentwood; but I did not renew my tenancy. By that time we had settled, and found for ourselves a pleasant home of our own.

I must add that when the doctor defies me, I can always bring back gravity to his countenance, and a pause in his railing, when I remind him of the juniper-bush. To me that was a matter of little importance. I could believe I was mistaken. I did not care about it one way or other; but on his mind the effect was different. The miserable voice, the spirit in pain, he could think of as the result of ventriloquism, or reverberation, or—anything you please: an elaborate prolonged hoax executed somehow by the tramp that had found a lodging in the old tower. But the juniper-bush staggered him. Things have effects so different on the minds of different men.

THE PORTRAIT

A T the period when the following incidents occurred I was living with my father at The Grove, a large old house in the immediate neighbourhood of a little town. This had been his home for a number of years; and I believe I was born in it. It was a kind of house which, notwithstanding all the red and white architecture, known at present by the name of Queen Anne, builders nowadays have forgotten how to build. It was straggling and irregular, with wide passages, wide staircases, broad landings; the rooms large but not very lofty; the arrangements leaving much to be desired, with no economy of space: a house belonging to a period when land was cheap, and, so far as that was concerned, there was no occasion to economise. Though it was so near the town, the clump of trees in which it was environed was a veritable grove. In the grounds in spring the primroses grew as thickly as in the forest. We had a few fields for the cows, and an excellent walled garden. The place is being pulled down at this moment to make room for more streets of mean little houses,—the kind of thing, and not a dull house of faded gentry, which perhaps the neighbourhood requires. The house was dull, and so were we, its last inhabitants; and the furniture was faded, even a little dingy,—nothing to brag of. I do not, however, intend to convey a suggestion that we were faded gentry, for that was not the case. My father, indeed, was rich, and had no need to spare any expense in making his life and his house bright if he pleased; but he did not please, and I had not been long enough at home to exercise any special influence of my own. It was the only home I had ever known;

but except in my earliest childhood, and in my holidays as a schoolboy, I had in reality known but little of it. My mother had died at my birth, or shortly after, and I had grown up in the gravity and silence of a house without women. In my infancy, I believe, a sister of my father's had lived with us, and taken charge of the household and of me; but she, too, had died long, long ago, my mourning for her being one of the first things I could recollect. And she had no successor. There was, indeed, a house-keeper and some maids,—the latter of whom I only saw disappearing at the end of a passage, or whisking out of a room when one of "the gentle-men" appeared. Mrs Weir, indeed, I saw nearly every day; but a curtsey, a smile, a pair of nice round arms which she caressed while folding them across her ample waist, and a large white apron, were all I knew of her. This was the only female influence in the house. The drawing-room I was aware of only as a place of deadly good order, into which nobody ever entered. It had three long windows opening on the lawn, and com-municated at the upper end, which was rounded like a great bay, with the conservatory. Sometimes I gazed into it as a child from without, won-dering at the needlework on the chairs, the screens, the looking-glasses which never reflected any living face. My father did not like the room, which probably was not wonderful, though it never occurred to me in those early days to inquire why.

I may say here, though it will probably be disappointing to those who form a sentimental idea of the capabilities of children, that it did not occur to me either, in these early days, to make any inquiry about my mother. There was no room in life, as I knew it, for any such person; nothing sug-gested to my mind either the fact that she must have existed, or that there was need of her in the house. I accepted, as I believe most children do, the facts of existence, on the basis with which I had first made acquaintance with them, without question or remark. As a matter of fact, I was aware that it was rather dull at home; but neither by comparison with the books I read, nor by the communications received from my school-fellows, did this seem to me anything remarkable. And I was possibly somewhat dull too by nature, for I did not mind. I was fond of reading, and for that there was unbounded opportunity. I had a little ambition in respect to work, and that too could be prosecuted undisturbed. When I went to the university, my society lay almost entirely among men; but by that time and afterwards, matters had of course greatly changed with me, and though I recognised women as part of the economy of nature, and did not indeed by any means dislike or avoid them, yet the idea of connecting them at all with my own home never entered into my head. That continued to be as it had always been, when at intervals I descended upon the cool, grave, colourless place, in the midst of my traffic with the world: always very still, well-ordered, serious—the cooking very good, the comfort perfect—old Morphew, the butler, a little older (but very little older, perhaps on the whole less old, since in my childhood I had thought him a kind of Methuselah), and Mrs Weir, less active, covering up her arms in sleeves, but folding and caressing them just as always. I remember looking in from the lawn through the windows upon that deadly-orderly drawing-room, with a humorous recollection of my childish admiration and wonder, and feeling that it must be kept so for ever and ever, and that to go into it would break some sort of amusing mock mystery, some pleasantly ridiculous spell.

But it was only at rare intervals that I went home. In the long vacation, as in my school holidays, my father often went abroad with me, so that we had gone over a great deal of the Continent together very pleasantly. He was old in proportion to the age of his son, being a man of sixty when I was twenty, but that did not disturb the pleasure of the relations between us. I don't know that they were ever very confidential. On my side there was but little to communicate, for I did not get into scrapes nor fall in love, the two predicaments which demand sympathy and confidences. And as for my father himself, I was never aware what there could be to communicate on his side. I knew his life exactly—what he did almost at every hour of the day; under what circumstances of the temperature he would ride and when walk; how often and with what guests he would indulge in the occasional break of a dinner-party, a serious pleasure,—perhaps, indeed, less a pleasure than a duty. All this I knew as well as he did, and also his views on public matters, his political opinions, which naturally were different from mine. What ground, then, remained for confidence? I did not know any. We were both of us of a reserved nature, not apt to enter into our religious feelings, for instance. There are many people who think reticence on such subjects a sign of the most reverential way of contemplating them. Of this I am far from being sure; but, at all events, it was the practice most congenial to my own mind.

And then I was for a long time absent, making my own way in the world I did not make it very successfully. I accomplished the natural fate of an Englishman, and went out to the Colonies; then to India in a semi-diplomatic position; but returned home after seven or eight years, invalided, in bad health and not much better spirits, tired and disappointed with my first trial of life. I had, as people say, "no occasion" to insist on making my way. My father was rich, and had never given me the slightest reason to believe that he did not intend me to be his heir. His allowance to me was not illiberal, and though he did not oppose the carrying out of my own plans, he by no means urged me to exertion. When I came home he received me very affectionately, and expressed his satisfaction in my return. "Of course," he said, "I am not glad that you are disappointed, Philip, or that your health is broken; but otherwise it is an ill wind, you know, that blows nobody good—and I am very glad to have you at home. I am growing an old man—"

"I don't see any difference, sir," said I; "everything here seems exactly the same as when I went away—"

He smiled, and shook his head. "It is true enough," he said, "after we have reached a certain age we seem to go on for a long time on a plane, and feel no great difference from year to year; but it is an inclined plane—and the longer we go on, the more sudden will be the fall at the end. But at all events it will be a great comfort to me to have you here."

"If I had known that," I said, "and that you wanted me, I should have come in any circumstances. As there are only two of us in the world—"

"Yes," he said, "there are only two of us in the world; but still I should not have sent for you, Phil, to interrupt your career."

"It is as well, then, that it has interrupted itself," I said, rather bitterly; for disappointment is hard to bear.

He patted me on the shoulder, and repeated, "It is an ill wind that blows nobody good," with a look of real pleasure which gave me a certain gratification too; for, after all, he was an old man, and the only one in all the world to whom I owed any duty. I had not been without dreams of warmer affections, but they had come to nothing—not tragically, but in the ordinary way. I might perhaps have had love which I did not want, but not that which I did want,—which was not a thing to make any unmanly moan about, but in the ordinary course of events. Such disappointments happen every day; indeed, they are more common than anything else, and sometimes it is apparent afterwards that it is better it was so.

However, here I was at thirty stranded—yet wanting for nothing, in a position to call forth rather envy than pity from the greater part of my contemporaries,—for I had an assured and comfortable existence, as much money as I wanted, and the prospect of an excellent fortune for the future. On the other hand, my health was still low, and I had no occupation. The neighbourhood of the town was a drawback rather than an advantage. I felt myself tempted, instead of taking the long walk into the country which my doctor recommended, to take a much shorter one through the High Street, across the river, and back again, which was not a walk but a lounge. The country was silent and full of thoughts—thoughts not always very agreeable—whereas there were always the humours of the little urban population to glance at, the news to be heard, all those petty matters which so often make up life in a very impoverished version for the idle man. I did not like it, but I felt myself yielding to it, not having energy enough to make a stand. The rector and the leading lawyer of the place asked me to dinner. I might have glided into the society, such as it was, had I been disposed for that—everything about me began to close over me as if I had been fifty, and fully contented with my lot.

It was possibly my own want of occupation which made me observe with surprise, after a while, how much occupied my father was. He had expressed himself glad of my return; but now that I had returned, I saw very little of him. Most of his time was spent in his library, as had always been the case. But on the few visits I paid him there, I could not but perceive that the aspect of the library was much changed. It had acquired the look of a business-room, almost an office. There were large business-like books on the table, which I could not associate with anything he could naturally have to do; and his correspondence was very large. I thought he closed one of those books hurriedly as I came in, and pushed it away, as if he did not wish me to see it. This surprised me at the moment, without arousing any other feeling; but afterwards I remembered it with a clearer sense of what it meant. He was more absorbed altogether than I had been used to see him. He was visited by men sometimes not of very prepossessing appearance. Surprise grew in my mind without any very distinct idea of the reason of it; and it was not till after a chance conversation with Morphew that my vague uneasiness began to take definite shape. It was begun without any special intention on my part. Morphew had informed me that master was very busy, on some occasion when I wanted to see him. And I was a little annoyed to be thus put off. "It appears to me that my father is always busy," I said, hastily. Morphew then began very oracularly to nod his head in assent.

"A deal too busy, sir, if you take my opinion," he said.

This startled me much, and I asked hurriedly, "What do you mean?" without reflecting that to ask for private information from a servant about my father's habits was as bad as investigating into a stranger's affairs. It did not strike me in the same light.

"Mr Philip," said Morphew, "a thing 'as 'appened as 'appens more often than it ought to. Master has got awful keen about money in his old age."

"That's a new thing for him," I said.

"No, sir, begging your pardon, it ain't a new thing. He was once broke of it, and that wasn't easy done; but it's come back, if you'll excuse me saying so. And I don't know as he'll ever be broke of it again at his age."

I felt more disposed to be angry than disturbed by this. "You must be making some ridiculous mistake," I said. "And if you were not so old a friend as you are, Morphew, I should not have allowed my father to be so spoken of to me."

The old man gave me a half-astonished, half-contemptuous look. "He's been my master a deal longer than he's been your father," he said, turning on his heel. The assumption was so comical that my anger could not stand in face of it. I went out, having been on my way to the door when this conversation occurred, and took my usual lounge about, which was not a satisfactory sort of amusement. Its vanity and empti- ness appeared to be more evident than usual today. I met half-a-dozen people I knew, and had as many pieces of news confided to me. I went up and down the length of the High Street. I made a small purchase or two. And then I turned homeward—despising myself, yet finding no alternative within my reach. Would a long country walk have been more virtuous?—it would at least have been more wholesome—but that was all that could be said. My mind did not dwell on Morphew's communi- cation. It seemed without sense or meaning to me; and after the excellent joke about his superior interest in his master to mine in my father, was dismissed lightly enough from my mind. I tried to invent some way of telling this to my father without letting him perceive that Morphew had been finding faults in him, or I listening; for it seemed a pity to lose so good a joke. However, as I returned home, something happened which put the joke entirely out of my head. It is curious when a new subject of trouble or anxiety has been suggested to the mind in an unexpected way, how often a second advertisement follows immediately after the first, and gives to that a potency which in itself it had not possessed.

I was approaching our own door, wondering whether my father had gone, and whether, on my return, I should find him at leisure—for I had several little things to say to him—when I noticed a poor woman lingering about the closed gates. She had a baby sleeping in her arms. It was a spring night, the stars shining in the twilight, and everything soft and dim; and the woman's figure was like a shadow, flitting about, now here, now there, on one side or another of the gate. She stopped when she saw me approaching, and hesitated for a moment, then seemed to take a sudden resolution. I watched her without knowing, with a prevision that she was going to address me, though with no sort of idea as to the subject of her address. She came up to me doubtfully, it seemed, yet certainly, as I felt, and when she was close to me, dropped a sort of hesitating curtsey, and said, "It's Mr Philip?" in a low voice.

"What do you want with me?" I said.

Then she poured forth suddenly, without warning or preparation, her long speech—a flood of words which must have been all ready and waiting at the doors of her lips for utterance. "Oh, sir, I want to speak to you! I can't believe you'll be so hard, for you're young; and I can't believe he'll be so hard if so be as his own son, as I've always heard he had but one, 'll speak up for us. Oh, gentleman, it is easy for the likes of you, that, if you ain't comfortable in one room, can just walk into another; but if one room is all you have, and every bit of furniture you have taken out of it, and nothing but the four walls left—not so much as the cradle for the child, or a chair for your man to sit down upon when he comes from his work, or a saucepan to cook him his supper—"

"My good woman," I said, "who can have taken all that from you? surely nobody can be so cruel?"

"You say it's cruel!" she cried with a sort of triumph. "Oh, I knowed you would, or any true gentleman that don't hold with screwing poor folks. Just go and say that to him inside there, for the love of God. Tell him to think what he's doing, driving poor creatures to despair. Summer's coming, the Lord be praised, but yet it's bitter cold at night with your counterpane gone; and when you've been working hard all day, and nothing but four bare walls to come home to, and all your poor little sticks of furniture that you've saved up for, and got together one by one, all gone—and you no better than when you started, or rather worse, for then you was young. Oh, sir!" the woman's voice rose into a sort of passionate wail. And then she added, beseechingly, recovering herself—"Oh, speak for us—he'll not refuse his own son—"

"To whom am I to speak? who is it that has done this to you?" I said.

The woman hesitated again, looking keenly in my face—then repeated with a slight faltering, "It's Mr Philip?" as if that made everything right.

"Yes; I am Philip Canning," I said; "but what have I to do with this? and to whom am I to speak?"

She began to whimper, crying and stopping herself. "Oh, please sir! it's Mr Canning as owns all the house property about—it's him that our court and the lane and everything belongs to. And he's taken the bed from under us, and the baby's cradle, although it's said in the Bible as you're not to take poor folks's bed."

"My father!" I cried in spite of myself—"then it must be some agent, some one else in his name. You may be sure he knows nothing of it. Of course I shall speak to him at once."

"Oh, God bless you, sir," said the woman. But then she added, in a lower tone—"It's no agent. It's one as never knows trouble. It's him that lives in that grand house." But this was said under her breath, evidently not for me to hear.

Morphew's words flashed through my mind as she spoke. What was this? Did it afford an explanation of the much occupied hours, the big books, the strange visitors? I took the poor woman's name, and gave her something to procure a few comforts for the night, and went indoors disturbed and troubled. It was impossible to believe that my father himself would have acted thus; but he was not a man to brook interference, and I did not see how to introduce the subject, what to say. I could but hope that, at the moment of broaching it, words would be put into my mouth, which often happens in moments of necessity, one knows not how, even when one's theme is not so all-important as that for which such help has been promised. As usual, I did not see my father till dinner. I have said that our dinners were very good, luxurious in a simple way, everything excellent in its kind, well cooked, well served, the perfection of comfort without show—which is a combination very dear to the English heart. I said nothing till Morphew, with his solemn attention to everything that was going, had retired—and then it was with some strain of courage that I began.

"I was stopped outside the gate today by a curious sort of petitioner—a poor woman, who seems to be one of your tenants, sir, but whom your agent must have been rather too hard upon."

"My agent? who is that?" said my father, quietly.

"I don't know his name, and I doubt his competence. The poor creature seems to have had everything taken from her—her bed, her child's cradle."

"No doubt she was behind with her rent."

"Very likely, sir. She seemed very poor," said I.

"You take it coolly," said my father, with an upward glance, half-amused, not in the least shocked by my statement. "But when a man, or a woman either, takes a house, I suppose you will allow that they ought to pay rent for it."

"Certainly, sir," I replied, "when they have got anything to pay."

"I don't allow the reservation," he said. But he was not angry, which I had feared he would be.

"I think," I continued, "that your agent must be too severe. And this emboldens me to say something which has been in my mind for some time"—(these were the words, no doubt, which I had hoped would be put into my mouth; they were the suggestion of the moment, and yet as I said them it was with the most complete conviction of their truth)—"and that is this: I am doing nothing; my time hangs heavy on my hands. Make me your agent. I will see for myself, and save you from such mistakes; and it will be an occupation—"

"Mistakes? What warrant have you for saying these are mistakes?" he said testily; then after a moment: "This is a strange proposal from you, Phil. Do you know what it is you are offering?—to be a collector of rents, going about from door to door, from week to week; to look after wretched little bits of repairs, drains, &c.; to get paid, which, after all, is the chief thing, and not to be taken in by tales of poverty."

"Not to let you be taken in by men without pity," I said.

He gave me a strange glance, which I did not very well understand, and said, abruptly, a thing which, so far as I remember, he had never in my life said before, "You've become a little like your mother, Phil—"

"My mother!" The reference was so unusual—nay, so unprecedented—that I was greatly startled. It seemed to me like the sudden introduction of a quite new element in the stagnant atmosphere, as well as a new party to our conversation. My father looked across the table, as if with some astonishment at my tone of surprise.

"Is that so very extraordinary?" he said.

"No; of course it is not extraordinary that I should resemble my mother. Only—I have heard very little of her—almost nothing."

"That is true." He got up and placed himself before the fire, which was very low, as the night was not cold—had not been cold heretofore at least; but it seemed to me now that a little chill came into the dim and faded room. Perhaps it looked more dull from the suggestion of a something brighter, warmer, that might have been. "Talking of mistakes," he said, "perhaps that was one: to sever you entirely from her side of the house. But I did not care for the connection. You will understand how it is that I speak of it now when I tell you—" He stopped here, however, said nothing more for a minute or so, and then rang the bell. Morphew came, as he always did, very deliberately, so that some time elapsed in silence, during which my surprise grew. When the old man appeared at the door—"Have you put the lights in the drawing-room, as I told you?" my father said.

"Yes, sir; and opened the box, sir; and it's a—it's a speaking likeness—"

This the old man got out in a great hurry, as if afraid that his master would stop him. My father did so with a wave of his hand.

"That's enough. I asked no information. You can go now."

The door closed upon us, and there was again a pause. My subject had floated away altogether like a mist, though I had been so concerned about it. I tried to resume, but could not. Something seemed to arrest my very breathing: and yet in this dull respectable house of ours, where everything breathed good character and integrity, it was certain that there could be no shameful mystery to reveal. It was some time before my father spoke, not from any purpose that I could see, but apparently because his mind was busy with probably unaccustomed thoughts.

"You scarcely know the drawing-room, Phil," he said at last.

"Very little. I have never seen it used. I have a little awe of it, to tell the truth."

"That should not be. There is no reason for that. But a man by himself, as I have been for the greater part of my life, has no occasion for a drawing-room. I always, as a matter of preference, sat among my books; however, I ought to have thought of the impression on you."

"Oh, it is not important," I said; "the awe was childish. I have not thought of it since I came home."

"It never was anything very splendid at the best," said he. He lifted the lamp from the table with a sort of abstraction, not remarking even my offer to take it from him, and led the way. He was on the verge of seventy, and looked his age: but it was a vigorous age, with no symptoms of giving way. The circle of light from the lamp lit up his white hair, and keen blue eyes, and clear complexion; his forehead was like old ivory, his cheek warmly coloured: an old man, yet a man in full strength. He was taller than I was, and still almost as strong. As he stood for a moment with the lamp in his hand, he looked like a tower in his great height and bulk. I reflected as I looked at him that I knew him intimately, more intimately than any other creature in the world,—I was familiar with every detail of his outward life; could it be that in reality I did not know him at all?

The drawing-room was already lighted with a flickering array of candles upon the mantelpiece and along the walls, producing the pretty starry effect which candles give without very much light. As I had not the smallest idea what I was about to see, for Morphew's "speaking likeness" was very hurriedly said, and only half comprehensible in the bewilderment of my faculties, my first glance was at this very unusual illumination, for which I could assign no reason. The next showed me a large full-length portrait, still in the box in which apparently it had travelled, placed upright, supported against a table in the centre of the room. My father walked straight up to it, motioned to me to place a smaller table close to the picture on the left side, and put his lamp upon that. Then he waved his hand towards it, and stood aside that I might see.

It was a full-length portrait of a very young woman—I might say a girl, scarcely twenty—in a white dress, made in a very simple old fashion, though I was too little accustomed to female costume to be able to fix the date. It might have been a hundred years old, or twenty, for aught I knew.

The face had an expression of youth, candour, and simplicity more than any face I had ever seen,—or so, at least, in my surprise, I thought. The eyes were a little wistful, with something which was almost anxiety—which at least was not content—in them; a faint, almost imperceptible, curve in the lids. The complexion was of a dazzling fairness, the hair light, but the eyes dark, which gave individuality to the face. It would have been as lovely had the eyes been blue—probably more so—but their darkness gave a touch of character, a slight discord, which made the harmony finer. It was not, perhaps, beautiful in the highest sense of the word. The girl must have been too young, too slight, too little developed for actual beauty; but a face which so invited love and confidence I never saw. One smiled at it with instinctive affection. "What a sweet face!" I said. "What a lovely girl! Who is she? Is this one of the relations you were speaking of on the other side?"

My father made me no reply. He stood aside, looking at it as if he knew it too well to require to look,—as if the picture was already in his eyes. "Yes," he said, after an interval, with a long-drawn breath, "she was a lovely girl, as you say."

"Was?—then she is dead. What a pity!" I said; "what a pity! so young and so sweet!"

We stood gazing at her thus, in her beautiful stillness and calm—two men, the younger of us full grown and conscious of many experiences, the other an old man—before this impersonation of tender youth. At length he said, with a slight tremulousness in his voice, "Does nothing suggest to you who she is, Phil?"

I turned round to look at him with profound astonishment, but he turned away from my look. A sort of quiver passed over his face. "That is your mother," he said, and walked suddenly away, leaving me there.

My mother!

I stood for a moment in a kind of consternation before the white-robed innocent creature, to me no more than a child; then a sudden laugh broke from me, without any will of mine: something ludicrous, as well as something awful, was in it. When the laugh was over, I found myself with tears in my eyes, gazing, holding my breath. The soft features seemed to melt, the lips to move, the anxiety in the eyes to become a personal inquiry. Ah, no! nothing of the kind; only because of the water in mine. My mother! oh, fair and gentle creature, scarcely woman—how could any man's voice call her by that name! I had little idea enough of what it meant,—had heard it laughed at, scoffed at, reverenced, but never had learned to place it even among the ideal powers of life. Yet, if it meant anything at all, what it meant was worth thinking of. What did she ask, looking at me with those eyes? what would she have said if "those lips had language"? If I had known her only as Cowper did—with a child's recollection—there might have been some thread, some faint but comprehensible link, between us; but now all that I felt was the curious incongruity. Poor child! I said to myself; so sweet a creature: poor little tender soul! as if she had been a little sister, a child of mine,—but my mother! I cannot tell how long I stood looking at her, studying the candid, sweet face, which surely had germs in it of everything that was good and beautiful; and sorry, with a profound regret, that she had died and never carried these promises to fulfilment. Poor girl! poor people who had loved her! These were my thoughts: with a curious vertigo and giddiness of my whole being in the sense of a mysterious relationship, which it was beyond my power to understand.

Presently my father came back: possibly because I had been a long time unconscious of the passage of the minutes, or perhaps because he was himself restless in the strange disturbance of his habitual calm. He came in and put his arm within mine, leaning his weight partially upon me, with an affectionate suggestion which went deeper than words. I pressed his arm to my side: it was more between us two grave Englishmen than any embracing.

"I cannot understand it," I said.

"No. I don't wonder at that; but if it is strange to you, Phil, think how much more strange to me! That is the partner of my life. I have never had another—or thought of another. That—girl! If we are to meet again, as I have always hoped we should meet again, what am I to say to her—I, an old man? Yes; I know what you mean. I am not an old man for my years; but my years are threescore and ten, and the play is nearly played out. How am I to meet that young creature? We used to say to each other that it was forever, that we never could be but one, that it was for life and death. But what—what am I to say to her, Phil, when I meet her again, that—that angel? No, it is not her being an angel that troubles me; but she is so young! She is like my—my grand-daughter," he cried, with a burst of what was half sobs, half laughter; "and she is my wife,—and I am an old man—an old man! And so much has happened that she could not understand."

I was too much startled by this strange complaint to know what to say. It was not my own trouble, and I answered it in the conventional way.

"They are not as we are, sir," I said; "they look upon us with larger, other eyes than ours."

"Ah! you don't know what I mean," he said quickly; and in the interval he had subdued his emotion. "At first, after she died, it was my consolation to think that I should meet her again—that we never could be really parted. But, my God, how I have changed since then! I am another man—I am a different being. I was not very young even then—twenty years older than she was: but her youth renewed mine. I was not an unfit partner; she asked no better: and knew as much more than I did in some things—being so much nearer the source—as I did in others that were of the world. But I have gone a long way since then, Phil—a long way; and there she stands just where I left her."

I pressed his arm again. "Father," I said, which was a title I seldom used, "we are not to suppose that in a higher life the mind stands still."

I did not feel myself qualified to discuss such topics, but something one must say.

"Worse, worse!" he replied; "then she too will be like me, a different being, and we shall meet as what? as strangers, as people who have lost sight of each other, with a long past between us—we who parted, my God! with—with—"

His voice broke and ended for a moment: then while, surprised and almost shocked by what he said, I cast about in my mind what to reply, he withdrew his arm suddenly from mine, and said in his usual tone, "Where shall we hang the picture, Phil? It must be here in this room. What do you think will be the best light?"

This sudden alteration took me still more by surprise, and gave me almost an additional shock; but it was evident that I must follow the changes of his mood, or at least the sudden repression of sentiment which he originated. We went into that simpler question with great seriousness, consulting which would be the best light. "You know I can scarcely advise," I said; "I have never been familiar with this room. I should like to put off, if you don't mind, till daylight."

"I think," he said, "that this would be the best place." It was on the other side of the fireplace, on the wall which faced the windows,—not the best light, I knew enough to be aware, for an oil-painting. When I said so, however, he answered me with a little impatience,—"It does not matter very much about the best light. There will be nobody to see it but you and me. I have my reasons—" There was a small table standing against the wall at this spot, on which he had his hand as he spoke. Upon it stood a little basket in very fine lace-like wickerwork. His hand must have trembled, for the table shook, and the basket fell, its contents turning out upon the carpet,—little bits of needlework, coloured silks, a small piece of knitting half done. He laughed as they rolled out at his feet, and tried to stoop to collect them, then tottered to a chair, and covered for a moment his face with his hands.

No need to ask what they were. No woman's work had been seen in the house since I could recollect it. I gathered them up reverently and put them back. I could see, ignorant as I was, that the bit of knitting was something for an infant. What could I do less than put it to my lips? It had been left in the doing—for me.

"Yes, I think this is the best place," my father said a minute after, in his usual tone.

We placed it there that evening with our own hands. The picture was large, and in a heavy frame, but my father would let no one help me but himself. And then, with a superstition for which I never could give any reason even to myself, having removed the packings, we closed and locked the door, leaving the candles about the room, in their soft strange illumination lighting the first night of her return to her old place.

That night no more was said. My father went to his room early, which was not his habit. He had never, however, accustomed me to sit late with him in the library. I had a little study or smoking-room of my own, in which all my special treasures were, the collections of my travels and my favourite books—and where I always sat after prayers, a ceremonial which was regularly kept up in the house. I retired as usual this night to my room, and as usual read—but tonight somewhat vaguely, often pausing to think. When it was quite late, I went out by the glass door to the lawn, and walked round the house, with the intention of looking in at the drawing-room windows, as I had done when a child. But I had forgotten that these windows were all shuttered at night, and nothing but a faint penetration of the light within through the crevices bore witness to the instalment of the new dweller there.

In the morning my father was entirely himself again. He told me without emotion of the manner in which he had obtained the picture. It had belonged to my mother's family, and had fallen eventually into the hands of a cousin of hers, resident abroad—"A man whom I did not like, and who did not like me," my father said; "there was, or had been, some rivalry, he thought: a mistake, but he was never aware of that. He refused all my requests to have a copy made. You may suppose, Phil, that I wished this very much. Had I succeeded, you would have been acquainted, at least, with your mother's appearance, and need not have sustained this shock. But he would not consent. It gave him, I think, a certain pleasure to think that he had the only picture. But now he is dead—and out of remorse, or with some other intention, has left it to me."

"That looks like kindness," said I.

"Yes; or something else. He might have thought that by so doing he was establishing a claim upon me," my father said: but he did not seem disposed to add any more. On whose behalf he meant to establish a claim I did not know, nor who the man was who had laid us under so great an obligation on his deathbed. He *had* established a claim on me at least: though, as he was dead, I could not see on whose behalf it was. And my father said nothing more. He seemed to dislike the subject. When I attempted to return to it, he had recourse to his letters or his newspapers. Evidently he had made up his mind to say no more.

Afterwards I went into the drawing-room to look at the picture once more. It seemed to me that the anxiety in her eyes was not so evident as I had thought it last night. The light possibly was more favourable. She stood just above the place where, I make no doubt, she had sat in life, where her little work-basket was—not very much above it. The picture was full-length, and we had hung it low, so that she might have been stepping into the room, and was little above my own level as I stood and looked at her again. Once more I smiled at the strange thought that this young creature, so young, almost childish, could be my mother; and once more my eyes grew wet looking at her. He was a benefactor, indeed, who had given her back to us. I said to myself, that if I could ever do anything for him or his, I would certainly do, for my—for this lovely young creature's sake.

And with this in my mind, and all the thoughts that came with it, I am obliged to confess that the other matter, which I had been so full of on the previous night, went entirely out of my head.

It is rarely, however, that such matters are allowed to slip out of one's mind. When I went out in the afternoon for my usual stroll—or rather when I returned from that stroll—I saw once more before me the woman with her baby whose story had filled me with dismay on the previous evening. She was waiting at the gate as before, and—"Oh, gentleman, but haven't you got some news to give me?" she said.

"My good woman—I—have been greatly occupied. I have had—no time to do anything."

"Ah!" she said, with a little cry of disappointment, "my man said not to make too sure, and that the ways of the gentlefolks is hard to know."

"I cannot explain to you," I said, as gently as I could, "what it is that has made me forget you. It was an event that can only do you good in the end. Go home now, and see the man that took your things from you, and tell him to come to me. I promise you it shall all be put right."

The woman looked at me in astonishment, then burst forth, as it seemed, involuntarily,—"What! without asking no questions?" After this there came a storm of tears and blessings, from which I made haste to escape, but not without carrying that curious commentary on my rashness away with me—"Without asking no questions?" It might be foolish, perhaps: but after all how slight a matter. To make the poor creature comfortable at the cost of what—a box or two of cigars, perhaps, or some other trifle. And if it should be her own fault, or her husband's—what then? Had I been punished for all my faults, where should I have been now. And if the advantage should be only temporary, what then? To be relieved and comforted even for a day or two, was not that something to count in life? Thus I quenched the fiery dart of criticism which my *protégée* herself had thrown into the transaction, not without a certain sense of the humour of it. Its effect, however, was to make me less anxious to see my father, to repeat my proposal to him, and to call his attention to the cruelty performed in his name. This one case I had taken out of the category of wrongs to be righted, by assuming arbitrarily the position of Providence in my own person—for, of course, I had bound myself to pay the poor creature's rent as well as redeem her goods—and, whatever might happen to her in the future, had taken the past into my own hands. The man came presently to see me who, it seems, had acted as my father's agent in the matter. "I don't know, sir, how Mr Canning will take it," he said. "He don't want none of those irregular, bad-paying one's in his property. He always says as to look over it and let the rent run on is making things worse in the end. His rule is, 'Never more than a month, Stevens:' that's what Mr Canning says to me, sir. He says, 'More than that they can't pay. It's no use trying.' And it's a good rule; it's a very good rule. He won't hear none of their stories, sir. Bless you, you'd never get a penny of rent from them small houses if you listened to their tales. But if so be as you'll pay Mrs Jordan's rent, it's none of my business how it's paid, so long as it's paid, and I'll send her back her things. But they'll just have to be took next time," he added, composedly. "Over and over: it's always the same story with them sort of poor folks—they're too poor for anything, that's the truth," the man said.

Morphew came back to my room after my visitor was gone. "Mr Philip," he said, "you'll excuse me, sir, but if you're going to pay all the poor folk's rent as have distresses put in, you may just go into the court at once, for it's without end—"

"I am going to be the agent myself, Morphew, and manage for my father: and we'll soon put a stop to that," I said, more cheerfully than I felt.

"Manage for—master," he said, with a face of consternation. "You, Mr Philip!"

"You seem to have a great contempt for me, Morphew."

He did not deny the fact. He said with excitement, "Master, sir—master don't let himself be put a stop to by any man. Master's—not one to be managed. Don't you quarrel with master, Mr Philip, for the love of God." The old man was quite pale.

"Quarrel!" I said. "I have never quarrelled with my father, and I don't mean to begin now."

Morphew dispelled his own excitement by making up the fire, which was dying in the grate. It was a very mild spring evening, and he made up a great blaze which would have suited December. This is one of many ways in which an old servant will relieve his mind. He muttered all the time as he threw on the coals and wood. "He'll not like it—we all know as he'll not like it. Master won't stand no meddling, Mr Philip,"—this last he discharged at me like a flying arrow as he closed the door.

I soon found there was truth in what he said. My father was not angry; he was even half amused. "I don't think that plan of yours will hold water, Phil. I hear you have been paying rents and redeeming furniture—that's an expensive game, and a very profitless one. Of course, so long as you are a benevolent gentleman acting for your own pleasure, it makes no difference to me. I am quite content if I get my money, even out of your pockets—so long as it amuses you. But as my collector, you know, which you are good enough to propose to be—"

"Of course I should act under your orders," I said; "but at least you might be sure that I would not commit you to any—to any—" I paused for a word.

"Act of oppression," he said with a smile—"piece of cruelty, exaction—there are half-a-dozen words—"

"Sir—" I cried.

"Stop, Phil, and let us understand each other. I hope I have always been a just man. I do my duty on my side, and I expect it from others. It is your benevolence that is cruel. I have calculated anxiously how much credit it is safe to allow; but I will allow no man, or woman either, to go beyond what he or she can make up. My law is fixed. Now you understand. My agents, as you call them, originate nothing—they execute only what I decide—"

"But then no circumstances are taken into account—no bad luck, no evil chances, no loss unexpected."

"There are no evil chances," he said, "there is no bad luck—they reap as they sow. No, I don't go among them to be cheated by their stories, and spend quite unnecessary emotion in sympathising with them. You will find it much better for you that I don't. I deal with them on a general rule, made, I assure you, not without a great deal of thought."

"And must it always be so?" I said. "Is there no way of ameliorating or bringing in a better state of things?"

"It seems not," he said; "we don't get 'no forrarder' in that direction so far as I can see." And then he turned the conversation to general matters.

I retired to my room greatly discouraged that night. In former ages— or so one is led to suppose—and in the lower primitive classes who still linger near the primeval type, action of any kind was, and is, easier than amid the complications of our higher civilisation. A bad man is a distinct entity, against whom you know more or less what steps to take. A tyrant, an oppressor, a bad landlord, a man who lets miserable tenements at a rack-rent (to come down to particulars), and exposes his wretched tenants to all those abominations of which we have heard so much—well! he is more or less a satisfactory opponent. There he is, and there is nothing to be said for him—down with him! and let there be an end of his wickedness. But when, on the contrary, you have before you a good man, a just man, who has considered deeply a question which you allow to be full of difficulty; who regrets, but cannot, being human, avert, the miseries which to some unhappy individuals follow from the very wisdom of his rule,—what can you do—what is to be done? Individual benevolence at haphazard may baulk him here and there, but what have you to put in the place of his well-considered scheme? Charity which makes paupers? or what else? I had not considered the question deeply, but it seemed to me that I now came to a blank wall, which my vague human sentiment of pity and scorn could find no way to breach. There must be wrong somewhere—but where? There must be some change for the better to be made—but how?

I was seated with a book before me on the table, with my head supported on my hands. My eyes were on the printed page, but I was not reading—my mind was full of these thoughts, my heart of great discouragement and despondency, a sense that I could do nothing, yet that there surely must and ought, if I but knew it, be something to do. The fire which Morphew had built up before dinner was dying out, the shaded lamp on my table left all the corners in a mysterious twilight. The house was perfectly still, no one moving: my father in the library, where, after the habit of many solitary years, he liked to be left alone, and I here in my retreat, preparing for the formation of similar habits. I thought all at once of the third member of the party, the new-comer, alone too in the room that had been hers; and there suddenly occurred to me a strong desire to take up my lamp and go to the drawing-room and visit her, to see whether her soft angelic face would give any inspiration. I restrained, however, this futile impulse—for what could the picture say?—and instead wondered what might have been had she lived, had she been there, warmly enthroned beside the warm domestic centre, the hearth which would have been a common sanctuary, the true home. In that case what might have been? Alas! the question was no more simple to answer than the other: she might have been there alone too, her husband's business, her son's thoughts, as far from her as now, when her silent representative held her old place in the silence and darkness. I had known it so, often enough. Love itself does not always give comprehension and sympathy. It might be that she was more to us there, in the sweet image of her undeveloped beauty, than she might have been had she lived and grown to maturity and fading, like the rest.

I cannot be certain whether my mind was still lingering on this not very cheerful reflection, or if it had been left behind, when the strange occurrence came of which I have now to tell: can I call it an occurrence? My eyes were on my book, when I thought I heard the sound of a door opening and shutting, but so far away and faint that if real at all it must have been in a far corner of the house. I did not move except to lift my eyes from the book, as one does instinctively the better to listen; when— But I cannot tell, nor have I ever been able to describe exactly what it was. My heart made all at once a sudden leap in my breast. I am aware that this language is figurative, and that the heart cannot leap: but it is a figure so entirely justified by sensation, that no one will have any difficulty in understanding what I mean. My heart leapt up and began beating wildly in my throat, in my ears, as if my whole being had received a sudden and intolerable shock. The sound went through my head like the dizzy sound of some strange mechanism, a thousand wheels and springs, circling, echoing, working in my brain. I felt the blood bound in my veins, my mouth became dry, my eyes hot, a sense of something insupportable took possession of me. I sprang to my feet, and then I sat down again. I cast a quick glance round me beyond the brief circle of the lamplight, but there was nothing there to account in any way for this sudden extraordinary rush of sensation—nor could I feel any meaning in it, any suggestion, any moral impression. I thought I must be going to be ill, and got out my watch and felt my pulse: it was beating furiously, about 125 throbs in a minute. I knew of no illness that could come on like this without warning, in a moment, and I tried to subdue myself, to say to myself that it was nothing, some flutter of the nerves, some physical disturbance. I laid myself down upon my sofa to try if rest would help me, and kept still—as long as the thumping and throbbing of this wild excited mechanism within, like a wild beast plunging and struggling, would let me. I am quite aware of the confusion of the metaphor—the reality was just so. It was like a mechanism deranged, going wildly with ever-increasing precipitation, like those horrible wheels that from time to time catch a helpless human being in them and tear him to pieces: but at the same time it was like a maddened living creature making the wildest efforts to get free.

When I could bear this no longer I got up and walked about my room; then having still a certain command of myself, though I could not master the commotion within me, I deliberately took down an exciting book from the shelf, a book of breathless adventure which had always interested me, and tried with that to break the spell. After a few minutes, however, I flung the book aside; I was gradually losing all power over myself. What I should be moved to do,—to shout aloud, to struggle with I know not what; or if I was going mad altogether, and next moment must be a raving lunatic,—I could not tell. I kept looking round, expecting I don't know what: several times, with the corner of my eye I seemed to see a movement, as if some one was stealing out of sight; but when I looked straight, there was never anything but the plain outlines of the wall and carpet, the chairs standing in good order. At last I snatched up the lamp in my hand and went out of the room. To look at the picture? which had been faintly showing in my imagination from time to time, the eyes, more anxious than ever, looking at me from out the silent air. But no; I passed the door of that room swiftly, moving, it seemed, without any volition of my own, and before I knew where I was going, went into my father's library with my lamp in my hand.

He was still sitting there at his writing-table; he looked up astonished to see me hurrying in with my light. "Phil!" he said, surprised. I remember that I shut the door behind me, and came up to him, and set down the lamp on his table. My sudden appearance alarmed him. "What is the matter?" he cried. "Philip, what have you been doing with yourself?"

I sat down on the nearest chair and gasped, gazing at him. The wild commotion ceased, the blood subsided into its natural channels, my heart resumed its place. I use such words as mortal weakness can to express the sensations I felt. I came to myself thus, gazing at him, confounded, at once by the extraordinary passion which I had gone through, and its sudden cessation. "The matter?" I cried; "I don't know what is the matter."

My father had pushed his spectacles up from his eyes. He appeared to me as faces appear in a fever, all glorified with light which is not in them—his eyes glowing, his white hair shining like silver; but his look was severe. "You are not a boy, that I should reprove you; but you ought to know better," he said.

Then I explained to him, so far as I was able, what had happened. Had happened? nothing had happened. He did not understand me—nor did I, now that it was over, understand myself; but he saw enough to make him aware that the disturbance in me was serious, and not caused by any folly of my own. He was very kind as soon as he had assured himself of this, and talked, taking pains to bring me back to unexciting subjects. He had a letter in his hand with a very deep border of black when I came in. I observed it, without taking any notice or associating it with anything I knew. He had many correspondents, and although we were excellent friends, we had never been on those confidential terms which warrant one man in asking another from whom a special letter has come. We were not so near to each other as this, though we were father and son. After a while I went back to my own room, and finished the evening in my usual way, without any return of the excitement which, now that it was over, looked to me like some extraordinary dream. What had it meant? had it meant anything? I said to myself that it must be purely physical, something gone temporarily amiss, which had righted itself. It was physical; the excitement did not affect my mind. I was independent of it all the time, a spectator of my own agitation—a clear proof that, whatever it was, it had affected my bodily organisation alone.

Next day I returned to the problem which I had not been able to solve. I found out my petitioner in the back street, and that she was happy in the recovery of her possessions, which to my eyes indeed did not seem very worthy either of lamentation or delight. Nor was her house the tidy house which injured virtue should have when restored to its humble rights. She was not injured virtue, it was clear. She made me a great many curtseys, and poured forth a number of blessings. Her "man" came in while I was there, and hoped in a gruff voice that God would reward me, and that the old gentleman 'd let 'em alone. I did not like the looks of the man. It seemed to me that in the dark lane behind the house of a winter's night he would not be a pleasant person to find in one's way. Nor was this all: when I went out into the little street which it appeared was all, or almost all, my father's property, a number of groups formed in my way, and at least half-a-dozen applicants sidled up. "I've more claims nor Mary Jordan any day," said one; "I've lived on Squire Canning's property, one place and another, this twenty year." "And what do you say to me," said another; "I've six children to her two, bless you, sir, and ne'er a father to do for them." I believed in my father's rule before I got out of the street, and approved his wisdom in keeping himself free from personal contact with his tenants. Yet when I looked back upon the swarming thoroughfare, the mean little houses, the women at their doors all so open-mouthed, and eager to contend for my favour, my heart sank within me at the thought that out of their misery some portion of our wealth came—I don't care how small a portion: that I, young and strong, should be kept idle and in luxury, in some part through the money screwed out of their necessities, obtained sometimes by the sacrifice of everything they prized! Of course I know all the ordinary commonplaces of life as well as any one—that if you build a house with your hands or your money, and let it, the rent of it is your just due, and must be paid. But yet—

"Don't you think, sir," I said that evening at dinner, the subject being reintroduced by my father himself, "that we have some duty towards them when we draw so much from them?"

"Certainly," he said; "I take as much trouble about their drains as I do about my own."

"That is always something, I suppose."

"Something! it is a great deal—it is more than they get anywhere else. I keep them clean, as far as that's possible. I give them at least the means of keeping clean, and thus check disease, and prolong life—which is more, I assure you, than they've any right to expect."

I was not prepared with arguments as I ought to have been. That is all in the Gospel according to Adam Smith, which my father had been brought up in, but of which the tenets had begun to be less binding in my day. I wanted something more, or else something less; but my views were not so clear, nor my system so logical and well-built, as that upon which my father rested his conscience, and drew his percentage with a light heart.

Yet I thought there were signs in him of some perturbation. I met him one morning coming out of the room in which the portrait hung, as if he had gone to look at it stealthily. He was shaking his head, and saying "No, no," to himself, not perceiving me, and I stepped aside when I saw him so absorbed. For myself, I entered that room but little. I went outside, as I had so often done when I was a child, and looked through the windows into the still and now sacred place, which had always impressed me with a certain awe. Looked at so, the slight figure in its white dress seemed to be stepping down into the room from some slight visionary altitude, looking with that which had seemed to me at first anxiety, which I sometimes represented to myself now as a wistful curiosity, as if she were looking for the life which might have been hers. Where was the existence that had belonged to her, the sweet household place, the infant she had left? She would no more recognise the man who thus came to look at her as through a veil with a mystic reverence, than I could recognise her. I could never be her child to her, any more than she could be a mother to me.

*

Thus time passed on for several quiet days. There was nothing to make us give any special heed to the passage of time, life being very uneventful and its habits unvaried. My mind was very much preoccupied by my father's tenants. He had a great deal of property in the town which was so near us,—streets of small houses, the best-paying property (I was assured) of any. I was very anxious to come to some settled conclusion: on the one hand, not to let myself be carried away by sentiment; on the other, not to allow my strongly roused feelings to fall into the blank of routine, as his had done. I was seated one evening in my own sitting-room busy with this matter,—busy with calculations as to cost and profit, with an anxious desire to convince him, either that his profits were greater than justice allowed, or that they carried with them a more urgent duty than he had conceived.

It was night, but not late, not more than ten o'clock, the household still astir. Everything was quiet—not the solemnity of midnight silence, in which there is always something of mystery, but the soft-breathing quiet of the evening, full of the faint habitual sounds of a human dwelling, a consciousness of life about. And I was very busy with my figures, interested, feeling no room in my mind for any other thought. The singular experience which had startled me so much had passed over very quickly, and there had been no return. I had ceased to think of it: indeed I had never thought of it save for the moment, setting it down after it was over to a physical cause without much difficulty. At this time I was far too busy to have thoughts to spare for anything, or room for imagination: and when suddenly in a moment, without any warning, the first symptom returned, I started with it into determined resistance, resolute not to be fooled by any mock influence which could resolve itself into the action of nerves or ganglions. The first symptom, as before, was that my heart sprang up with a bound, as if a cannon had been fired at my ear. My whole being responded with a start. The pen fell out of my fingers, the figures went out of my head as if all faculty had departed: and yet I was conscious for a time at least of keeping my self-control. I was like the rider of a frightened horse, rendered almost wild by something which in the mystery of its voiceless being it has seen, something on the road which it will not pass, but wildly plunging, resisting every persuasion, turns from, with ever increasing passion. The rider himself after a time becomes infected with this inexplainable desperation of terror, and I suppose I must have done so: but for a time I kept the upper hand. I would not allow myself to spring up as I wished, as my impulse was, but sat there doggedly, clinging to my books, to my table, fixing myself on I did not mind what, to resist the flood of sensation, of emotion, which was sweeping through me, carrying me away. I tried to continue my calculations. I tried to stir myself up with recollections of the miserable sights I had seen, the poverty, the helplessness. I tried to work myself into indignation; but all through these efforts I felt the contagion growing upon me, my mind falling into sympathy with all those straining faculties of the body, startled, excited, driven wild by something I knew not what. It was not fear. I was like a ship at sea straining and plunging against wind and tide, but I was not afraid. I am obliged to use these metaphors, otherwise I could give no explanation of my condition, seized upon against my will, and torn from all those moorings of reason to which I clung with desperation—as long as I had the strength.

When I got up from my chair at last, the battle was lost, so far as my powers of self-control were concerned. I got up, or rather was dragged up, from my seat, clutching at these material things round me as with a last effort to hold my own. But that was no longer possible; I was overcome. I stood for a moment looking round me feebly, feeling myself begin to babble with stammering lips, which was the alternative of shrieking, and which I seemed to choose as a lesser evil. What I said was, "What am I to do?" and after a while, "What do you want me to do?" although throughout I saw no one, heard no voice, and had in reality not power enough in my dizzy and confused brain to know what I myself meant. I stood thus for a moment looking blankly round me for guidance, repeating the question, which seemed after a time to become almost mechanical. What do you want me to do? though I neither knew to whom I addressed it nor why I said it. Presently—whether in answer, whether in mere yielding of nature, I cannot tell—I became aware of a difference: not a lessening of the agitation, but a softening, as if my powers of resistance being exhausted, a gentler force, a more benignant influence, had room. I felt myself consent to whatever it was. My heart melted in the midst of the tumult; I seemed to give myself up, and move as if drawn by some one whose arm was in mine, as if softly swept along, not forcibly, but with an utter consent of all my faculties to do I knew not what, for love of I knew not whom. For love—that was how it seemed—not by force, as when I went before. But my steps took the same course: I went through the dim passages in an exaltation indescribable, and opened the door of my father's room.

He was seated there at his table as usual, the light of the lamp falling on his white hair: he looked up with some surprise at the sound of the opening door. "Phil," he said, and, with a look of wondering apprehension on his face, watched my approach. I went straight up to him, and put my hand on his shoulder. "Phil, what is the matter? What do you want with me? What is it?" he said.

"Father, I can't tell you. I come not of myself. There must be something in it, though I don't know what it is. This is the second time I have been brought to you here."

"Are you going—?" he stopped himself. The exclamation had been begun with an angry intention. He stopped, looking at me with a scared look, as if perhaps it might be true.

"Do you mean mad? I don't think so. I have no delusions that I know of. Father, think—do you know any reason why I am brought here? for some cause there must be."

I stood with my hand upon the back of his chair. His table was covered with papers, among which were several letters with the broad black border which I had before observed. I noticed this now in my excitement without any distinct associations of thoughts, for that I was not capable of; but the black border caught my eye. And I was conscious that he, too, gave a hurried glance at them, and with one hand swept them away.

"Philip," he said, pushing back his chair, "you must be ill, my poor boy. Evidently we have not been treating you rightly: you have been more ill all through than I supposed. Let me persuade you to go to bed."

"I am perfectly well," I said. "Father, don't let us deceive one another. I am neither a man to go mad nor to see ghosts. What it is that has got the command over me I can't tell: but there is some cause for it. You are doing something or planning something with which I have a right to interfere."

He turned round squarely in his chair with a spark in his blue eyes. He was not a man to be meddled with. "I have yet to learn what can give my son a right to interfere. I am in possession of all my faculties, I hope."

"Father," I cried, "won't you listen to me? no one can say I have been undutiful or disrespectful. I am a man, with a right to speak my mind, and I have done so; but this is different. I am not here by my own will. Something that is stronger than I has brought me. There is something in your mind which disturbs—others. I don't know what I am saying. This is not what I meant to say: but you know the meaning better than I. Some one—who can speak to you only by me—speaks to you by me; and I know that you understand."

He gazed up at me, growing pale, and his under lip fell. I, for my part, felt that my message was delivered. My heart sank into a stillness so sudden that it made me faint. The light swam in my eyes: everything went round with me. I kept upright only by my hold upon the chair; and in the sense of utter weakness that followed, I dropped on my knees I think first, then on the nearest seat that presented itself, and covering my face with my hands, had hard ado not to sob, in the sudden removal of that strange influence, the relaxation of the strain.

There was silence between us for some time; then he said, but with a voice slightly broken, "I don't understand you, Phil. You must have taken some fancy into your mind which my slower intelligence— Speak out what you want to say. What do you find fault with? Is it all—all that woman Jordan?"

He gave a short forced laugh as he broke off, and shook me almost roughly by the shoulder, saying, "Speak out! what—what do you want to say?"

"It seems, sir, that I have said everything." My voice trembled more than his, but not in the same way. "I have told you that I did not come by my own will—quite otherwise. I resisted as long as I could: now all is said. It is for you to judge whether it was worth the trouble or not."

He got up from his seat in a hurried way. "You would have me as— mad as yourself," he said, then sat down again as quickly. "Come, Phil: if it will please you, not to make a breach, the first breach, between us, you shall have your way. I consent to your looking into that matter about the poor tenants. Your mind shall not be upset about that, even though I don't enter into all your views."

"Thank you," I said; "but, father, that is not what it is."

"Then it is a piece of folly," he said, angrily. "I suppose you mean—but this is a matter in which I choose to judge for myself."

"You know what I mean," I said, as quietly as I could, "though I don't myself know; that proves there is good reason for it. Will you do one thing for me before I leave you? Come with me into the drawing-room—"

"What end," he said, with again the tremble in his voice, "is to be served by that?"

"I don't very well know; but to look at her, you and I together, will always do something for us, sir. As for breach, there can be no breach when we stand there."

He got up, trembling like an old man, which he was, but which he never looked like save at moments of emotion like this, and told me to take the light; then stopped when he had got half-way across the room. "This is a piece of theatrical sentimentality," he said. "No, Phil, I will not go. I will not bring her into any such— Put down the lamp, and if you will take my advice, go to bed."

"At least," I said, "I will trouble you no more, father, tonight. So long as you understand, there need be no more to say."

He gave me a very curt "good-night," and turned back to his papers— the letters with the black edge, either by my imagination or in reality, always keeping uppermost. I went to my own room for my lamp, and then alone proceeded to the silent shrine in which the portrait hung. I at least would look at her tonight. I don't know whether I asked myself, in so many words, if it were she who—or if it was any one—I knew nothing; but my heart was drawn with a softness—born, perhaps, of the great weakness in which I was left after that visitation—to her, to look at her, to see perhaps if there was any sympathy, any approval in her face. I set down my lamp on the table where her little work-basket still was: the light threw a gleam upward upon her,—she seemed more than ever to be stepping into the room, coming down towards me, coming back to her life. Ah no! her life was lost and vanished: all mine stood between her and the days she knew. She looked at me with eyes that did not change. The anxiety I had seen at first seemed now a wistful subdued question; but that difference was not in her look but in mine.

I need not linger on the intervening time. The doctor who attended us usually, came in next day "by accident," and we had a long conversation. On the following day a very impressive yet genial gentleman from town lunched with us—a friend of my father's, Dr Something; but the introduction was hurried, and I did not catch his name. He, too, had a long talk with me afterwards—my father being called away to speak to some one on business. Dr — drew me out on the subject of the dwellings of the poor. He said he heard I took great interest in this question, which had come so much to the front at the present moment. He was interested in it too, and wanted to know the view I took. I explained at considerable length that my view did not concern the general subject, on which I had scarcely thought, so much as the individual mode of management of my father's estate. He was a most patient and intelligent listener, agreeing with me on some points, differing in others; and his visit was very pleasant. I had no idea until after of its special object: though a certain puzzled look and slight shake of the head when my father returned, might have thrown some light upon it. The report of the medical experts in my case must, however, have been quite satisfactory, for I heard nothing more of them. It was, I think, a fortnight later when the next and last of these strange experiences came.

This time it was morning, about noon,—a wet and rather dismal spring day. The half-spread leaves seemed to tap at the window, with an appeal to be taken in; the primroses, that showed golden upon the grass at the roots of the trees, just beyond the smooth-shorn grass of the lawn, were all drooped and sodden among their sheltering leaves. The very growth seemed dreary—the sense of spring in the air making the feeling of winter a grievance, instead of the natural effect which it had conveyed a few months before. I had been writing letters, and was cheerful enough, going back among the associates of my old life, with, perhaps, a little longing for its freedom and independence, but at the same time a not ungrateful consciousness that for the moment my present tranquillity might be best.

This was my condition—a not unpleasant one—when suddenly the now well-known symptoms of the visitation to which I had become subject suddenly seized upon me,—the leap of the heart; the sudden, causeless, overwhelming physical excitement, which I could neither ignore nor allay. I was terrified beyond description, beyond reason, when I became conscious that this was about to begin over again: what purpose did it answer, what good was in it? My father indeed understood the meaning of it, though I did not understand: but it was little agreeable to be thus made a helpless instrument without any will of mine, in an operation of which I knew nothing; and to enact the part of the oracle unwillingly, with suffering and such a strain as it took me days to get over. I resisted, not as before, but yet desperately, trying with better knowledge to keep down the growing passion. I hurried to my room and swallowed a dose of a sedative which had been given me to procure sleep on my first return from India. I saw Morphew in the hall, and called him to talk to him, and cheat myself, if possible, by that means. Morphew lingered, however, and, before he came, I was beyond conversation. I heard him speak, his voice coming vaguely through the turmoil which was already in my ears, but what he said I have never known. I stood staring, trying to recover my power of attention, with an aspect which ended by completely frightening the man. He cried out at last that he was sure I was ill, that he must bring me something; which words penetrated more or less into my maddened brain. It became impressed upon me that he was going to get some one—one of my father's doctors, perhaps—to prevent me from acting, to stop my interference,—and that if I waited a moment longer I might be too late. A vague idea seized me at the same time, of taking refuge with the portrait—going to its feet, throwing myself there, perhaps, till the paroxysm should be over. But it was not there that my footsteps were directed. I can remember making an effort to open the door of the drawing-room, and feeling myself swept past it, as if by a gale of wind. It was not there that I had to go. I knew very well where I had to go,—once more on my confused and voiceless mission to my father, who understood, although I could not understand.

Yet as it was daylight, and all was clear, I could not help noting one or two circumstances on my way. I saw some one sitting in the hall as if waiting—a woman, a girl, a black-shrouded figure, with a thick veil over her face: and asked myself who she was, and what she wanted there? This question, which had nothing to do with my present condition, somehow got into my mind, and was tossed up and down upon the tumultuous tide like a stray log on the breast of a fiercely rolling stream, now submerged, now coming uppermost, at the mercy of the waters. It did not stop me for a moment, as I hurried towards my father's room, but it got upon the current of my mind. I flung open my father's door, and closed it again after me, without seeing who was there or how he was engaged. The full clearness of the daylight did not identify him as the lamp did at night. He looked up at the sound of the door, with a glance of apprehension; and rising suddenly, interrupting some one who was standing speaking to him with much earnestness and even vehemence, came forward to meet me. "I cannot be disturbed at present," he said quickly; "I am busy." Then seeing the look in my face, which by this time he knew, he too changed colour. "Phil," he said, in a low, imperative voice, "wretched boy, go away—go away; don't let a stranger see you—"

"I can't go away," I said. "It is impossible. You know why I have come. I cannot, if I would. It is more powerful than I—"

"Go, sir," he said; "go at once—no more of this folly. I will not have you in this room. Go—go!"

I made no answer. I don't know that I could have done so. There had never been any struggle between us before; but I had no power to do one thing or another. The tumult within me was in full career. I heard indeed what he said, and was able to reply; but his words, too, were like straws tossed upon the tremendous stream. I saw now with my feverish eyes who the other person present was. It was a woman, dressed also in mourning similar to the one in the hall; but this a middle-aged woman, like a respectable servant. She had been crying, and in the pause caused by this encounter between my father and myself, dried her eyes with a handkerchief, which she rolled like a ball in her hand, evidently in strong emotion. She turned and looked at me as my father spoke to me, for a moment with a gleam of hope, then falling back into her former attitude.

My father returned to his seat. He was much agitated too, though doing all that was possible to conceal it. My inopportune arrival was evidently a great and unlooked-for vexation to him. He gave me the only look of passionate displeasure I have ever had from him, as he sat down again: but he said nothing more.

"You must understand," he said, addressing the woman, "that I have said my last words on this subject. I don't choose to enter into it again in the presence of my son, who is not well enough to be made a party to any discussion. I am sorry that you should have had so much trouble in vain; but you were warned beforehand, and you have only yourself to blame. I acknowledge no claim, and nothing you can say will change my resolution. I must beg you to go away. All this is very painful and quite useless. I acknowledge no claim."

"Oh, sir," she cried, her eyes beginning once more to flow, her speech interrupted by little sobs. "Maybe I did wrong to speak of a claim. I'm not educated to argue with a gentleman. Maybe we have no claim. But if it's not by right, oh, Mr Canning, won't you let your heart be touched by pity? She don't know what I'm saying, poor dear. She's not one to beg and pray for herself, as I'm doing for her. Oh, sir, she's so young! She's so lone in this world—not a friend to stand by her, nor a house to take her in! You are the nearest to her of any one that's left in this world. She hasn't a relation—not one so near as you—oh!" she cried, with a sudden thought, turning quickly round upon me, "this gentleman's your son! Now I think of it, it's not your relation she is, but his, through his mother! That's nearer, nearer! Oh, sir! you're young; your heart should be more tender. Here is my young lady that has no one in the world to look to her. Your own flesh and blood: your mother's cousin—your mother's—"

My father called to her to stop, with a voice of thunder. "Philip, leave us at once. It is not a matter to be discussed with you."

And then in a moment it became clear to me what it was. It had been with difficulty that I had kept myself still. My breast was labouring with the fever of an impulse poured into me, more than I could contain. And now for the first time I knew why. I hurried towards him, and took his hand, though he resisted, into mine. Mine were burning, but his like ice: their touch burnt me with its chill, like fire. "This is what it is?" I cried. "I had no knowledge before. I don't know now what is being asked of you. But, father—understand! You know, and I know now, that some one sends me—some one—who has a right to interfere."

He pushed me away with all his might. "You are mad," he cried. "What right have you to think—? Oh, you are mad—mad! I have seen it coming on—"

The woman, the petitioner, had grown silent, watching this brief conflict with the terror and interest with which women watch a struggle between men. She started and fell back when she heard what he said, but did not take her eyes off me, following every movement I made. When I turned to go away, a cry of indescribable disappointment and remonstrance burst from her, and even my father raised himself up and stared at my withdrawal, astonished to find that he had overcome me so soon and easily. I paused for a moment, and looked back on them, seeing them large and vague through the mist of fever. "I am not going away," I said. "I am going for another messenger—one you can't gainsay."

My father rose. He called out to me threateningly, "I will have nothing touched that is hers. Nothing that is hers shall be profaned—"

I waited to hear no more: I knew what I had to do. By what means it was conveyed to me I cannot tell; but the certainty of an influence which no one thought of calmed me in the midst of my fever. I went out into the hall, where I had seen the young stranger waiting. I went up to her and touched her on the shoulder. She rose at once, with a little movement of alarm, yet with docile and instant obedience, as if she had expected the summons. I made her take off her veil and her bonnet, scarcely looking at her, scarcely seeing her, knowing how it was: I took her soft, small, cool, yet trembling hand into mine; it was so soft and cool, not cold, it refreshed me with its tremulous touch. All through I moved and spoke like a man in a dream, swiftly, noiselessly, all the complications of waking life removed, without embarrassment, without reflection, without the loss of a moment. My father was still standing up, leaning a little forward as he had done when I withdrew, threatening, yet terror-stricken, not knowing what I might be about to do, when I returned with my companion. That was the one thing he had not thought of. He was entirely undefended, unprepared. He gave her one look, flung up his arms above his head, and uttered a distracted cry, so wild that it seemed the last outcry of nature—"Agnes!" then fell back like a sudden ruin, upon himself, into his chair.

I had no leisure to think how he was, or whether he could hear what I said. I had my message to deliver. "Father," I said, labouring with my panting breath, "it is for this that heaven has opened, and one whom I never saw, one whom I know not, has taken possession of me. Had we been less earthly we should have seen her—herself, and not merely her image. I have not even known what she meant. I have been as a fool without understanding. This is the third time I have come to you with her message, without knowing what to say. But now I have found it out. This is her message. I have found it out at last."

There was an awful pause—pause in which no one moved or breathed. Then there came a broken voice out of my father's chair. He had not understood, though I think he heard what I said. He put out two feeble hands. "Phil—I think I am dying—has she—has she come for me?" he said.

We had to carry him to his bed. What struggles he had gone through before I cannot tell. He had stood fast, and had refused to be moved, and now he fell—like an old tower, like an old tree. The necessity there was for thinking of him saved me from the physical consequences which had prostrated me on a former occasion. I had no leisure now for any consciousness of how matters went with myself.

His delusion was not wonderful, but most natural. She was clothed in black from head to foot, instead of the white dress of the portrait. She had no knowledge of the conflict, of nothing but that she was called for, that her fate might depend on the next few minutes. In her eyes there was a pathetic question, a line of anxiety in the lids, an innocent appeal in the looks. And the face the same: the same lips, sensitive, ready to quiver; the same innocent, candid brow; the look of a common race, which is more subtle than mere resemblance. How I knew that it was so, I cannot tell, nor any man. It was the other—the elder—ah no! not elder; the ever young, the Agnes to whom age can never come—she who they say was the mother of a man who never saw her—it was she who led her kinswoman, her representative, into our hearts.

My father recovered after a few days: he had taken cold, it was said, the day before—and naturally, at seventy, a small matter is enough to upset the balance even of a strong man. He got quite well; but he was willing enough afterwards to leave the management of that ticklish kind of property which involves human wellbeing in my hands, who could move about more freely, and see with my own eyes how things were going on. He liked home better, and had more pleasure in his personal existence in the end of his life. Agnes is now my wife, as he had, of course, foreseen. It was not merely the disinclination to receive her father's daughter, or to take upon him a new responsibility, that had moved him, to do him justice. But both these motives had told strongly. I have never been told, and now will never be told, what his griefs against my mother's family, and specially against that cousin, had been; but that he had been very determined, deeply prejudiced, there can be no doubt. It turned out after, that the first occasion on which I had been mysteriously commissioned to him with a message which I did not understand, and which for that time he did not understand, was the evening of the day on which he had received the dead man's letter, appealing to him—to him, a man whom he had wronged—on behalf of the child who was about to be left friendless in the world. The second time, further letters, from the nurse who was the only guardian of the orphan, and the chaplain of the place where her father had died, taking it for granted that my father's house was her natural refuge—had been received. The third I have already described, and its results.

For a long time after, my mind was never without a lurking fear that the influence which had once taken possession of me might return again. Why should I have feared to be influenced—to be the messenger of a blessed creature, whose wishes could be nothing but heavenly? Who can say? Flesh and blood is not made for such encounters: they were more than I could bear. But nothing of the kind has ever occurred again.

Agnes had her peaceful domestic throne established under the picture. My father wished it to be so, and spent his evenings there in the warmth and light, instead of in the old library, in the narrow circle cleared by our lamp out of the darkness, as long as he lived. It is supposed by strangers that the picture on the wall is that of my wife; and I have always been glad that it should be so supposed. She who was my mother, who came back to me and became as my soul for three strange moments and no more, but with whom I can feel no credible relationship as she stands there, has retired for me into the tender regions of the unseen. She has passed once more into the secret company of those shadows, who can only become real in an atmosphere fitted to modify and harmonise all differences, and make all wonders possible—the light of the perfect day.

DIES IRÆ

"He that works me good with unmoved face,
Does it but half; he chills me while he aids,—
My benefactor, not my Brother-man."

—COLERIDGE

PART I

I HAD been very ill. I knew that. Strange whisperings had from time to time penetrated to my brain that were not intended for me to hear, and I knew from them that those in waiting upon me had given up all hope of my recovery.

At first I had rebelled, bitterly, clamorously. Still, as I appeared to lie, speechless, helpless, life was at fever-heat in my brain, and my soul was rising up in fierce rebellion. In the full tide of youth and health to be singled out from the multitude to… die! There was surely injustice, cruel injustice, in it. "Threescore and ten years," I quoted, and I had but lived twenty-five. Never yet had I been denied anything that life could give, and now the common blessing of life itself was to be taken from me at a stroke.

I knew, I did not deny that I knew, that Death had never been a respecter of ages; but "All men think all men mortal but themselves": and that it should be I against whom the decree had gone forth—it was incredible.

That phase had passed; my fruitless wrath had spent itself; a few salt tears had gathered, and lain in the hollow cups of my eyes, and those that watched had looked more sadly than before upon me.

165

"Hush! she is dying!" I heard them say, as the first cock crew.

So the "Supreme Moment" was at hand; and, strangely enough, I was now beyond caring for it. Probably I was too weak to care.

"It must be very near," I thought, as I saw my good pastor kneel by my bedside, a look of intense earnestness contracting his features.

"She must not die. She shall not die. There is much for her to do on earth yet."

What did he mean? Was it work that I had left undone, and was he going to wrestle for my soul from out the very grip of death; as had done Luther, centuries ago, for his friend?

Ah! I was weary… too weary to think more. Through dimming sight I could just see the hospital nurse, a kindly dark-eyed woman, who seemed all eyes and cap and spotless linen, move round me as in a dream. Was she praying now too? And my cousin, whom they had brought four hundred miles, because I had no nearer relative, was she too sinking on her knees?… I was growing faint… fainter… the air was stifling!… I was struggling… panting… striving… Free!… drawing, it seemed to me, a long, long breath.

Where was I?

Half-way through the room, half-way to the roof, turning with amazed eyes to look on the scene upon which I had just closed my eyes.

There was the kneeling pastor, with folded upraised hands and supplicating speech; there the nurse, with bent head but professional watchfulness; my little fair-haired cousin, her head buried on her hands; strangest of all, there lay a figure outstretched under a snowy counterpane, that it was impossible to help recognising as myself. For one moment I saw distinctly the white, drawn face, sharpening in the death-agony, the closed eyes, the cup-like hollows filled with the cruel tears I had shed, the white hand on the counterpane… A moment and all was dark. I knew no more.

*

Had I been asleep, or was I awake now?

I was in the open air, a great sense of space, of breath, of life about me.

Behind me lay a valley stretching into the dim distance, encompassed with white mist. Shadows of human beings were faintly discernible in its midst, moving to and fro, and a very distant hum of voices penetrated the air. Here and there I could see figures emerging from its white cloud; sometimes in little bands of three and four—sometimes alone. Was that the earth that lay so close to an encircling world?…

Yes, and it lay behind me now. What was beyond? I looked up with eager inquiry.

Before me rose in a long incline the green slope of a hillside that, through shaded ways, led to a level overshadowed by an amphitheatre of hills—hills whose peaks rose like great white crystals, roseate, golden-tipped, losing themselves in colour.

With bated breath and a strange thrill of expectancy, I asked myself, if perchance my feet had wandered to the threshold of Paradise; if these golden heights were where saints and angels congregated—where they "summered high in bliss upon the hills of God."

Nor did I fear that I had been deceived, when down the turf-clad path there moved towards me one, half-goddess, half-woman.

Where had I seen or heard of beauty such as hers before? Surely in some dream. Ah! I knew… How often had I repeated with untiring delight—

> "Her robe, ungirt from clasp to hem
>   No wrought flowers did adorn…
> Her hair, that lay along her back,
>   Was yellow, like ripe corn."

There, in all the glory of the poet's picturing, she stood: a Blessed Damozel; and her soft slow steps were surely bringing her to me.

She was close to me. I was looking up into the blue depths of her eyes.

Yes:

> "They were deeper than the depths
> Of water stilled at even."

But they were filled with a soft sadness that brought a shapeless fear to mingle with my wonder.

Was she sad for me, this Blessed Damozel? Her whole mien was one of gracious pity… Was it for me?…

A faint feeling began to gather at my heart. The "hills of God" seemed very far away.

PART II

We were slowly climbing the steep, the Blessed Damozel and I. Her hand clasped mine in familiar touch. Her words of welcome had been sweet to my soul, for in saying them, through the depth of sorrow in her eyes there had shone the purest light of love.

"You… love me!" I had said, surprised into speech.

"I have loved you," she had murmured, "all your life upon the earth."

"Then I will fear no evil," I had answered, reassured, and clung to her outstretched hand.

As we went I pointed to the crystal heights on which the glory lay.

"I know them. I have read of them. They are the 'hills of God.' Are we going there?"

She lifted a reverent gaze to the far-off peaks.

"These are the 'hills of Holiness,'" she answered, and with averted gaze pursued her way.

The old faint fear crept coldly round my heart, and my gaze went fearfully forward. Visions of Paradise were slowly melting away from me. In their place the *Dies Iræ* began to repeat itself in my brain.

That Day of Wrath! that dreadful day!...

What was before me?... What awaited me?...

Half-way up the slope a murmur behind made me turn curiously. A little company was just emerging from the mist-filled valley, and following in our steps. My guide looked behind.

"Shall we wait for them?" she asked, and drew me aside into the shade of a grove of trees.

Before long they were nearing us. A little woman led by the hand by a fair guide somewhat like my own, but of a very different type of beauty. The flowing hair was dark, the figure fuller, and there was a very marked difference in her expression. It was of one that triumphed, and in her large dark eyes a light of victory shone. A little company followed them. A widow with streaming eyes, leading by the hand a boy and girl; a maiden, pale-faced and worn; a hard-featured woman, speaking volubly to a deaf audience, but with tears in her eyes.

"Who is she?" I asked, my gaze going back to the small central figure.

"A little maiden lady of seventy years, who left the world this morning. No, she does not look her years. It is the 'youth of the soul' that is on her face—immortal youth."

"And those who are with her, are they all dead? They somehow look different."

"No; these are the forms of those who have loved her, and whose souls are longing after her so powerfully, that, unknown to themselves, they are here with her, testifying unconsciously to her love and sweet charity while among them."

"Did... did no one come with me?" I asked, shamed, I knew not why, before the question was well framed.

"She had seventy years of life, you only twenty-five," my friend answered, very sorrowfully. Her love would evidently fain cover a multitude of sins.

At this moment the group stopped almost opposite to us. The little face had the beauty of a child rather than that of an old woman.

"*She* has possessed her soul in innocency," I said, involuntarily. "But what does it all mean? I suppose she was kind to those people, but…"

"Keep your gaze fixed steadily upon her, and you will one by one see the different scenes of her life stand out in clear relief. I see them now, and as she moves up to higher planes, they will stand out in bolder and still bolder relief to every eye."

I steadied my gaze, and this is what I saw:—

I saw her as a girl seated at a piano, painfully imparting the most elementary knowledge of its use to a perplexed girl as old as herself.

"The girl has to win her bread by teaching. She is trying to fit her for the battle. She has no money. She is giving time… and love."

The scene had melted away.

Round her was a little house of mean appearance. She was "on household cares intent." A fretful woman was extended on a sofa, speaking in querulous tones.

I looked to my guide.

"The sick woman is a worn-out music-teacher, homeless, sick. She is no relative, not even a friend, has but the claim of weakness and want. The little maiden lady had very small means. She argued with herself that the only way by which she could help her was to do without any service herself, and to use the cost of service in housing and clothing this poor woman. Like Dr Johnson's dependants, the music-mistress too often used her opportunities to grumble at her benefactress. But she is worshipping her today."

The woman of voluble speech was indeed on her knees before the little lady. I could hear her murmured thanks, and the troubled protest in response.

When I looked again, she was in other surroundings. The young widow and the boy and girl, whose figures were now fading into the mist, were clustered round her, younger and poorer.

"When the querulous old music-mistress died," spoke my guide, "the little lady vowed that she would still share her home with the homeless. Out of the crowd came this young widow, penniless, with a boy and girl to rear. These are the mourners whose true sorrow follows her. The widow's gratitude was not confined to words. Look at the home she made for her."

I saw a bright and happy household, holding the head in loving reverence, and she growing old among them.

"Now," said my guide, bringing me back to the present, "she will have her reward."

At this moment her guide stopped, her face wreathed with smiles, took a crown she had been carefully carrying, and stooping over her with infinite tenderness, placed it on her brows.

She turned her face towards me, alight with soft surprise, and I saw plainly written in letters of gold:—

"I was a stranger, and ye took me in."

Then they passed away, to where sweet strains of music called. We were alone, I with the tears gathered thick in my eyes.

"And I," looking round in bewilderment—"I have loved none, helped none, except through others; denied myself for none. What of me?... Ah! God will for Christ's sake forgive me. I died trusting in Him."

"God will for Christ's sake forgive you," said my sweet Damozel, solemnly, "but..."

"But what? Sweet Damozel, answer me," for my guide was pursuing her way with sorrowful mien.

"Yet one thing thou lackest,"... she quoted.

"'One thing thou lackest,'" I repeated after her. "'Sell all that thou hast, and give to the poor.' But that… we were told that was not meant literally."

"Its 'spirit' giveth life."

"Its 'Spirit'!"…

"Its spirit is Love, and Love is Everlasting Life."

I was deeply bewildered.

"But"—a strange fear beginning to gather round my heart—"the pains of hell, they at least were an invention of narrow-minded men, of whom Calvin was the chief: not even for the wicked do they exist!"

"I can believe in no hell," I went on passionately, finding my guide slow to answer, "for with it there could be no heaven. I for one," daringly, being deeply imbued with the latest sentiments I had listened to on earth—"I could not be happy in the highest heaven if I knew there was one poor soul imprisoned in a hell."

I thought for a moment that my Blessed Damozel was breathing a prayer for me, so sad was the expression of her uplifted eyes, and slowly but surely the terrors of the Unknown began to encompass me about.

The air was growing colder, purer, more difficult of breath, and an excessive light was blinding me. We had reached the level.

It was, as I had seen from afar, an amphitheatre encircled by high hills; at first it seemed to be closed in entirely, but on looking closer and with straining gaze, I saw openings to right and to left.

With a flash of memory, words that had been familiar to me from childhood repeated themselves in my brain.

"*And He set the sheep on His right hand, and the goats on His left.*"

"Where… do they lead?" I asked, with a strange sinking of the heart.

"To God," answered my guide, solemnly.

Oh, Day of Wrath!… Oh, Dreadful Day!… rhymed on in my brain.

"Come!" said my guide; and, with a terror growing ever greater at my heart, I followed to where, as I gazed on the two parting roads, there, out of the light a shape slowly formed itself, terrible in its beauty to any erring child of earth, for its beauty was the beauty of Holiness.

I fell prostrate at its feet. I closed my eyes in the dust. All my complacency fell from me as a garment; all the fair colouring with which I had clothed myself in imagination, melted like a breath before that pure presence. Petty self-deceivings, multiplied self-excusings, they were as if they had never been.

I had but one cry:—

"*God have mercy upon me… Christ have mercy upon me.*"

Through the silence, and as if it were afar off, I heard the voice of my Blessed Damozel pleading for me.

"Lord, have pity upon her. She has sinned in ignorance."

…"*God have mercy upon me.*"

"She is yet of tender years. Only a third of the days allotted to man upon the earth have been granted to her."

…"*Christ have mercy upon me.*"

Strangely enough, although I lay prostrate as before, I could as plainly see my pleader and my Judge as if I had been standing upright before them; and although I did not once open my lips, a voice that yet seemed mine took up speech against me, almost without my will.

"*Mea culpa! mea culpa!*"…

"She brings none with her, it is true, but she lived in a charmed circle. Great wealth of this world's goods were bequeathed to her. She has known no poverty."

…"*God have mercy upon me.*"

"She has known no sorrow."

…"*Christ have mercy upon me.*"

"And," she went on, with pleading earnestness, "she has known no love."

Then I knew, from the light on my sweet guide's face, that this last plea had somehow brought amelioration of my sentence.

"Come!" she whispered low, and I kissed the hem of her garment as she gently raised me.

"Where... are you leading me?" I asked in a new humility, when we had gone some distance. "But I know,"... for she was slow to answer. "To Outer Darkness."

She stopped short, and wound her arms round my neck.

"It is indeed Outer Darkness," she answered, and made my spirit to fail with her word. "But, my love, you go on a quest that will end in victory... on a high and holy quest."

"What quest?" raising weary eyes.

"The quest after Love."

"Ah! you said I had never known that. I thought I had."

"It is one thing to love, another to be loved. On earth we too often crave for the second, and so miss the first. Yet the first is of God; the second of self."

"And when I find Love, shall I be safe?" sorrowfully enough.

Her eyes were very sad. "When you have ceased to ask after safety, you may come within reach of Love."

"Alas! you talk in riddles."

"Till the riddle is solved, you will not see God, for... 'God is Love.'"

I was sorely bewildered, and grievously faint at heart.

"Wherever I go, will you go with me?" I asked, clinging to her in a loneliness that was growing and growing in me.

"You will come back to me," she answered, her eyes filling slowly with tears as she bent over me. "From the day that you were born, I have had you in my care. Now I may keep you but a very little longer. Ah! I am sad exceedingly for you, for I too have trodden every step of the way. I, like you, came hither trusting in the Christ, but with the very first lessons of the 'Religion of Love' unlearned; and only when you have conquered, shall I be free to live the wider life that lies beyond."

"There is a wider life beyond?"

"Yes!" the joy of all the ages future shining in her eyes, till she was transfigured to a beauty that thrilled me through and through, "a wider life beyond and beyond, and for ever beyond. We shall share it together."

"I shall never be like you!" I cried, in despair.

"My love, you will one day awake in His likeness… so shall I… and we shall be satisfied."

But now and for me that Outer Darkness beckoned. Already I imagined that shadows were falling around us.

She read my thought.

"I shall wait for you at Dawn," she whispered.

"Have I then only one long night of horror and of pain before me?" I asked, with conscious relief.

"We count no time here. A night is as a thousand years; a thousand years as a night."

"You mean that Life is so intense, time is lost sight of."

"Yes."

"Why have you changed the word in the passage? why night instead of day?"

"There is no day where you go," she answered. "It is always night there."

I began to tremble exceedingly.

"But you will watch for me at Dawn?" in accents that were now piteous entreaty. "You will not fail me?"

"I shall watch with open arms for you at Dawn," she answered, and therewith fell on my neck and kissed me, mingling her tears with mine.

I thought I heard a sob, but it might have been my own sobbing breath, for my fears had overcome me, and I lay like a child in her arms, holding her fast.

As in a dream I felt the arms loosening slowly from round me, and then my own tenderly unclasped. I seemed to cling with all my might.

"Oh, Blessed Damozel!" I cried, "have pity!… Stay!"…

But it was of no avail. She was gone. I was alone, and swooning for fear and grief.

PART III

When I awoke, the shadows of night were indeed around me. Straining my gaze into their depths, I could distinguish blacker shadows of massive buildings rising higher and higher on every hand; buildings on buildings, dark, gloomy, with endless passages winding in and out among them—passages narrow, foul, and overshadowed with such darkness as lay on my very soul; for surely it was not the darkness of Nature alone that brooded over that ghostly city.

From a height I looked down on it with ever-quickening gaze. Could these be human beings that crowded storey after storey of the towering masses of stone, and swarmed in swaying multitudes in every darkened passage? They did indeed seem to take shape to my curious gaze. Figures of old and young, sickly infants, and tottering old women, men and women of all ages, mixed in a motley crowd; and ever and anon, to my shrinking ear, from the whole came up a confused wailing of many voices, sounding, it seemed to me, every note of pain, from the feeble wail of infancy to that of torture unendurable, while loud-mouthed curses, that made my very flesh creep for fear, mingled from time to time with the sounds.

It is, I think, Jean Paul Richter who has recorded his belief that of all Hells the Hell of sound is the worst; and I knew then, as I had never known before, what he meant. It was no long time till, after listening to cry after cry, I put my hands to my ears in the vain endeavour to escape from it all. But no device of earth availed here. There was no closing of the ears. The increasing wail waxed ever louder and more bitter; I even grew to distinguish a horrible laughter mingling itself with it, till, when at last a terror-filled shriek rang and rang through the darkened air, I could bear it no longer. I threw myself on my knees and added my cry to theirs.

"God in Heaven, what have they done, to be so tormented?" I cried. "Is there no mercy in heaven or earth to help them?"

A voice, stern, resolute, sounded in my ear. It bade me rise; and looking up, I found by my side one of terrible aspect, awful in a majesty that made me cower before him.

"Who art thou?" I did not dare to ask, but he had read and answered my thought.

"I am the Avenging Angel," he answered.

"To these poor people," I said, with an indignant thrill.

"Of these poor people," he answered.

And although I knew not what he meant, I shrank before him.

"You are… their…"

But even as I spoke, another of those terror-laden shrieks rent the air and startled me out of all self-control.

"What does it mean?" I sobbed, in almost equal terror.

"It means that cruelty is rampant, and there is none to check it; that lust is unbridled, and the innocent flee before it; that avarice stalks unheeded throughout the land, leaving famine and desolation behind. Look and learn."

They were words my Blessed Damozel had used; but they were repeated now with a sternness of tone that made me tremble as before a judge. No compassion shone in the eyes of the Avenging Angel as he bent them on me.

I turned my gaze where he directed, and found that by some strange means he had contrived to throw a strong light down on a pair of figures in the far depth of the valley—a pair clasped in each other's arms; a husband and wife. The woman was wan and worn to a shadow; the man scarcely better.

"Avarice has been on their track for years," said my guide. "She is slowly dying, but she has possessed her soul in patience. She will be at rest tonight."

"But why are they here at all? What sin did they commit?"

There was no answer. The thoughts of the Avenging Angel were far from me.

"Tomorrow at dawn I shall set her free, and she shall sleep till then. But… 'woe to him by whom the offence cometh.'"

Why should all the graciousness pass from his face when he turned to me? Why should I have to shrink again into the attitude of a culprit? I did not dare to ask the question I was longing to have answered. Did death reign here as in the world? for no such possibility had entered my imagination. But questioning was lost sight of in a new terror.

A cry as of a hunted animal rent the air and startled me into a new agony of fear.

"What?… what is that?"

For answer the strange light fell with lurid gleam on a fleeing maiden of tender years and a monster in human shape pursuing.

My heart stood still, then leapt with sudden horror.

"O God, he gains on her!… Stop him!… You are an angel! Oh…"

My shrieks were mingling with the maiden's as I fell on my face to shut out the hideous horror.

It was long before I raised streaming eyes to my companion.

"You could have helped, you would not move."

"I am her Avenger," he answered, grimly.

"You will hurl her destroyer to the lowest hell," I said.

"Nay, not him alone."

"On whom will vengeance fall?" I asked, eagerly.

"These are the hidden things of God," he answered, solemnly. "Each goeth to his own place."

Each to his own place, and I was here. What had such scenes as those I was witnessing to do with me?...

Even as we spoke a great hum of angry voices was coming again within hearing, swelling as it rose and rose, ever nearer, and bringing with it a new horror before which my spirit quailed. Was there to be no rest for me through all this weary night? I shrank before the ever-growing tumult: children crying, women shrilly calling, men cursing.

"Oh, I cannot bear more!... The night is hideous with sound. A moment, I pray you, of rest. Shut out the sounds from my ears but for one brief moment. Let me dream, were it only for a moment, that I am again back in my old home, all barbarous sounds shut out... I am a weak and tenderly reared girl... Such sights and sounds as I have seen and heard tonight, I have never even dreamt of. What... what is happening now?... Ah, spare me! No more light, I pray. But, my God, what is that?..."

"Cruelty rampant: the victims are at its mercy."

"Is there none to help? none to answer to such cries?"

"The few help; the many disregard. But the Lord will avenge," solemnly, "and I am His servant."

He was awful as he spoke, for the valley rang with execrations, strange oaths, piteous weeping.

I went back to my pleading.

"A moment of respite, I pray you... I am sick at heart."...

What was happening? A strange light was spreading far and wide in a large semicircle, leaving the valley below in deeper gloom than before. The night was become light about us. I gazed as one in a dream at fair gardens stretching down gentle slopes, at stately mansions, at delicate women and strong-limbed men, strolling through softly carpeted rooms or lounging on low settees. Children like to little angels played merrily, and soft laughter welled out to us.

As I looked, recognition slowly came to me. I had got my prayer.

"It is what I left behind!" I cried, in rapture. "Ah, how good it was!"

For a brief moment I gazed, forgetting all the horrors I had gone through. Alas! it was only for a moment. My guide touched me on the shoulder.

"How good it was!" I repeated, ere I responded.

His face was sterner than before as he looked down on me. Slowly raising his hand with an ominous gesture, he pointed to the deep Valley of Shadow I had for the moment been allowed to forget.

"And what of them?" he asked.

I followed his gaze. I was growing truly bewildered.

"What!… Do they lie so near?"

"So near that although those in the Valley cannot climb to those who 'dwell at ease,' yet those dwellers at ease can go to the weary and tormented and save them if they will."

"If they will!" I cried, indignantly. "Who would rest if they could help that struggling multitude?"…

… A curious thing was happening. Slowly the mists enshrouding the Valley were rolling away before my eyes, and as they lifted themselves, the place was assuming a strangely familiar shape. Were not these the towers and fastnesses of my own town rising out of the crowd? Was that streak of grey not the river with its bridges, that separated the old town from the new? Could it be? Was that Valley of wicked strife and dire poverty and cruel disease indeed the picturesque valley in the midst of my childhood's home? Was this the Valley of Shadow unspeakable I had been contemplating?

It was night. The gas-lit streets were swarming with a swaying multitude, the crowded houses still poured forth their inmates… They were recognisable for such men and women and children as I had grown up among. At this moment the old town clock I had known from a child tolled out the hour. I counted the strokes mechanically.

"Twelve o'clock!… Midnight!" I said, without thinking.

"Midnight!" repeated my guide, as the last stroke died away. "It is now the 'Day of Rest.'"

Oh! hideous mockery.

"And that is…"

"The town where you and they were born."

"And these are…"

"Your sisters… and brothers."

"It has been a morbid dream," I cried. "I have had a nightmare."

But almost before I had dared to uplift my voice, the mists fell as before on all around. I was standing alone with my guide on the mountain-side. Below us stretched the darkened Valley like a Lake of Gloom in the heart of the pretty town: worse than all, that wail of all the weary, that cry of all the suffering, was filling again the void.

"Where are the watchmen?" I asked, with a tone of earth in my voice, which my guide must have recognised.

"In the fray," answered my guide, "adding to it, saving some, too late for others. They perhaps are least likely to think your dream morbid."

And, indeed, with that weary, weary wail in my ears, it was difficult to repeat my words.

"My God, it is too awful!" I cried in despair, for sight was now being added to sound; and when I would fain have closed both eyes and ears, it was to find as before that no such escape was possible. "It is too awful! It is hell indeed!"

And so saying, I sank to earth.

"No happiness was possible for you in Heaven, while one poor spirit lay in Hell," gibed a mocking voice in my ear.

Without looking up, I knew that my stern guide was gone, and that his place had been taken by an imp of darkness, who was grinning at my discomfiture.

"Beautiful dreamer of fair sentiments!" reviled another voice. "Imaginative sympathy is so fine a thing. And so easy."…

"Learn what this meaneth," spoke one solemnly in passing; "'I will have mercy, and not sacrifice.'"...

... "'And though I bestow all my goods to feed the poor... and have not Love,'" quoted another sorrowfully, "'it profiteth me nothing.'"...

PART IV

"One night is as a thousand years."...

I was in the arms of my Blessed Damozel, sobbing my heart out on her breast.

"At last... At last the day had dawned and set me free, and, as I had never doubted she would be, there, waiting on the fair hillside, had stood my sweet and blessed Lady, the first rays of sunshine lying on her golden hair, her white arms outstretched, her eyes full of tenderest sympathy, and deep with unforgotten sorrow."

I could not speak. I could not bring before her mind one picture of the horrors I had undergone. I could only cling to her neck and sob... and sob.

"I know it all," she whispered. "I too have gone every step of the way."

It seemed too cruel. She too, my Blessed Damozel.

"No! Not cruel, love."... Did ever saint or angel say that word as did my sweet lady? It fell as balm on the wounded spirit. "Not cruel. I... listen, love,"... for indeed I was refusing to listen—"I would go through every pang of that time to gain what I have gained."

It was a spiritless questioning I undertook.

"What was your gain?"

"The Crown of Life: Love," she answered.

I had forgotten. It was a quest after Love I had been supposed to be sent forth on. I had not even once remembered it.

"I... have gained nothing," I answered.

"Ah, yes, you have."…

"What?"

"Knowledge."…

I was too weary for answer. I dropped my head upon her fair bosom. She understood, and presently we reclined on the slope together, I held fast in her arms, the soft air of summer wrapping us round, the trill of birds in our ear, the clear trickling of a brook close by. But what were they all to the loving embrace that held me: tender, true, for all the Eternity that lay before us?

We were "as the angels of God."

PART V

"A thousand years is as a day."

It had seemed no more than a day, a too short day, till again the shadows were falling thick around me, and I stood alone with reluctant feet at the entrance to that world of darkness I had learned to name hell.

A force it was useless to resist was impelling me forward, and yet it was only to be met by sounds and sights that as strongly seemed to force me back at every step. Ah, for a door of escape!… And yet… One glimmer of intelligence shone like a star in a dark firmament, where all was blackness before.

My Blessed Damozel had trodden every step of the way—nay, Christ Himself had trodden it… I could never be as Christ, or even as my sweet lady, but there might be for me also sweet to be gained by the bitter.

I was moving ever down the slope, nearer and nearer to the black masses of people, deeper into the shadow of gloom, till I was at length myself one of the multitude that swayed this way and that, in the narrow alleys and in the open squares.

Caught into the stream, I had small time given me to think. There at my feet was a little child, disfigured, marred in visage, probably all that was criminal in embryo, but still a child, weak, helpless; and a reeling madman, emerging from the darkness, had his foot raised to kick. With the old cry of pain, I sprang to interpose, but it was only to discover what I had for the moment forgotten, that I was not now of Earth. I could interpose no human body between; the child fell with a moan, and a passer-by lifted it, while another promptly implanted a blow on the drunken wretch, which he was too insensible to feel.

I turned and fled. The old horrors of my night were indeed begun. It was as if all the peaceful homes were hidden from my sight, and light, a strange lurid light, that of itself lent a horrible clearness to the pictures, was poured down on every revolting sight that a city at its lowest can show. Nothing that was not of Earth, and already familiar to me through the newspaper columns of the day; it was only that the light detached them from the whole, and for a time I was made to see them, and only them, in a succession of horrors that was agonising.

Yes, they were all familiar.

That, before which I shrieked, would tomorrow be reported as a murder "under peculiarly revolting circumstances;" that which made me sicken to the verge of unconsciousness would be included in the annual statistics of the Society for Prevention of Cruelty to Children as one of the ten thousand cases that had been brought under their notice; and this, where I had stood at the girl's elbow, and wept, and implored her to turn from the temptation before her, would be mentioned as a sad case of suicide.

That fair young girl had moved me greatly. A cloud rested on her brain. Temporary illness had some months before stopped the weekly wage for which she worked, and, in her need, she had fallen behind in her payments. The burden of debt had ever since pressed heavily upon her; in the enfeebled state of her health, it had taken undue hold of her imagination, till now, with darkened vision, she stood like a creature at bay, on the brink of the Unknown.

"Help will come tomorrow," I had pleaded.

"There have been a great many tomorrows," had been her answer, "and no help came."

"They do not know," I pleaded, for the girl looked fiercely up at the gardened slopes where the helpers lay.

"They do not seek to know."

"Oh yes, they do. If I had known."…

"They know that we are here, and that we have not bread. They know that where there is not bread there is hunger, and sickness, and bitterness, and loss of self-restraint."

"They do not know that you have not bread."

But as I spoke, my confidence melted from me. I remembered that it was only the week before my illness, that I had sat at my comfortable drawing-room fire, brooding over the latest results of inquiries in East London. Twenty-five, if not thirty per cent, of the people living that day below the Poverty Line, one in four not knowing where "Daily Bread" was to come from: one in every ten "Very poor". This very girl must have been one of these. I had had a week to do it in. Why had I not gone down on the spot into the dark gully, on whose banks we had builded our pleasant homes—why had I not gone down, and putting my arms round her, said to her, "Sister, you must know no more want, while I am here to share with you"?

O God, if I had but done it, if I could but do it now! No one could possibly object to charity like that; they could not say it was "demoralising." For that had been my great "problem" in these now far-off days. I laughed my problem to scorn as I stood close to my poor sister.

"Sweet, my love," I said to her, my whole heart going out in a strange yearning that it had never known before, "have patience but a little while. I know good women over there who would be shocked beyond measure if they thought you were on the point of taking away your own life, because of hunger, and cold, and misery. Let me but have time to go to them, and awake them from their slumber, and you will see what life can be yet."

She smiled bitterly at what she thought was her own better nature speaking.

"Ah, yes, I know well," she answered, with impatience in her voice, and her eye alight with a pained bewilderment, "that if I could bring myself to be a beggar and go from door to door, I should gather half-crowns in plenty; but 'to beg I am ashamed.'… Yet bread I must have or I cannot live. And my work does not suffice. My flesh fails for very weariness before I have coppers enough to buy more food to give strength for more work. Why should I go on?… I have none to care whether I live or die… There is rest here!"… pointing to the flood below.

"Oh, it is awful!" I said. "So much given, and yet blood at our doors."

"It is not money we want," she answered, almost fiercely, her intellect waking up with sudden flash to its clearest. "Yes, indeed, showers of half-crowns are falling, and the scramble for them is not good to see. More and more joining the clamouring crowd."… She suddenly laughed a horrible laugh. "Four coffins finding their way to one man's deathbed, sent by four different societies!—one will be enough for me… Ah! I am sick, sick, weary of it all. The scramble for the falling coins, the 'crumbs from the rich man's table,' and those who have no heart or too much pride for the scramble… dying. Listen!" her eye gleaming fire, as she laid her hand on an imaginary listener—or was vision lent to her, that she could see as well as hear me?—"I tell you, tell you truly, what we want is not money but… Love. One loving woman to one struggling sister; one loving brother to one fallen comrade in the fight. One and one alone: caring as a sister would care, not once leaving her till she sees all her wrongs righted, or till her weakness or poverty is a thing of the past. Ah!" looking up to the gardened slopes, passionate pity gathering in her eyes, "were I ever to become rich, would it be possible for me, I wonder, to forget it all; to forget my toiling sisters, going wearily home after hours of sunshine spent in close rooms, home to bare meals, too tired to be amused, if there were amusement provided; only too thankful if kindly sleep await them, instead of perplexing care, care of how the week's debts are to be met? Would it be possible for me to forget, I wonder, that there must be many and many doing as I have so often done, toiling in spirit with the weary car-horses, feeling that life with them and with me was much the same: on and on: the whip of want, if one threatens to stop? Ah! if I were but one of these," again looking up to the gardens above, tears in her voice and gathering in her eyes, "I would take one at least from this sorry den and make her life so fair for her; and she should know no want any more, nor care any more,—just as if I were her true sister,—nor bitterness of dependence, for there is no bitterness where Love is, nor shame of beggary. But… it is easy to dream dreams. If I were as they, I should no doubt grow self-absorbed and self-sufficient even as they. Ah!… what nonsense it all is! Only, if my dream came to pass, there could be no talk then of 'over-lapping Charity!'" and she laughed a laugh that was not good to hear. "Oh!" raising her hands to her head, "I shall be glad when my ears are deafened that I cannot hear; the mockery of it all is too great."

And once more there settled down upon her brain the cloud I now knew myself powerless to combat.

"Let me be your sister," I would fain have said; but I knew, before the words were spoken, that it was in vain. My punishment was, that I could not give her help. My love and longing had come all too late.

Yet I had deemed myself a follower of Him who said: "Love one another, as I have loved you."

I sought excuses. It was truly the sin of ignorance. My youth!… Had I then been so young? If one is not to rise to gracious womanhood in twenty-five years, when will the awakening come? I had surely not been too young to know what women of my own age were suffering.

"How old are you?" I found myself asking.

"Twenty-five. My birthday falls tomorrow."

Twenty-five, and weary of life: weary of disappointment rather; for of life, bright, beautiful, young life, with its joy in colour and movement, this sister of mine had known nothing.

Just then one passed close by us, in satin and pearls, with rouged cheek and glittering white teeth, that laughed us to scorn.

She was a N A N A, let loose as a scourge on the weaklings of the day, scattering fortunes as a child scatters *bonbons*, sending youths forth stripped penniless, as the fruit of a week's folly; but for herself, all the pleasures a life of sin could give were hers. My companion lifted her head at sound of the laughter, and shuddered as she passed. There was again a flash of sanity.

"I was once as beautiful as she."

"But you were not tempted…"

"Never. This," pointing to the flowing tide, "is better than that."

I stooped to hide the blinding tears.

"Sister!…" I said, "I am not worthy… Ah!…"

She had not heard me. Like a bird she had flashed through the gloom into the tide below, and the water had opened to receive her.

What angel would greet *her* as she emerged from the mist? I thanked heaven that she went into God's good keeping, and, as the shrill laughter of the woman of sin came again on the still air, once more I thanked God for her.

Turning slowly back to the crowded maze, with weeping eyes and humbled heart, I was conscious of a curious change in myself. What was it? The lagging step was gone, the intense unwillingness to move forward. The bitter outcry that the burden laid upon me was more than I could bear was no more. In its place there had come a strong impulse forward into the heart of the crowd; a great longing to take some one of them to me, the weaker the better, and push the way for him or her and myself out from the shadow into the light. I had forgotten even my Blessed Damozel in the strong interest that had sprung up in my heart… Yes! in my heart… that was then the secret.

My heart was awake… at last! Awake in its own regal right… asking nothing… giving all…

"And if I love thee, what is that to thee?" rang down a century's length and was understood.

And pity as an emotion was swallowed up in pity as a motive.

Instead of closing my ears to the continuous wail of pain, my eyes to the saddening sights, my arms seemed to stretch themselves out in pure yearning towards that sorrowing multitude, my feet were swift to take me into the heart of it.

One loving woman to one struggling sister!… that at least was within reach: to have her and hold her, and care for her and love her… for ever! That at least… what more the future might unfold… I could leave.

Alas! I had forgotten… I was not of earth, and could help have come from heaven, these poor souls had been helped long ere now. No such heaven opened before me as I had been picturing. It was to be my fate to wander sadly, helpless, prayerful, in ever-present pain of powerlessness, among that weary multitude—suffering with them, learning from them, feeling myself unworthy to tie the shoe-latchet of the least of them. It was they who were to save me, not I them.

PART VI

The sorrow was all gone from my sweet lady's eyes as they rested lovingly on mine. For the day had dawned once more, the shadows had melted away from about me, and I was standing in the early sunshine, my hands in hers, in a strong grasp of new strength and comradeship. Was I dreaming, or was that the same light of triumph on her countenance which had so impressed me in the dark-eyed saint who had led the little old lady of seventy to her Lord, and was she triumphing for me?...

But my heart was too full of enlarged life to allow me to linger for more than a moment on this new impression. I hastened to share it with her.

"Sweet sister..." I did not notice the new equality... "I have found it. I know... what it is to love."

The grasp on my hands grew tighter.

"And although there," glancing back, "and for a little time, it is indeed sorrow... for all eternity it will be joy."

Ah! the deep, deep joy that glowed in the eyes of my listener!

"They are coming, are they not... one by one; all those who have one spark of the Divine in them? And I know now why you pleaded for me so earnestly as my excuse that I had not known poverty, for indeed 'Hardly shall they that have riches enter into the Kingdom.' It is poverty that has taught many of these poor souls that lesson of self-forgetfulness, which I altogether failed in learning. And sorrow is teaching others; and all... all except that lowest grade of all, that one in every hundred, which none yet have had power to raise or help—all are living nearer to the lessons of life, than are many of the dwellers at ease on the hillside."

No word would she speak in answer, but her look was eloquent of triumph at every word I spoke, and pleaded for more... more...

"Yes, they are surely closer to each other in their struggling and striving, failing and winning, than are the rich they envy. It is true, they stretch out weary limbs at night, and aching frames are laid on hard couches; but often and often, even then, their hearts 'make holiday.' For often, too tired to sleep, they allow their minds to dwell on the hard task completed, the righteous debt paid, want once more tided over for some one dearer than self! Yes, through it all, round the hearts of the loving among them—and there are many such—there never ceases to play that warmth of tender feeling, that only stern workers know who toil for those they love. Ah! to stand in the breach for the weak!… above all, for the weak that we love!… I have learned, sweet sister, from that struggling multitude, that there is no joy on earth to compare with that; there is, there can be, no joy in earth or heaven greater than that.".…

Upon which my Blessed Damozel loosened suddenly her grasp of my hands, put her arms round my neck, and our lips met in a kiss that was full of promise. It told that we were one in intent and purpose: that we loved one another, but we loved humanity more; and the joy of the future would be, that, hand in hand, we would go forth together, as "ministers of grace" to "do His pleasure."

"God bless all those who are trying to add to the sum of human happiness; God bless all those who are trying to lessen the sum of human pain," had prayed Sunday after Sunday the clergyman of our parish.

Ah! we should be henceforth among "the blessed of God."

When she drew it back, my Blessed Damozel's face shone with such beauty that I found myself saying in fresh wonderment, "How very beautiful you are!"

She smiled. "Come," she said.

And she led me to a lake clear as crystal.

"Look."

I bent and saw reflected in it two faces side by side. One was that of my companion, smiling back at me with a beauty that again filled me with a great sense of gladness. I loved beauty. I loved her beauty.

Then I turned to the other, and as I looked my wonder grew and grew; and as my wonder grew, the eyes in the looking-glass we had found grew larger and softer and softer, till they filled with tears.

"I… cannot be… like that.".…

"You are like that," whispered my sister; "for that is 'the beauty of Holiness.'"

"But I am not holy!" said I, in still deeper amazement.

"Holiness is… an Infinite Sympathy for others," she whispered again. "You remember?"…

Yes, I remembered a sister on Earth had spoken that, and I had thought it very beautiful.

While I was still pondering I felt my companion turn from me, and wafted on the soft air, there came from the direction in which she turned a distant sound of rejoicing.

I raised my head and turned with her. "What… is it?" I asked.

"The 'Songs of them that triumph,'" said my Blessed Damozel, her eye lighting, her body swaying forward; "'the Shouts of them that feast.' Hark! they are calling to us, calling to you and to me… Come."

With a long, long sigh I was awaking.

Awaking to what? To the twilight of a darkened chamber, to the far, far-off sound of familiar voices: now to the sight of a familiar face.

It was the hospital nurse. She took my hand.

I could hear her speak. I could catch what she was saying.

"She is conscious, I am sure. She pressed my hand."

Another far-off voice: our clergyman's. "It was prayer that brought her back. For a moment the soul seemed separate from the body, but I was intent she should not die; with her powers, her riches, her youth, she had so much to do in the world yet… I *would* not let her go."

I struggled for utterance.

"So much to do in the world yet! One loving woman to one struggling sister… to have her and hold her… and care for her and love her,—above all… to love her… for ever."…

"She is wandering again," said the nurse.

Was I wandering? Am I wandering still?… Has it been a dream, a dream and nothing more?

THE END

THE LIBRARY WINDOW

WAS not aware at first of the many discussions which had gone
on about that window. It was almost opposite one of the windows
of the large old-fashioned drawing-room of the house in which I
spent that summer, which was of so much importance in my life. Our
house and the library were on opposite sides of the broad High Street
of St Rule's, which is a fine street, wide and ample, and very quiet, as
strangers think who come from noisier places; but in a summer evening
there is much coming and going, and the stillness is full of sound—the
sound of footsteps and pleasant voices, softened by the summer air.
There are even exceptional moments when it is noisy: the time of the
fair, and on Saturday night sometimes, and when there are excursion
trains. Then even the softest sunny air of the evening will not smooth
the harsh tones and the stumbling steps; but at these unlovely moments
we shut the windows, and even I, who am so fond of that deep recess
where I can take refuge from all that is going on inside, and make myself
a spectator of all the varied story out of doors, withdraw from my watch-
tower. To tell the truth, there never was very much going on inside. The
house belonged to my aunt, to whom (she says, Thank God!) nothing
ever happens. I believe that many things have happened to her in her
time; but that was all over at the period of which I am speaking, and she
was old, and very quiet. Her life went on in a routine never broken. She
got up at the same hour every day, and did the same things in the same
rotation, day by day the same. She said that this was the greatest support

in the world, and that routine is a kind of salvation. It may be so; but it is a very dull salvation, and I used to feel that I would rather have incident, whatever kind of incident it might be. But then at that time I was not old, which makes all the difference.

At the time of which I speak the deep recess of the drawing-room window was a great comfort to me. Though she was an old lady (perhaps because she was so old) she was very tolerant, and had a kind of feeling for me. She never said a word, but often gave me a smile when she saw how I had built myself up, with my books and my basket of work. I did very little work, I fear—now and then a few stitches when the spirit moved me, or when I had got well afloat in a dream, and was more tempted to follow it out than to read my book, as sometimes happened. At other times, and if the book were interesting, I used to get through volume after volume sitting there, paying no attention to anybody. And yet I did pay a kind of attention. Aunt Mary's old ladies came in to call, and I heard them talk, though I very seldom listened; but for all that, if they had anything to say that was interesting, it is curious how I found it in my mind afterwards, as if the air had blown it to me. They came and went, and I had the sensation of their old bonnets gliding out and in, and their dresses rustling; and now and then had to jump up and shake hands with some one who knew me, and asked after my papa and mamma. Then Aunt Mary would give me a little smile again, and I slipped back to my window. She never seemed to mind. My mother would not have let me do it, I know. She would have remembered dozens of things there were to do. She would have sent me upstairs to fetch something which I was quite sure she did not want, or downstairs to carry some quite unnecessary message to the housemaid. She liked to keep me running about. Perhaps that was one reason why I was so fond of Aunt Mary's drawing-room, and the deep recess of the window, and the curtain that fell half over it, and the broad window-seat, where one could collect so many things

without being found fault with for untidiness. Whenever we had anything the matter with us in these days, we were sent to St Rule's to
get up our strength. And this was my case at the time of which I am
going to speak.

Everybody had said, since ever I learned to speak, that I was fantastic and fanciful and dreamy, and all the other words with which a girl
who may happen to like poetry, and to be fond of thinking, is so often
made uncomfortable. People don't know what they mean when they say
fantastic. It sounds like Madge Wildfire or something of that sort. My
mother thought I should always be busy, to keep nonsense out of my
head. But really I was not at all fond of nonsense. I was rather serious
than otherwise. I would have been no trouble to anybody if I had been
left to myself. It was only that I had a sort of second-sight, and was
conscious of things to which I paid no attention. Even when reading the
most interesting book, the things that were being talked about blew in to
me; and I heard what the people were saying in the streets as they passed
under the window. Aunt Mary always said I could do two or indeed
three things at once—both read and listen, and see. I am sure that I did
not listen much, and seldom looked out, of set purpose—as some people
do who notice what bonnets the ladies in the street have on; but I did
hear what I couldn't help hearing, even when I was reading my book, and
I did see all sorts of things, though often for a whole half-hour I might
never lift my eyes.

This does not explain what I said at the beginning, that there were
many discussions about that window. It was, and still is, the last window
in the row, of the College Library, which is opposite my aunt's house in
the High Street. Yet it is not exactly opposite, but a little to the west, so
that I could see it best from the left side of my recess. I took it calmly
for granted that it was a window like any other till I first heard the talk
about it which was going on in the drawing-room. "Have you never
made up your mind, Mrs Balcarres," said old Mr Pitmilly, "whether that

window opposite is a window or no?" He said Mistress Balcarres—and he was always called Mr Pitmilly, Morton: which was the name of his place.

"I am never sure of it, to tell the truth," said Aunt Mary, "all these years."

"Bless me!" said one of the old ladies, "and what window may that be?"

Mr Pitmilly had a way of laughing as he spoke, which did not please me; but it was true that he was not perhaps desirous of pleasing me. He said, "Oh, just the window opposite," with his laugh running through his words; "our friend can never make up her mind about it, though she has been living opposite it since—"

"You need never mind the date," said another; "the Leebrary window! Dear me, what should it be but a window? up at that height it could not be a door."

"The question is," said my aunt, "if it is a real window with glass in it, or if it is merely painted, or if it once was a window, and has been built up. And the oftener people look at it, the less they are able to say."

"Let me see this window," said old Lady Carnbee, who was very active and strong-minded; and then they all came crowding upon me—three or four old ladies, very eager, and Mr Pitmilly's white hair appearing over their heads, and my aunt sitting quiet and smiling behind.

"I mind the window very well," said Lady Carnbee; "ay: and so do more than me. But in its present appearance it is just like any other window; but has not been cleaned, I should say, in the memory of man."

"I see what ye mean," said one of the others. "It is just a very dead thing without any reflection in it; but I've seen as bad before."

"Ay, it's dead enough," said another, "but that's no rule; for these hizzies of women-servants in this ill age—"

"Nay, the women are well enough," said the softest voice of all, which was Aunt Mary's. "I will never let them risk their lives cleaning the outside of mine. And there are no women-servants in the Old Library: there is maybe something more in it than that."

They were all pressing into my recess, pressing upon me, a row of old faces, peering into something they could not understand. I had a sense in my mind how curious it was, the wall of old ladies in their old satin gowns all glazed with age, Lady Carnbee with her lace about her head. Nobody was looking at me or thinking of me; but I felt unconsciously the contrast of my youngness to their oldness, and stared at them as they stared over my head at the Library window. I had given it no attention up to this time. I was more taken up with the old ladies than with the thing they were looking at.

"The framework is all right at least, I can see that, and pented black—"

"And the panes are pented black too. It's no window, Mrs Balcarres. It has been filled in, in the days of the window duties: you will mind, Leddy Carnbee."

"Mind!" said that oldest lady. "I mind when your mother was marriet, Jeanie: and that's neither the day nor yesterday. But as for the window, it's just a delusion: and that is my opinion of the matter, if you ask me."

"There's a great want of light in that muckle room at the college," said another. "If it was a window, the Leebrary would have more light."

"One thing is clear," said one of the younger ones, "it cannot be a window to see through. It may be filled in or it may be built up, but it is not a window to give light."

"And who ever heard of a window that was no to see through?" Lady Carnbee said. I was fascinated by the look on her face, which was a curious scornful look as of one who knew more than she chose to say: and then my wandering fancy was caught by her hand as she held it up, throwing back the lace that drooped over it. Lady Carnbee's lace was the chief thing about her—heavy black Spanish lace with large flowers. Everything she wore was trimmed with it. A large veil of it hung over her old bonnet. But her hand coming out of this heavy lace was a curious thing to see. She had very long fingers, very taper, which had been much admired in her youth; and her hand was very white, or rather more than white, pale, bleached, and bloodless, with large blue veins standing up upon the back; and she wore some fine rings, among others a big diamond in an ugly old claw setting. They were too big for her, and were wound round and round with yellow silk to make them keep on: and this little cushion of silk, turned brown with long wearing, had twisted round so that it was more conspicuous than the jewels; while the big diamond blazed underneath in the hollow of her hand, like some dangerous thing hiding and sending out darts of light. The hand, which seemed to come almost to a point, with this strange ornament underneath, clutched at my half-terrified imagination. It too seemed to mean far more than was said. I felt as if it might clutch me with sharp claws, and the lurking, dazzling creature bite—with a sting that would go to the heart.

Presently, however, the circle of the old faces broke up, the old ladies returned to their seats, and Mr Pitmilly, small but very erect, stood up in the midst of them, talking with mild authority like a little oracle among the ladies. Only Lady Carnbee always contradicted the neat, little old gentleman. She gesticulated, when she talked, like a Frenchwoman, and darted forth that hand of hers with the lace hanging over it, so that I always caught a glimpse of the lurking diamond. I thought she looked like a witch among the comfortable little group which gave such attention to everything Mr Pitmilly said.

"For my part, it is my opinion there is no window there at all," he said. "It's very like the thing that's called in scienteefic language an optical illusion. It arises generally, if I may use such a word in the presence of ladies, from a liver that is not just in the perfitt order and balance that organ demands—and then you will see things—a blue dog, I remember, was the thing in one case, and in another—"

"The man has gane gyte," said Lady Carnbee; "I mind the windows in the Auld Leebrary as long as I mind anything. Is the Leebrary itself an optical illusion too?"

"Na, na," and "No, no," said the old ladies; "a blue dogue would be a strange vagary: but the Library we have all kent from our youth," said one. "And I mind when the Assemblies were held there one year when the Town Hall was building," another said.

"It is just a great divert to me," said Aunt Mary: but what was strange was that she paused there, and said in a low tone, "now": and then went on again, "for whoever comes to my house, there are aye discussions about that window. I have never just made up my mind about it myself. Sometimes I think it's a case of these wicked window duties, as you said, Miss Jeanie, when half the windows in our houses were blocked up to save the tax. And then, I think, it may be due to that blank kind of building like the great new buildings on the Earthen Mound in Edinburgh, where the windows are just ornaments. And then whiles I am sure I can see the glass shining when the sun catches it in the afternoon."

"You could so easily satisfy yourself, Mrs Balcarres, if you were to—"

"Give a laddie a penny to cast a stone, and see what happens," said Lady Carnbee.

"But I am not sure that I have any desire to satisfy myself," Aunt Mary said. And then there was a stir in the room, and I had to come out from my recess and open the door for the old ladies and see them downstairs, as they all went away following one another. Mr Pitmilly gave his arm to Lady Carnbee, though she was always contradicting him; and so the tea-party dispersed. Aunt Mary came to the head of the stairs with her guests in an old-fashioned gracious way, while I went down with them to see that the maid was ready at the door. When I came back Aunt Mary was still standing in the recess looking out. Returning to my seat she said, with a kind of wistful look, "Well, honey: and what is your opinion?"

"I have no opinion. I was reading my book all the time," I said.

"And so you were, honey, and no' very civil; but all the same I ken well you heard every word we said."

II

It was a night in June; dinner was long over, and had it been winter the maids would have been shutting up the house, and my Aunt Mary preparing to go upstairs to her room. But it was still clear daylight, that daylight out of which the sun has been long gone, and which has no longer any rose reflections, but all has sunk into a pearly neutral tint—a light which is daylight yet is not day. We had taken a turn in the garden after dinner, and now we had returned to what we called our usual occupations. My aunt was reading. The English post had come in, and she had got her *Times*, which was her great diversion. The *Scotsman* was her morning reading, but she liked her *Times* at night.

As for me, I too was at my usual occupation, which at that time was doing nothing. I had a book as usual, and was absorbed in it: but I was conscious of all that was going on all the same. The people strolled along the broad pavement, making remarks as they passed under the open window which came up into my story or my dream, and sometimes made me laugh. The tone and the faint singsong, or rather chant, of the accent, which was "a wee Fifish," was novel to me, and associated with holiday, and pleasant; and sometimes they said to each other something that was amusing, and often something that suggested a whole story; but presently they began to drop off, the footsteps slackened, the voices died away. It was getting late, though the clear soft daylight went on and on. All through the lingering evening, which seemed to consist of interminable hours, long but not weary, drawn out as if the spell of the light and the outdoor life might never end, I had now and then, quite unawares, cast a glance at the mysterious window which my aunt and her friends had discussed, as I felt, though I dared not say it even to myself, rather foolishly. It caught my eye without any intention on my part, as I paused, as it were, to take breath, in the flowing and current of undistinguishable thoughts and things from without and within which carried me along. First it occurred to me, with a little sensation of discovery, how absurd to say it was not a window, a living window, one to see through! Why, then, had they never *seen* it, these old folk? I saw as I looked up suddenly the faint greyness as of visible space within—a room behind, certainly—dim, as it was natural a room should be on the other side of the street—quite indefinite: yet so clear that if some one were to come to the window there would be nothing surprising in it. For certainly there was a feeling of space behind the panes which these old half-blind ladies had disputed about whether they were glass or only fictitious panes marked on the wall. How silly! when eyes that could see could make it out in a minute. It was only a greyness at present, but it was unmistakable, a space that went back into gloom, as every room does when you look into it across a street. There were no curtains to show whether it was inhabited or not; but a room—oh, as distinctly as ever room was! I was pleased with myself, but said nothing, while Aunt Mary rustled her paper, waiting for a favourable moment to announce a discovery which settled her problem at once. Then I was carried away upon the stream again, and forgot the window, till somebody threw unawares a word from the outer world, "I'm goin' hame; it'll soon be dark." Dark! what was the fool thinking of? it never would be dark if one waited out, wandering in the soft air for hours longer; and then my eyes, acquiring easily that new habit, looked across the way again.

Ah, now! nobody indeed had come to the window; and no light had been lighted, seeing it was still beautiful to read by—a still, clear, colourless light; but the room inside had certainly widened. I could see the grey space and air a little deeper, and a sort of vision, very dim, of a wall, and something against it; something dark, with the blackness that a solid article, however indistinctly seen, takes in the lighter darkness that is only space—a large, black, dark thing coming out into the grey. I looked more intently, and made sure it was a piece of furniture, either a writing-table or perhaps a large bookcase. No doubt it must be the last, since this was part of the old library. I never visited the old College Library, but I had seen such places before, and I could well imagine it to myself. How curious that for all the time these old people had looked at it, they had never seen this before!

It was more silent now, and my eyes, I suppose, had grown dim with gazing, doing my best to make it out, when suddenly Aunt Mary said, "Will you ring the bell, my dear? I must have my lamp."

"Your lamp?" I cried, "when it is still daylight." But then I gave another look at my window, and perceived with a start that the light had indeed changed: for now I saw nothing. It was still light, but there was so much change in the light that my room, with the grey space and the large shadowy bookcase, had gone out, and I saw them no more: for even a Scotch night in June, though it looks as if it would never end, does darken at the last. I had almost cried out, but checked myself, and rang the bell for Aunt Mary, and made up my mind I would say nothing till next morning, when to be sure naturally it would be more clear.

Next morning I rather think I forgot all about it—or was busy: or was more idle than usual: the two things meant nearly the same. At all events I thought no more of the window, though I still sat in my own, opposite to it, but occupied with some other fancy. Aunt Mary's visitors came as usual in the afternoon; but their talk was of other things, and for a day or two nothing at all happened to bring back my thoughts into this channel. It might be nearly a week before the subject came back, and once more it was old Lady Carnbee who set me thinking; not that she said anything upon that particular theme. But she was the last of my aunt's afternoon guests to go away, and when she rose to leave she threw up her hands, with those lively gesticulations which so many old Scotch ladies have. "My faith!" said she, "there is that bairn there still like a dream. Is the creature bewitched, Mary Balcarres? and is she bound to sit there by night and by day for the rest of her days? You should mind that there's things about, uncanny for women of our blood."

I was too much startled at first to recognise that it was of me she was speaking. She was like a figure in a picture, with her pale face the colour of ashes, and the big pattern of the Spanish lace hanging half over it, and her hand held up, with the big diamond blazing at me from the inside of her uplifted palm. It was held up in surprise, but it looked as if it were raised in malediction; and the diamond threw out darts of light and glared and twinkled at me. If it had been in its right place it would not have mattered; but there, in the open of the hand! I started up, half in terror, half in wrath. And then the old lady laughed, and her hand dropped. "I've wakened you to life, and broke the spell," she said, nodding her old head at me, while the large black silk flowers of the lace waved and threatened. And she took my arm to go downstairs, laughing and bidding me be steady, and no' tremble and shake like a broken reed. "You should be as steady as a rock at your age. I was like a young tree," she said, leaning so heavily that my willowy girlish frame quivered—"I was a support to virtue, like Pamela, in my time."

"Aunt Mary, Lady Carnbee is a witch!" I cried, when I came back.

"Is that what you think, honey? well: maybe she once was," said Aunt Mary, whom nothing surprised.

And it was that night once more after dinner, and after the post came in, and the *Times*, that I suddenly saw the Library window again. I had seen it every day—and noticed nothing; but tonight, still in a little tumult of mind over Lady Carnbee and her wicked diamond which wished me harm, and her lace which waved threats and warnings at me, I looked across the street, and there I saw quite plainly the room opposite, far more clear than before. I saw dimly that it must be a large room, and that the big piece of furniture against the wall was a writing-desk. That in a moment, when first my eyes rested upon it, was quite clear: a large old-fashioned escritoire, standing out into the room: and I knew by the shape of it that it had a great many pigeon-holes and little drawers in the back, and a large table for writing. There was one just like it in my father's library at home. It was such a surprise to see it all so clearly that I closed my eyes, for the moment almost giddy, wondering how papa's desk could have come here—and then when I reminded myself that this was nonsense, and that there were many such writing-tables besides papa's, and looked again—lo! it had all become quite vague and indistinct as it was at first; and I saw nothing but the blank window, of which the old ladies could never be certain whether it was filled up to avoid the window tax, or whether it had ever been a window at all.

This occupied my mind very much, and yet I did not say anything to Aunt Mary. For one thing, I rarely saw anything at all in the early part of the day; but then that is natural: you can never see into a place from out-side, whether it is an empty room or a looking-glass, or people's eyes, or anything else that is mysterious, in the day. It has, I suppose, something to do with the light. But in the evening in June in Scotland—then is the time to see. For it is daylight, yet it is not day, and there is a quality in it which I cannot describe, it is so clear, as if every object was a reflection of itself.

I used to see more and more of the room as the days went on. The large escritoire stood out more and more into the space: with sometimes white glimmering things, which looked like papers, lying on it: and once or twice I was sure I saw a pile of books on the floor close to the writing-table, as if they had gilding upon them in broken specks, like old books. It was always about the time when the lads in the street began to call to each other that they were going home, and sometimes a shriller voice would come from one of the doors, bidding somebody to "cry upon the laddies" to come back to their suppers. That was always the time I saw best, though it was close upon the moment when the veil seemed to fall and the clear radiance became less living, and all the sounds died out of the street, and Aunt Mary said in her soft voice, "Honey! will you ring for the lamp?" She said honey as people say darling: and I think it is a prettier word.

Then finally, while I sat one evening with my book in my hand, looking straight across the street, not distracted by anything, I saw a little movement within. It was not any one visible—but everybody must know what it is to see the stir in the air, the little disturbance—you cannot tell what it is, but that it indicates some one there, even though you can see no one. Perhaps it is a shadow making just one flicker in the still place. You may look at an empty room and the furniture in it for hours, and then suddenly there will be the flicker, and you know that something has come into it. It might only be a dog or a cat; it might be, if that were possible, a bird flying across; but it is some one, something living, which is so different, so completely different, in a moment from the things that are not living. It seemed to strike right through me, and I gave a little cry. Then Aunt Mary stirred a little, and put down the huge newspaper that almost covered her from sight, and said, "What is it, honey?" I cried "Nothing," with a little gasp, quickly, for I did not want to be disturbed just at this moment when somebody was coming! But I suppose she was not satisfied, for she got up and stood behind to see what it was, putting her hand on my shoulder. It was the softest touch in the world, but I could have flung it off angrily: for that moment everything was still again, and the place grew grey and I saw no more.

"Nothing," I repeated, but I was so vexed I could have cried. "I told you it was nothing, Aunt Mary. Don't you believe me, that you come to look—and spoil it all!"

I did not mean of course to say these last words; they were forced out of me. I was so much annoyed to see it all melt away like a dream: for it was no dream, but as real as—as real as—myself or anything I ever saw.

She gave my shoulder a little pat with her hand. "Honey," she said, "were you looking at something? Is't that? is't that?" "Is it what?" I wanted to say, shaking off her hand, but something in me stopped me: for I said nothing at all, and she went quietly back to her place. I suppose she must have rung the bell herself, for immediately I felt the soft flood of the light behind me, and the evening outside dimmed down, as it did every night, and I saw nothing more.

It was next day, I think, in the afternoon that I spoke. It was brought on by something she said about her fine work. "I get a mist before my eyes," she said; "you will have to learn my old lace stitches, honey—for I soon will not see to draw the threads."

"Oh, I hope you will keep your sight," I cried, without thinking what I was saying. I was then young and very matter-of-fact. I had not found out that one may mean something, yet not half or a hundredth part of what one seems to mean: and even then probably hoping to be contradicted if it is anyhow against one's self.

"My sight!" she said, looking up at me with a look that was almost angry; "there is no question of losing my sight—on the contrary, my eyes are very strong. I may not see to draw fine threads, but I see at a distance as well as ever I did—as well as you do."

"I did not mean any harm, Aunt Mary," I said. "I thought you said— But how can your sight be as good as ever when you are in doubt about that window? I can see into the room as clear as—" My voice wavered, for I had just looked up and across the street, and I could have sworn that there was no window at all, but only a false image of one painted on the wall.

"Ah!" she said, with a little tone of keenness and of surprise: and she half rose up, throwing down her work hastily, as if she meant to come to me: then, perhaps seeing the bewildered look on my face, she paused and hesitated—"Ay, honey!" she said, "have you got so far ben as that?"

What did she mean? Of course I knew all the old Scotch phrases as well as I knew myself; but it is a comfort to take refuge in a little ignorance, and I know I pretended not to understand whenever I was put out. "I don't know what you mean by 'far ben,'" I cried out, very impatient. I don't know what might have followed, but some one just then came to call, and she could only give me a look before she went forward, putting out her hand to her visitor. It was a very soft look, but anxious, and as if she did not know what to do: and she shook her head a very little, and I thought, though there was a smile on her face, there was something wet about her eyes. I retired into my recess, and nothing more was said.

But it was very tantalising that it should fluctuate so; for sometimes I saw that room quite plain and clear—quite as clear as I could see papa's library, for example, when I shut my eyes. I compared it naturally to my father's study, because of the shape of the writing-table, which, as I tell you, was the same as his. At times I saw the papers on the table quite plain, just as I had seen his papers many a day. And the little pile of books on the floor at the foot—not ranged regularly in order, but put down one above the other, with all their angles going different ways, and a speck of the old gilding shining here and there. And then again at other times I saw nothing, absolutely nothing, and was no better than the old ladies who had peered over my head, drawing their eyelids together, and arguing that the window had been shut up because of the old long-abolished window tax, or else that it had never been a window at all. It annoyed me very much at those dull moments to feel that I too puckered up my eyelids and saw no better than they.

Aunt Mary's old ladies came and went day after day while June went on. I was to go back in July, and I felt that I should be very unwilling indeed to leave until I had quite cleared up—as I was indeed in the way of doing—the mystery of that window which changed so strangely and appeared quite a different thing, not only to different people, but to the same eyes at different times. Of course I said to myself it must simply be an effect of the light. And yet I did not quite like that explanation either, but would have been better pleased to make out to myself that it was some superiority in me which made it so clear to me, if it were only the great superiority of young eyes over old—though that was not quite enough to satisfy me, seeing it was a superiority which I shared with every little lass and lad in the street. I rather wanted, I believe, to think that there was some particular insight in me which gave clearness to my sight—which was a most impertinent assumption, but really did not mean half the harm it seems to mean when it is put down here in black and white. I had several times again, however, seen the room quite plain, and made out that it was a large room, with a great picture in a dim gilded frame hanging on the farther wall, and many other pieces of solid furniture making a blackness here and there, besides the great escritoire against the wall, which had evidently been placed near the window for the sake of the light. One thing became visible to me after another, till I almost thought I should end by being able to read the old lettering on one of the big volumes which projected from the others and caught the light; but this was all preliminary to the great event which happened about Midsummer Day—the day of St John, which was once so much thought of as a festival, but now means nothing at all in Scotland any more than any other of the saints' days: which I shall always think a great pity and loss to Scotland, whatever Aunt Mary may say.

III

It was about midsummer, I cannot say exactly to a day when, but near that time, when the great event happened. I had grown very well acquainted by this time with that large dim room. Not only the escritoire, which was very plain to me now, with the papers upon it, and the books at its foot, but the great picture that hung against the farther wall, and various other shadowy pieces of furniture, especially a chair which one evening I saw had been moved into the space before the escritoire,—a little change which made my heart beat, for it spoke so distinctly of some one who must have been there, the some one who had already made me start, two or three times before, by some vague shadow of him or thrill of him which made a sort of movement in the silent space: a movement which made me sure that next minute I must see something or hear something which would explain the whole—if it were not that something always happened outside to stop it, at the very moment of its accomplishment. I had no warning this time of movement or shadow. I had been looking into the room very attentively a little while before, and had made out everything almost clearer than ever; and then had bent my attention again on my book, and read a chapter or two at a most exciting period of the story: and consequently had quite left St Rule's, and the High Street, and the College Library, and was really in a South American forest, almost throttled by the flowery creepers, and treading softly lest I should put my foot on a scorpion or a dangerous snake. At this moment something suddenly calling my attention to the outside, I looked across, and then, with a start, sprang up, for I could not contain myself. I don't know what I said, but enough to startle the people in the room, one of whom was old Mr Pitmilly. They all looked round upon me to ask what was the matter. And when I gave my usual answer of "Nothing," sitting down again shamefaced but very much excited, Mr Pitmilly got up and came forward, and looked out, apparently to see what was the cause. He saw nothing, for he went back again, and I could hear him telling Aunt Mary not to be alarmed, for Missy had fallen into a doze with the heat, and had startled herself waking up, at which they all laughed: another time I could have killed him for his impertinence, but my mind was too much taken up now to pay any attention. My head was throbbing and my heart beating. I was in such high excitement, how-ever, that to restrain myself completely, to be perfectly silent, was more easy to me then than at any other time of my life. I waited until the old gentleman had taken his seat again, and then I looked back. Yes, there he was! I had not been deceived. I knew then, when I looked across, that this was what I had been looking for all the time—that I had known he was there, and had been waiting for him, every time there was that flicker of movement in the room—him and no one else. And there at last, just as I had expected, he was. I don't know that in reality I ever had expected him, or any one: but this was what I felt when, suddenly looking into that curious dim room, I saw him there.

He was sitting in the chair, which he must have placed for himself, or which some one else in the dead of night when nobody was looking must have set for him, in front of the escritoire—with the back of his head towards me, writing. The light fell upon him from the left hand, and therefore upon his shoulders and the side of his head, which, how-ever, was too much turned away to show anything of his face. Oh, how strange that there should be some one staring at him as I was doing, and he never to turn his head, to make a movement! If any one stood and looked at me, were I in the soundest sleep that ever was, I would wake, I would jump up, I would feel it through everything. But there he sat and never moved. You are not to suppose, though I said the light fell upon him from the left hand, that there was very much light. There never is in a room you are looking into like that across the street; but there was enough to see him by—the outline of his figure dark and solid, seated in the chair, and the fairness of his head visible faintly, a clear spot against the dimness. I saw this outline against the dim gilding of the frame of the large picture which hung on the farther wall.

I sat all the time the visitors were there, in a sort of rapture, gazing at this figure. I knew no reason why I should be so much moved. In an ordinary way, to see a student at an opposite window quietly doing his work might have interested me a little, but certainly it would not have moved me in any such way. It is always interesting to have a glimpse like this of an unknown life—to see so much and yet know so little, and to wonder, perhaps, what the man is doing, and why he never turns his head. One would go to the window—but not too close, lest he should see you and think you were spying upon him—and one would ask, Is he still there? is he writing, writing always? I wonder what he is writing! And it would be a great amusement: but no more. This was not my feeling at all in the present case. It was a sort of breathless watch, an absorption. I did not feel that I had eyes for anything else, or any room in my mind for another thought. I no longer heard, as I generally did, the stories and the wise remarks (or foolish) of Aunt Mary's old ladies or Mr Pitmilly. I heard only a murmur behind me, the interchange of voices, one softer, one sharper; but it was not as in the time when I sat reading and heard every word, till the story in my book, and the stories they were telling (what they said almost always shaped into stories), were all mingled into each other, and the hero in the novel became somehow the hero (or more likely heroine) of them all. But I took no notice of what they were saying now. And it was not that there was anything very interesting to look at, except the fact that he was there. He did nothing to keep up the absorption of my thoughts. He moved just so much as a man will do when he is very busily writing, thinking of nothing else. There was a faint turn of his head as he went from one side to another of the page he was writing; but it appeared to be a long long page which never wanted turning. Just a little inclination when he was at the end of the line, outward, and then a little inclination inward when he began the next. That was little enough to keep one gazing. But I suppose it was the gradual course of events leading up to this, the finding out of one thing after another as the eyes got accustomed to the vague light: first the room itself, and then the writing-table, and then the other furniture, and last of all the human inhabitant who gave it all meaning. This was all so interesting that it was like a country which one had discovered. And then the extraordinary blindness of the other people who disputed among themselves whether it was a window at all! I did not, I am sure, wish to be disrespectful, and I was very fond of my Aunt Mary, and I liked Mr Pitmilly well enough, and I was afraid of Lady Carnbee. But yet to think of the—I know I ought not to say stupidity—the blindness of them, the foolishness, the insensibility! discussing it as if a thing that your eyes could see was a thing to discuss! It would have been unkind to think it was because they were old and their faculties dimmed. It is so sad to think that the faculties grow dim, that such a woman as my Aunt Mary should fail in seeing, or hearing, or feeling, that I would not have dwelt on it for a moment, it would have seemed so cruel! And then such a clever old lady as Lady Carnbee, who could see through a millstone, people said—and Mr Pitmilly, such an old man of the world. It did indeed bring tears to my eyes to think that all those clever people, solely by reason of being no longer young as I was, should have the simplest things shut out from them; and for all their wisdom and their knowledge be unable to see what a girl like me could see so easily. I was too much grieved for them to dwell upon that thought, and half ashamed, though perhaps half proud too, to be so much better off than they.

All those thoughts flitted through my mind as I sat and gazed across the street. And I felt there was so much going on in that room across the street! He was so absorbed in his writing, never looked up, never paused for a word, never turned round in his chair, or got up and walked about the room as my father did. Papa is a great writer, everybody says: but he would have come to the window and looked out, he would have drummed with his fingers on the pane, he would have watched a fly and helped it over a difficulty, and played with the fringe of the curtain, and done a dozen other nice, pleasant, foolish things, till the next sentence took shape. "My dear, I am waiting for a word," he would say to my mother when she looked at him, with a question why he was so idle, in her eyes; and then he would laugh, and go back again to his writing-table. But He over there never stopped at all. It was like a fascination. I could not take my eyes from him and that little scarcely perceptible movement he made, turning his head. I trembled with impatience to see him turn the page, or perhaps throw down his finished sheet on the floor, as somebody looking into a window like me once saw Sir Walter do, sheet after sheet. I should have cried out if this Unknown had done that. I should not have been able to help myself, whoever had been present; and gradually I got into such a state of suspense waiting for it to be done that my head grew hot and my hands cold. And then, just when there was a little movement of his elbow, as if he were about to do this, to be called away by Aunt Mary to see Lady Carnbee to the door! I believe I did not hear her till she had called me three times, and then I stumbled up, all flushed and hot, and nearly crying. When I came out from the recess to give the old lady my arm (Mr Pitmilly had gone away some time before), she put up her hand and stroked my cheek. "What ails the bairn?" she said; "she's fevered. You must not let her sit her lane in the window, Mary Balcarres. You and me know what comes of that." Her old fingers had a strange touch, cold like something not living, and I felt that dreadful diamond sting me on the cheek.

I do not say that this was not just a part of my excitement and suspense; and I know it is enough to make any one laugh when the excitement was all about an unknown man writing in a room on the other side of the way, and my impatience because he never came to an end of the page. If you think I was not quite as well aware of this as any one could be! but the worst was that this dreadful old lady felt my heart beating against her arm that was within mine. "You are just in a dream," she said to me, with her old voice close at my ear as we went downstairs. "I don't know who it is about, but it's bound to be some man that is not worth it. If you were wise you would think of him no more."

"I am thinking of no man!" I said, half crying. "It is very unkind and dreadful of you to say so, Lady Carnbee. I never thought of—any man, in all my life!" I cried in a passion of indignation. The old lady clung tighter to my arm, and pressed it to her, not unkindly.

"Poor little bird," she said, "how it's strugglin' and flutterin'! I'm not saying but what it's more dangerous when it's all for a dream."

She was not at all unkind; but I was very angry and excited, and would scarcely shake that old pale hand which she put out to me from her carriage window when I had helped her in. I was angry with her, and I was afraid of the diamond, which looked up from under her finger as if it saw through and through me; and whether you believe me or not, I am certain that it stung me again—a sharp malignant prick, oh full of meaning! She never wore gloves, but only black lace mittens, through which that horrible diamond gleamed. I ran upstairs—she had been the last to go—and Aunt Mary too had gone to get ready for dinner, for it was late. I hurried to my place, and looked across, with my heart beating more than ever. I made quite sure I should see the finished sheet lying white upon the floor. But what I gazed at was only the dim blank of that window which they said was no window. The light had changed in some wonderful way during that five minutes I had been gone, and there was nothing, nothing, not a reflection, not a glimmer. It looked exactly as they all said, the blank form of a window painted on the wall. It was too much: I sat down in my excitement and cried as if my heart would break. I felt that they had done something to it, that it was not natural, that I could not bear their unkindness—even Aunt Mary. They thought it not good for me! not good for me! and they had done something—even Aunt Mary herself—and that wicked diamond that hid itself in Lady Carnbee's hand. Of course I knew all this was ridiculous as well as you could tell me; but I was exasperated by the disappointment and the sudden stop to all my excited feelings, and I could not bear it. It was more strong than I.

I was late for dinner, and naturally there were some traces in my eyes that I had been crying when I came into the full light in the dining-room, where Aunt Mary could look at me at her pleasure, and I could not run away. She said, "Honey, you have been shedding tears. I'm loth, loth that a bairn of your mother's should be made to shed tears in my house."

"I have not been made to shed tears," cried I; and then, to save myself another fit of crying, I burst out laughing and said, "I am afraid of that dreadful diamond on old Lady Carnbee's hand. It bites—I am sure it bites! Aunt Mary, look here."

"You foolish lassie," Aunt Mary said; but she looked at my cheek under the light of the lamp, and then she gave it a little pat with her soft hand. "Go away with you, you silly bairn. There is no bite; but a flushed cheek, my honey, and a wet eye. You must just read out my paper to me after dinner when the post is in: and we'll have no more thinking and no more dreaming for tonight."

"Yes, Aunt Mary," said I. But I knew what would happen; for when she opens up her *Times*, all full of the news of the world, and the speeches and things which she takes an interest in, though I cannot tell why—she forgets. And as I kept very quiet and made not a sound, she forgot tonight what she had said, and the curtain hung a little more over me than usual, and I sat down in my recess as if I had been a hundred miles away. And my heart gave a great jump, as if it would have come out of my breast; for he was there. But not as he had been in the morning—I suppose the light, perhaps, was not good enough to go on with his work without a lamp or candles—for he had turned away from the table and was fronting the window, sitting leaning back in his chair, and turning his head to me. Not to me—he knew nothing about me. I thought he was not looking at anything; but with his face turned my way. My heart was in my mouth: it was so unexpected, so strange! though why it should have seemed strange I know not, for there was no communication between him and me that it should have moved me; and what could be more natural than that a man, wearied of his work, and feeling the want perhaps of more light, and yet that it was not dark enough to light a lamp, should turn round in his own chair, and rest a little, and think—perhaps of nothing at all? Papa always says he is thinking of nothing at all. He says things blow through his mind as if the doors were open, and he has no responsibility. What sort of things were blowing through this man's mind? or was he thinking, still thinking, of what he had been writing and going on with it still? The thing that troubled me most was that I could not make out his face. It is very difficult to do so when you see a person only through two windows, your own and his. I wanted very much to recognise him afterwards if I should chance to meet him in the street. If he had only stood up and moved about the room, I should have made out the rest of his figure, and then I should have known him again; or if he had only come to the window (as papa always did), then I should have seen his face clearly enough to have recognised him. But, to be sure, he did not see any need to do anything in order that I might recognise him, for he did not know I existed; and probably if he had known I was watching him, he would have been annoyed and gone away.

But he was as immovable there facing the window as he had been seated at the desk. Sometimes he made a little faint stir with a hand or a foot, and I held my breath, hoping he was about to rise from his chair—but he never did it. And with all the efforts I made I could not be sure of his face. I puckered my eyelids together as old Miss Jeanie did who was shortsighted, and I put my hands on each side of my face to concentrate the light on him: but it was all in vain. Either the face changed as I sat staring, or else it was the light that was not good enough, or I don't know what it was. His hair seemed to me light—certainly there was no dark line about his head, as there would have been had it been very dark—and I saw, where it came across the old gilt frame on the wall behind, that it must be fair: and I am almost sure he had no beard. Indeed I am sure that he had no beard, for the outline of his face was distinct enough; and the daylight was still quite clear out of doors, so that I recognised perfectly a baker's boy who was on the pavement opposite, and whom I should have known again whenever I had met him: as if it was of the least importance to recognise a baker's boy! There was one thing, however, rather curious about this boy. He had been throwing stones at something or somebody. In St Rule's they have a great way of throwing stones at each other, and I suppose there had been a battle. I suppose also that he had one stone in his hand left over from the battle, and his roving eye took in all the incidents of the street to judge where he could throw it with most effect and mischief. But apparently he found nothing worthy of it in the street, for he suddenly turned round with a flick under his leg to show his cleverness, and aimed it straight at the window. I remarked without remarking that it struck with a hard sound and without any breaking of glass, and fell straight down on the pavement. But I took no notice of this even in my mind, so intently was I watching the figure within, which moved not nor took the slightest notice, and remained just as dimly clear, as perfectly seen, yet as indistinguishable, as before. And then the light began to fail a little, not diminishing the prospect within, but making it still less distinct than it had been.

Then I jumped up, feeling Aunt Mary's hand upon my shoulder. "Honey," she said, "I asked you twice to ring the bell; but you did not hear me."

"Oh, Aunt Mary!" I cried in great penitence, but turning again to the window in spite of myself.

"You must come away from there: you must come away from there," she said, almost as if she were angry: and then her soft voice grew softer, and she gave me a kiss: "never mind about the lamp, honey; I have rung myself, and it is coming; but, silly bairn, you must not aye be dreaming—your little head will turn."

All the answer I made, for I could scarcely speak, was to give a little wave with my hand to the window on the other side of the street.

She stood there patting me softly on the shoulder for a whole minute or more, murmuring something that sounded like, "She must go away, she must go away." Then she said, always with her hand soft on my shoulder, "Like a dream when one awaketh." And when I looked again, I saw the blank of an opaque surface and nothing more.

Aunt Mary asked me no more questions. She made me come into the room and sit in the light and read something to her. But I did not know what I was reading, for there suddenly came into my mind and took possession of it, the thud of the stone upon the window, and its descent straight down, as if from some hard substance that threw it off: though I had myself seen it strike upon the glass of the panes across the way.

IV

I am afraid I continued in a state of great exaltation and commotion of mind for some time. I used to hurry through the day till the evening came, when I could watch my neighbour through the window opposite. I did not talk much to any one, and I never said a word about my own questions and wonderings. I wondered who he was, what he was doing, and why he never came till the evening (or very rarely); and I also wondered much to what house the room belonged in which he sat. It seemed to form a portion of the old College Library, as I have often said. The window was one of the line of windows which I understood lighted the large hall; but whether this room belonged to the library itself, or how its occupant gained access to it, I could not tell. I made up my mind that it must open out of the hall, and that the gentleman must be the Librarian or one of his assistants, perhaps kept busy all the day in his official duties, and only able to get to his desk and do his own private work in the evening. One has heard of so many things like that—a man who had to take up some other kind of work for his living, and then when his leisure-time came, gave it all up to something he really loved—some study or some book he was writing. My father himself at one time had been like that. He had been in the Treasury all day, and then in the evening wrote his books, which made him famous. His daughter, however little she might know of other things, could not but know that! But it discouraged me very much when somebody pointed out to me one day in the street an old gentleman who wore a wig and took a great deal of snuff, and said, That's the Librarian of the old College. It gave me a great shock for a moment; but then I remembered that an old gentleman has generally assistants, and that it must be one of them.

Gradually I became quite sure of this. There was another small window above, which twinkled very much when the sun shone, and looked a very kindly bright little window, above that dullness of the other which hid so much. I made up my mind this was the window of his other room, and that these two chambers at the end of the beautiful hall were really beautiful for him to live in, so near all the books, and so retired and quiet, that nobody knew of them. What a fine thing for him! and you could see what use he made of his good fortune as he sat there, so constant at his writing for hours together. Was it a book he was writing, or could it be perhaps Poems? This was a thought which made my heart beat; but I concluded with much regret that it could not be Poems, because no one could possibly write Poems like that, straight off, without pausing for a word or a rhyme. Had they been Poems he must have risen up, he must have paced about the room or come to the window as papa did—not that papa wrote Poems: he always said, "I am not worthy even to speak of such prevailing mysteries," shaking his head—which gave me a wonderful admiration and almost awe of a Poet, who was thus much greater even than papa. But I could not believe that a poet could have kept still for hours and hours like that. What could it be then? perhaps it was history; that is a great thing to work at, but you would not perhaps need to move nor to stride up and down, or look out upon the sky and the wonderful light.

He did move now and then, however, though he never came to the window. Sometimes, as I have said, he would turn round in his chair and turn his face towards it, and sit there for a long time musing when the light had begun to fail, and the world was full of that strange day which was night, that light without colour, in which everything was so clearly visible, and there were no shadows. "It was between the night and the day, when the fairy folk have power." This was the after-light of the wonderful, long, long summer evening, the light without shadows. It had a spell in it, and sometimes it made me afraid: and all manner of strange thoughts seemed to come in, and I always felt that if only we had a little more vision in our eyes we might see beautiful folk walking about in it, who were not of our world. I thought most likely he saw them, from the way he sat there looking out: and this made my heart expand with the most curious sensation, as if of pride that, though I could not see, he did, and did not even require to come to the window, as I did, sitting close in the depth of the recess, with my eyes upon him, and almost seeing things through his eyes.

I was so much absorbed in these thoughts and in watching him every evening—for now he never missed an evening, but was always there—that people began to remark that I was looking pale and that I could not be well, for I paid no attention when they talked to me, and did not care to go out, nor to join the other girls for their tennis, nor to do anything that others did; and some said to Aunt Mary that I was quickly losing all the ground I had gained, and that she could never send me back to my mother with a white face like that. Aunt Mary had begun to look at me anxiously for some time before that, and, I am sure, held secret consultations over me, sometimes with the doctor, and sometimes with her old ladies, who thought they knew more about young girls than even the doctors. And I could hear them saying to her that I wanted diversion, that I must be diverted, and that she must take me out more, and give a party, and that when the summer visitors began to come there would perhaps be a ball or two, or Lady Carnbee would get up a picnic. "And there's my young lord coming home," said the old lady whom they called Miss Jeanie, "and I never knew the young lassie yet that would not cock up her bonnet at the sight of a young lord."

But Aunt Mary shook her head. "I would not lippen much to the young lord," she said. "His mother is sore set upon siller for him; and my poor bit honey has no fortune to speak of. No, we must not fly so high as the young lord; but I will gladly take her about the country to see the old castles and towers. It will perhaps rouse her up a little."

"And if that does not answer we must think of something else," the old lady said.

I heard them perhaps that day because they were talking of me, which is always so effective a way of making you hear—for latterly I had not been paying any attention to what they were saying; and I thought to myself how little they knew, and how little I cared about even the old castles and curious houses, having something else in my mind. But just about that time Mr Pitmilly came in, who was always a friend to me, and, when he heard them talking, he managed to stop them and turn the conversation into another channel. And after a while, when the ladies were gone away, he came up to my recess, and gave a glance right over my head. And then he asked my Aunt Mary if ever she had settled her question about the window opposite, "that you thought was a window sometimes, and then not a window, and many curious things," the old gentleman said.

My Aunt Mary gave me another very wistful look; and then she said, "Indeed, Mr Pitmilly, we are just where we were, and I am quite as unsettled as ever; and I think my niece she has taken up my views, for I see her many a time looking across and wondering, and I am not clear now what her opinion is."

"My opinion!" I said, "Aunt Mary." I could not help being a little scornful, as one is when one is very young. "I have no opinion. There is not only a window but there is a room, and I could show you—" I was going to say, "show you the gentleman who sits and writes in it," but I stopped, not knowing what they might say, and looked from one to another. "I could tell you—all the furniture that is in it," I said. And then I felt something like a flame that went over my face, and that all at once my cheeks were burning. I thought they gave a little glance at each other, but that may have been folly. "There is a great picture, in a big dim frame," I said, feeling a little breathless, "on the wall opposite the window—"

"Is there so?" said Mr Pitmilly, with a little laugh. And he said, "Now I will tell you what we'll do. You know that there is a conversation party, or whatever they call it, in the big room tonight, and it will be all open and lighted up. And it is a handsome room, and two-three things well worth looking at. I will just step along after we have all got our dinner, and take you over to the pairty, madam—Missy and you—"

"Dear me!" said Aunt Mary. "I have not gone to a pairty for more years than I would like to say—and never once to the Library Hall." Then she gave a little shiver, and said quite low, "I could not go there."

"Then you will just begin again tonight, madam," said Mr Pitmilly, taking no notice of this, "and a proud man will I be leading in Mistress Balcarres that was once the pride of the ball."

"Ah, once!" said Aunt Mary, with a low little laugh and then a sigh. "And we'll not say how long ago;" and after that she made a pause, looking always at me: and then she said, "I accept your offer, and we'll put on our braws; and I hope you will have no occasion to think shame of us. But why not take your dinner here?"

That was how it was settled, and the old gentleman went away to dress, looking quite pleased. But I came to Aunt Mary as soon as he was gone, and besought her not to make me go. "I like the long bonnie night and the light that lasts so long. And I cannot bear to dress up and go out, wasting it all in a stupid party. I hate parties, Aunt Mary!" I cried, "and I would far rather stay here."

"My honey," she said, taking both my hands, "I know it will maybe be a blow to you,—but it's better so."

"How could it be a blow to me?" I cried; "but I would far rather not go."

"You'll just go with me, honey, just this once: it is not often I go out. You will go with me this one night, just this one night, my honey sweet."

I am sure there were tears in Aunt Mary's eyes, and she kissed me between the words. There was nothing more that I could say; but how I grudged the evening! A mere party, a conversazione (when all the College was away, too, and nobody to make conversation!), instead of my enchanted hour at my window and the soft strange light, and the dim face looking out, which kept me wondering and wondering what was he thinking of, what was he looking for, who was he? all one wonder and mystery and question, through the long, long, slowly fading night!

It occurred to me, however, when I was dressing—though I was so sure that he would prefer his solitude to everything—that he might perhaps, it was just possible, be there. And when I thought of that, I took out my white frock—though Janet had laid out my blue one—and my little pearl necklace which I had thought was too good to wear. They were not very large pearls, but they were real pearls, and very even and lustrous though they were small; and though I did not think much of my appearance then, there must have been something about me—pale as I was but apt to colour in a moment, with my dress so white, and my pearls so white, and my hair all shadowy—perhaps, that was pleasant to look at: for even old Mr Pitmilly had a strange look in his eyes, as if he was not only pleased but sorry too, perhaps thinking me a creature that would have troubles in this life, though I was so young and knew them not. And when Aunt Mary looked at me, there was a little quiver about her mouth. She herself had on her pretty lace and her white hair very nicely done, and looking her best. As for Mr Pitmilly, he had a beautiful fine French cambric frill to his shirt, plaited in the most minute plaits, and with a diamond pin in it which sparkled as much as Lady Carnbee's ring; but this was a fine frank kindly stone, that looked you straight in the face and sparkled, with the light dancing in it as if it were pleased to see you, and to be shining on that old gentleman's honest and faithful breast: for he had been one of Aunt Mary's lovers in their early days, and still thought there was nobody like her in the world.

I had got into quite a happy commotion of mind by the time we set out across the street in the soft light of the evening to the Library Hall. Perhaps, after all, I should see him, and see the room which I was so well acquainted with, and find out why he sat there so constantly and never was seen abroad. I thought I might even hear what he was working at, which would be such a pleasant thing to tell papa when I went home. A friend of mine at St Rule's—oh, far, far more busy than you ever were, papa!—and then my father would laugh as he always did, and say he was but an idler and never busy at all.

The room was all light and bright, flowers wherever flowers could be, and the long lines of the books that went along the walls on each side, lighting up wherever there was a line of gilding or an ornament, with a little response. It dazzled me at first all that light: but I was very eager, though I kept very quiet, looking round to see if perhaps in any corner, in the middle of any group, he would be there. I did not expect to see him among the ladies. He would not be with them,—he was too studious, too silent: but perhaps among that circle of grey heads at the upper end of the room—perhaps—

No: I am not sure that it was not half a pleasure to me to make quite sure that there was not one whom I could take for him, who was at all like my vague image of him. No: it was absurd to think that he would be here, amid all that sound of voices, under the glare of that light. I felt a little proud to think that he was in his room as usual, doing his work, or thinking so deeply over it, as when he turned round in his chair with his face to the light.

I was thus getting a little composed and quiet in my mind, for now that the expectation of seeing him was over, though it was a disappointment, it was a satisfaction too—when Mr Pitmilly came up to me, holding out his arm. "Now," he said, "I am going to take you to see the curiosities." I thought to myself that after I had seen them and spoken to everybody I knew, Aunt Mary would let me go home, so I went very willingly, though I did not care for the curiosities. Something, however, struck me strangely as we walked up the room. It was the air, rather fresh and strong, from an open window at the east end of the hall. How should there be a window there? I hardly saw what it meant for the first moment, but it blew in my face as if there was some meaning in it, and I felt very uneasy without seeing why.

Then there was another thing that startled me. On that side of the wall which was to the street there seemed no windows at all. A long line of bookcases filled it from end to end. I could not see what that meant either, but it confused me. I was altogether confused. I felt as if I was in a strange country, not knowing where I was going, not knowing what I might find out next. If there were no windows on the wall to the street, where was my window? My heart, which had been jumping up and calming down again all the time, gave a great leap at this, as if it would have come out of me—but I did not know what it could mean.

Then we stopped before a glass case, and Mr Pitmilly showed me some things in it. I could not pay much attention to them. My head was going round and round. I heard his voice going on, and then myself speaking with a queer sound that was hollow in my ears; but I did not know what I was saying or what he was saying. Then he took me to the very end of the room, the east end, saying something that I caught—that I was pale, that the air would do me good. The air was blowing full on me, lifting the lace of my dress, lifting my hair, almost chilly. The window opened into the pale daylight, into the little lane that ran by the end of the building. Mr Pitmilly went on talking, but I could not make out a word he said. Then I heard my own voice speaking through it, though I did not seem to be aware that I was speaking. "Where is my window?—where, then, is my window?" I seemed to be saying, and I turned right round, dragging him with me, still holding his arm. As I did this my eye fell upon something at last which I knew. It was a large picture in a broad frame, hanging against the farther wall.

What did it mean? Oh, what did it mean? I turned round again to the open window at the east end, and to the daylight, the strange light without any shadow, that was all round about this lighted hall, holding it like a bubble that would burst, like something that was not real. The real place was the room I knew, in which that picture was hanging, where the writing-table was, and where he sat with his face to the light. But where was the light and the window through which it came? I think my senses must have left me. I went up to the picture which I knew, and then I walked straight across the room, always dragging Mr Pitmilly, whose face was pale, but who did not struggle but allowed me to lead him, straight across to where the window was—where the window was not;—where there was no sign of it. "Where is my window?—where is my window?" I said. And all the time I was sure that I was in a dream, and these lights were all some theatrical illusion, and the people talking; and nothing real but the pale, pale, watching, lingering day standing by to wait until that foolish bubble should burst.

"My dear," said Mr Pitmilly, "my dear! Mind that you are in public. Mind where you are. You must not make an outcry and frighten your Aunt Mary. Come away with me. Come away, my dear young lady! and you'll take a seat for a minute or two and compose yourself; and I'll get you an ice or a little wine." He kept patting my hand, which was on his arm, and looking at me very anxiously. "Bless me! bless me! I never thought it would have this effect," he said.

But I would not allow him to take me away in that direction. I went to the picture again and looked at it without seeing it: and then I went across the room again, with some kind of wild thought that if I insisted I should find it. "My window—my window!" I said.

There was one of the professors standing there, and he heard me. "The window!" said he. "Ah, you've been taken in with what appears outside. It was put there to be in uniformity with the window on the stair. But it never was a real window. It is just behind that bookcase. Many people are taken in by it," he said.

His voice seemed to sound from somewhere far away, and as if it would go on for ever; and the hall swam in a dazzle of shining and of noises round me; and the daylight through the open window grew greyer, waiting till it should be over, and the bubble burst.

v

It was Mr Pitmilly who took me home; or rather it was I who took him, pushing him on a little in front of me, holding fast by his arm, not waiting for Aunt Mary or any one. We came out into the daylight again outside, I, without even a cloak or a shawl, with my bare arms, and uncovered head, and the pearls round my neck. There was a rush of the people about, and a baker's boy, that baker's boy, stood right in my way and cried, "Here's a braw ane!" shouting to the others: the words struck me somehow, as his stone had struck the window, without any reason. But I did not mind the people staring, and hurried across the street, with Mr Pitmilly half a step in advance. The door was open, and Janet standing at it, looking out to see what she could see of the ladies in their grand dresses. She gave a shriek when she saw me hurrying across the street; but I brushed past her, and pushed Mr Pitmilly up the stairs, and took him breathless to the recess, where I threw myself down on the seat, feeling as if I could not have gone another step farther, and waved my hand across to the window. "There! there!" I cried. Ah! there it was—not that senseless mob—not the theatre and the gas, and the people all in a murmur and clang of talking. Never in all these days had I seen that room so clearly. There was a faint tone of light behind, as if it might have been a reflection from some of those vulgar lights in the hall, and he sat against it, calm, wrapped in his thoughts, with his face turned to the window. Nobody but must have seen him. Janet could have seen him had I called her upstairs. It was like a picture, all the things I knew, and the same attitude, and the atmosphere, full of quietness, not disturbed by anything. I pulled Mr Pitmilly's arm before I let him go,—"You see, you see!" I cried. He gave me the most bewildered look, as if he would have liked to cry. He saw nothing! I was sure of that from his eyes. He was an old man, and there was no vision in him. If I had called up Janet, she would have seen it all. "My dear!" he said. "My dear!" waving his hands in a helpless way.

"He has been there all these nights," I cried, "and I thought you could tell me who he was and what he was doing; and that he might have taken me in to that room, and showed me, that I might tell papa. Papa would understand, he would like to hear. Oh, can't you tell me what work he is doing, Mr Pitmilly? He never lifts his head as long as the light throws a shadow, and then when it is like this he turns round and thinks, and takes a rest!"

Mr Pitmilly was trembling, whether it was with cold or I know not what. He said, with a shake in his voice, "My dear young lady—my dear—" and then stopped and looked at me as if he were going to cry. "It's peetiful, it's peetiful," he said; and then in another voice, "I am going across there again to bring your Aunt Mary home; do you understand, my poor little thing, my—I am going to bring her home—you will be better when she is here." I was glad when he went away, as he could not see anything: and I sat alone in the dark which was not dark, but quite clear light—a light like nothing I ever saw. How clear it was in that room! not glaring like the gas and the voices, but so quiet, everything so visible, as if it were in another world. I heard a little rustle behind me, and there was Janet, standing staring at me with two big eyes wide open. She was only a little older than I was. I called to her, "Janet, come here, come here, and you will see him,—come here and see him!" impatient that she should be so shy and keep behind. "Oh, my bonnie young leddy!" she said, and burst out crying. I stamped my foot at her, in my indignation that she would not come, and she fled before me with a rustle and swing of haste, as if she were afraid. None of them, none of them! not even a girl like myself, with the sight in her eyes, would understand. I turned back again, and held out my hands to him sitting there, who was the only one that knew. "Oh," I said, "say something to me! I don't know who you are, or what you are: but you're lonely and so am I; and I only—feel for you. Say something to me!" I neither hoped that he would hear, nor expected any answer. How could he hear, with the street between us, and his window shut, and all the murmuring of the voices and the people standing about? But for one moment it seemed to me that there was only him and me in the whole world.

But I gasped with my breath, that had almost gone from me, when I saw him move in his chair! He had heard me, though I knew not how. He rose up, and I rose too, speechless, incapable of anything but this mechanical movement. He seemed to draw me as if I were a puppet moved by his will. He came forward to the window, and stood looking across at me. I was sure that he looked at me. At last he had seen me: at last he had found out that somebody, though only a girl, was watching him, looking for him, believing in him. I was in such trouble and commotion of mind and trembling, that I could not keep on my feet, but dropped kneeling on the window-seat, supporting myself against the window, feeling as if my heart were being drawn out of me. I cannot describe his face. It was all dim, yet there was a light on it: I think it must have been a smile; and as closely as I looked at him he looked at me. His hair was fair, and there was a little quiver about his lips. Then he put his hands upon the window to open it. It was stiff and hard to move; but at last he forced it open with a sound that echoed all along the street. I saw that the people heard it, and several looked up. As for me, I put my hands together, leaning with my face against the glass, drawn to him as if I could have gone out of myself, my heart out of my bosom, my eyes out of my head. He opened the window with a noise that was heard from the West Port to the Abbey. Could any one doubt that?

And then he leaned forward out of the window, looking out. There was not one in the street but must have seen him. He looked at me first, with a little wave of his hand, as if it were a salutation—yet not exactly that either, for I thought he waved me away; and then he looked up and down in the dim shining of the ending day, first to the east, to the old Abbey towers, and then to the west, along the broad line of the street where so many people were coming and going, but so little noise, all like enchanted folk in an enchanted place. I watched him with such a melting heart, with such a deep satisfaction as words could not say; for nobody could tell me now that he was not there,—nobody could say I was dreaming any more. I watched him as if I could not breathe—my heart in my throat, my eyes upon him. He looked up and down, and then he looked back to me. I was the first, and I was the last, though it was not for long: he did know, he did see, who it was that had recognised him and sympathised with him all the time. I was in a kind of rapture, yet stupor too; my look went with his look, following it as if I were his shadow; and then suddenly he was gone, and I saw him no more.

I dropped back again upon my seat, seeking something to support me, something to lean upon. He had lifted his hand and waved it once again to me. How he went I cannot tell, nor where he went I cannot tell; but in a moment he was away, and the window standing open, and the room fading into stillness and dimness, yet so clear, with all its space, and the great picture in its gilded frame upon the wall. It gave me no pain to see him go away. My heart was so content, and I was so worn out and satisfied—for what doubt or question could there be about him now? As I was lying back as weak as water, Aunt Mary came in behind me, and flew to me with a little rustle as if she had come on wings, and put her arms round me, and drew my head on to her breast. I had begun to cry a little, with sobs like a child. "You saw him, you saw him!" I said. To lean upon her, and feel her so soft, so kind, gave me a pleasure I cannot describe, and her arms round me, and her voice saying "Honey, my honey!"—as if she were nearly crying too. Lying there I came back to myself, quite sweetly, glad of everything. But I wanted some assurance from them that they had seen him too. I waved my hand to the window that was still standing open, and the room that was stealing away into the faint dark. "This time you saw it all?" I said, getting more eager. "My honey!" said Aunt Mary, giving me a kiss: and Mr Pitmilly began to walk about the room with short little steps behind, as if he were out of patience. I sat straight up and put away Aunt Mary's arms. "You cannot be so blind, so blind!" I cried. "Oh, not tonight, at least not tonight!" But neither the one nor the other made any reply. I shook myself quite free, and raised myself up. And there, in the middle of the street, stood the baker's boy like a statue, staring up at the open window, with his mouth open and his face full of wonder—breathless, as if he could not believe what he saw. I darted forward, calling to him, and beckoned him to come to me. "Oh, bring him up! bring him, bring him to me!" I cried.

Mr Pitmilly went out directly, and got the boy by the shoulder. He did not want to come. It was strange to see the little old gentleman, with his beautiful frill and his diamond pin, standing out in the street, with his hand upon the boy's shoulder, and the other boys round, all in a little crowd. And presently they came towards the house, the others all following, gaping and wondering. He came in unwilling, almost resisting, looking as if we meant him some harm. "Come away, my laddie, come and speak to the young lady," Mr Pitmilly was saying. And Aunt Mary took my hands to keep me back. But I would not be kept back.

"Boy," I cried, "you saw it too: you saw it: tell them you saw it! It is that I want, and no more."

He looked at me as they all did, as if he thought I was mad. "What's she wantin' wi' me?" he said; and then, "I did nae harm, even if I did throw a bit stane at it—and it's nae sin to throw a stane."

"You rascal!" said Mr Pitmilly, giving him a shake; "have you been throwing stones? You'll kill somebody some of these days with your stones." The old gentleman was confused and troubled, for he did not understand what I wanted, nor anything that had happened. And then Aunt Mary, holding my hands and drawing me close to her, spoke. "Laddie," she said, "answer the young lady, like a good lad. There's no intention of finding fault with you. Answer her, my man, and then Janet will give ye your supper before you go."

"Oh speak, speak!" I cried; "answer them and tell them! you saw that window opened, and the gentleman look out and wave his hand?"

"I saw nae gentleman," he said, with his head down, "except this wee gentleman here."

"Listen, laddie," said Aunt Mary. "I saw ye standing in the middle of the street staring. What were ye looking at?"

"It was naething to make a wark about. It was just yon windy yonder in the library that is nae windy. And it was open—as sure's death. You may laugh if you like. Is that a' she's wantin' wi' me?"

"You are telling a pack of lies, laddie," Mr Pitmilly said.

"I'm tellin' nae lees—it was standin' open just like ony ither windy. It's as sure's death. I couldna believe it mysel'; but it's true."

"And there it is," I cried, turning round and pointing it out to them with great triumph in my heart. But the light was all grey, it had faded, it had changed. The window was just as it had always been, a sombre break upon the wall.

I was treated like an invalid all that evening, and taken upstairs to bed, and Aunt Mary sat up in my room the whole night through.

Whenever I opened my eyes she was always sitting there close to me, watching. And there never was in all my life so strange a night. When I would talk in my excitement, she kissed me and hushed me like a child. "Oh, honey, you are not the only one!" she said. "Oh whisht, whisht, bairn! I should never have let you be there!"

"Aunt Mary, Aunt Mary, you have seen him too?"

"Oh whisht, whisht, honey!" Aunt Mary said: her eyes were shining—there were tears in them. "Oh whisht, whisht! Put it out of your mind, and try to sleep. I will not speak another word," she cried.

But I had my arms round her, and my mouth at her ear. "Who is he there?—tell me that and I will ask no more—"

"Oh honey, rest, and try to sleep! It is just—how can I tell you?—a dream, a dream! Did you not hear what Lady Carnbee said?—the women of our blood—"

"What? what? Aunt Mary, oh Aunt Mary—"

"I canna tell you," she cried in her agitation, "I canna tell you! How can I tell you, when I know just what you know and no more? It is a longing all your life after—it is a looking—for what never comes."

"He will come," I cried. "I shall see him tomorrow—that I know, I know!"

She kissed me and cried over me, her cheek hot and wet like mine. "My honey, try if you can sleep—try if you can sleep: and we'll wait to see what tomorrow brings."

"I have no fear," said I; and then I suppose, though it is strange to think of, I must have fallen asleep—I was so worn-out, and young, and not used to lying in my bed awake. From time to time I opened my eyes, and sometimes jumped up remembering everything; but Aunt Mary was always there to soothe me, and I lay down again in her shelter like a bird in its nest.

But I would not let them keep me in bed next day. I was in a kind of fever, not knowing what I did. The window was quite opaque, without the least glimmer in it, flat and blank like a piece of wood. Never from the first day had I seen it so little like a window. "It cannot be wondered at," I said to myself, "that seeing it like that, and with eyes that are old, not so clear as mine, they should think what they do." And then I smiled to myself to think of the evening and the long light, and whether he would look out again, or only give me a signal with his hand. I decided I would like that best: not that he should take the trouble to come forward and open it again, but just a turn of his head and a wave of his hand. It would be more friendly and show more confidence,—not as if I wanted that kind of demonstration every night.

I did not come down in the afternoon, but kept at my own window upstairs alone, till the tea-party should be over. I could hear them making a great talk; and I was sure they were all in the recess staring at the window, and laughing at the silly lassie. Let them laugh! I felt above all that now. At dinner I was very restless, hurrying to get it over; and I think Aunt Mary was restless too. I doubt whether she read her *Times* when it came; she opened it up so as to shield her, and watched from a corner. And I settled myself in the recess, with my heart full of expectation. I wanted nothing more than to see him writing at his table, and to turn his head and give me a little wave of his hand, just to show that he knew I was there. I sat from half-past seven o'clock to ten o'clock: and the daylight grew softer and softer, till at last it was as if it was shining through a pearl, and not a shadow to be seen. But the window all the time was as black as night, and there was nothing, nothing there.

Well: but other nights it had been like that; he would not be there every night only to please me. There are other things in a man's life, a great learned man like that. I said to myself I was not disappointed. Why should I be disappointed? There had been other nights when he was not there. Aunt Mary watched me, every movement I made, her eyes shining, often wet, with a pity in them that almost made me cry: but I felt as if I were more sorry for her than for myself. And then I flung myself upon her, and asked her, again and again, what it was, and who it was, imploring her to tell me if she knew? and when she had seen him, and what had happened? and what it meant about the women of our blood? She told me that how it was she could not tell, nor when: it was just at the time it had to be; and that we all saw him in our time—"that is," she said, "the ones that are like you and me." What was it that made her and me different from the rest? but she only shook her head and would not tell me. "They say," she said, and then stopped short. "Oh, honey, try and forget all about it—if I had but known you were of that kind! They say—that once there was one that was a Scholar, and liked his books more than any lady's love. Honey, do not look at me like that. To think I should have brought all this on you!"

"He was a Scholar?" I cried.

"And one of us, that must have been a light woman, not like you and me— But maybe it was just in innocence; for who can tell? She waved to him and waved to him to come over: and yon ring was the token: but he would not come. But still she sat at her window and waved and waved—till at last her brothers heard of it, that were stirring men; and then—oh, my honey, let us speak of it no more!"

"They killed him!" I cried, carried away. And then I grasped her with my hands, and gave her a shake, and flung away from her. "You tell me that to throw dust in my eyes—when I saw him only last night: and he as living as I am, and as young!"

"My honey, my honey!" Aunt Mary said.

After that I would not speak to her for a long time; but she kept close to me, never leaving me when she could help it, and always with that pity in her eyes. For the next night it was the same; and the third night. That third night I thought I could not bear it any longer. I would have to do something—if only I knew what to do! If it would ever get dark, quite dark, there might be something to be done. I had wild dreams of stealing out of the house and getting a ladder, and mounting up to try if I could not open that window, in the middle of the night—if perhaps I could get the baker's boy to help me; and then my mind got into a whirl, and it was as if I had done it; and I could almost see the boy put the ladder to the window, and hear him cry out that there was nothing there. Oh, how slow it was, the night! and how light it was, and everything so clear—no darkness to cover you, no shadow, whether on one side of the street or on the other side! I could not sleep, though I was forced to go to bed. And in the deep midnight, when it is dark dark in every other place, I slipped very softly downstairs, though there was one board on the landing-place that creaked—and opened the door and stepped out. There was not a soul to be seen, up or down, from the Abbey to the West Port: and the trees stood like ghosts, and the silence was terrible, and everything as clear as day. You don't know what silence is till you find it in the light like that, not morning but night, no sun-rising, no shadow, but everything as clear as the day.

It did not make any difference as the slow minutes went on: one o'clock, two o'clock. How strange it was to hear the clocks striking in that dead light when there was nobody to hear them! But it made no difference. The window was quite blank; even the marking of the panes seemed to have melted away. I stole up again after a long time, through the silent house, in the clear light, cold and trembling, with despair in my heart.

I am sure Aunt Mary must have watched and seen me coming back, for after a while I heard faint sounds in the house; and very early, when there had come a little sunshine into the air, she came to my bedside with a cup of tea in her hand; and she, too, was looking like a ghost. "Are you warm, honey—are you comfortable?" she said. "It doesn't matter," said I. I did not feel as if anything mattered; unless if one could get into the dark somewhere—the soft, deep dark that would cover you over and hide you—but I could not tell from what. The dreadful thing was that there was nothing, nothing to look for, nothing to hide from—only the silence and the light.

That day my mother came and took me home. I had not heard she was coming; she arrived quite unexpectedly, and said she had no time to stay, but must start the same evening so as to be in London next day, papa having settled to go abroad. At first I had a wild thought I would not go. But how can a girl say I will not, when her mother has come for her, and there is no reason, no reason in the world, to resist, and no right! I had to go, whatever I might wish or any one might say. Aunt Mary's dear eyes were wet; she went about the house drying them quietly with her handkerchief, but she always said, "It is the best thing for you, honey—the best thing for you!" Oh, how I hated to hear it said that it was the best thing, as if anything mattered, one more than another! The old ladies were all there in the afternoon, Lady Carnbee looking at me from under her black lace, and the diamond lurking, sending out darts from under her finger. She patted me on the shoulder, and told me to be a good bairn. "And never lippen to what you see from the window," she said. "The eye is deceitful as well as the heart." She kept patting me on the shoulder, and I felt again as if that sharp wicked stone stung me. Was that what Aunt Mary meant when she said yon ring was the token? I thought afterwards I saw the mark on my shoulder. You will say why? How can I tell why? If I had known, I should have been contented, and it would not have mattered any more.

I never went back to St Rule's, and for years of my life I never again looked out of a window when any other window was in sight. You ask me did I ever see him again? I cannot tell: the imagination is a great deceiver, as Lady Carnbee said: and if he stayed there so long, only to punish the race that had wronged him, why should I ever have seen him again? for I had received my share. But who can tell what happens in a heart that often, often, and so long as that, comes back to do its errand? If it was he whom I have seen again, the anger is gone from him, and he means good and no longer harm to the house of the woman that loved him. I have seen his face looking at me from a crowd. There was one time when I came home a widow from India, very sad, with my little children: I am certain I saw him there among all the people coming to welcome their friends. There was nobody to welcome me,—for I was not expected: and very sad was I, without a face I knew: when all at once I saw him, and he waved his hand to me. My heart leaped up again: I had forgotten who he was, but only that it was a face I knew, and I landed almost cheerfully, thinking here was some one who would help me. But he had disappeared, as he did from the window, with that one wave of his hand.

And again I was reminded of it all when old Lady Carnbee died—an old, old woman—and it was found in her will that she had left me that diamond ring. I am afraid of it still. It is locked up in an old sandal-wood box in the lumber-room in the little old country-house which belongs to me, but where I never live. If any one would steal it, it would be a relief to my mind. Yet I never knew what Aunt Mary meant when she said, "Yon ring was the token," nor what it could have to do with that strange window in the old College Library of St Rule's.

STORY SOURCES

"The Secret Chamber", first published in *Blackwood's Magazine*, December 1876 and was reworked into the novel *The Wizard's Son* (Macmillan, 1884).

"Earthbound", first published in *Fraser's Magazine*, January 1880.

"The Open Door", first published in *Blackwood's Magazine*, January 1882 and collected in *Two Stories of the Seen and Unseen* (Edinburgh: Blackwood, 1885).

"The Portrait", first published in *Blackwood's Magazine*, January 1885 and collected in *Two Stories of the Seen and Unseen* (Boston: Roberts Bros., 1885).

"*Dies Iræ*", first published as *Dies Iræ: The Story of a Spirit in Prison* (Edinburgh: Blackwood, 1895).

"The Library Window", first published in *Blackwood's Magazine*, January 1896 and collected in *Stories of the Seen and Unseen* (Edinburgh: Blackwood, 1902).